CLEARED FOR PLANTING

Janice Cole Hopkins

CLEARED FOR PLANTING

APPALACHIAN ROOTS – BOOK 1

JANICE COLE HOPKINS

Ambassador International
Greenville, South Carolina & Belfast, Northern Ireland
www.ambassador-international.com

Cleared for Planting
Appalachian Roots – Book 1

© 2015 by Janice Cole Hopkins
All rights reserved

Printed in the United States of America

ISBN: 978-1-62020-504-4
eISBN: 978-1-62020-408-5

All Scripture taken from the King James Version, the Authorized Version.

Cover Design and Page Layout by Hannah Nichols
Ebook Conversion by Anna Raats

AMBASSADOR INTERNATIONAL
Emerald House
427 Wade Hampton Blvd.
Greenville, SC 29609, USA
www.ambassador-international.com

AMBASSADOR BOOKS
The Mount
2 Woodstock Link
Belfast, BT6 8DD, Northern Ireland, UK
www.ambassadormedia.co.uk

The colophon is a trademark of Ambassador

*Until the spirit be poured upon us
from on high, and the wilderness
be a fruitful field . . .*

~ Isaiah 32:15a

PART ONE

EMMA AND EDGAR

CHAPTER ONE

The Move

Southeast of the North Carolina foothills – April 1804

Emmaline Cagle watched the scenery slowly pass from where she sat in the back of the farm wagon. Her two sisters sat near, but they'd grown quiet for a change. Christine even seemed to be nodding off. Francine, the oldest, looked from Christie to Emma and smiled. They both tried to look after their youngest sister. Emma had turned fourteen. Francie was two years older, and Christie was only ten.

Mama said this move gave them the opportunity for a new start. Emma hoped time would prove Mama correct, but she wondered. She hoped it would happen with all her being, but Papa hadn't changed in the past years. In fact, his drinking problem had gotten worse.

Emma loved Papa, but he sure could be mean when he got drunk. He seemed a reasonable man for the most part when he was sober, but that had become a rare occurrence—until he got the letter from Uncle Roy, Papa's older brother. Emma had never seen him because he lived in the mountains.

"My wife and boy have died of milk sickness," Uncle Roy had written. "I have no one, and I'm consumed with grief. I own my own cabin and a tract of land in the mountains near the Linville River. Won't you bring your family and join me here? I need you. It's going to be hard for me to work the land without my boy, and my cooking is hard to take. Bring your family and give me a reason to continue on."

Papa didn't know who Roy got to write the letter, because neither Papa nor Roy could read or write. Mama could, though, and Papa got excited when she read him the letter. He wanted to start out at once.

They didn't have their own place, and Papa had come close to wearing out his welcome as a tenant farmer. They'd no doubt be moving again soon anyway, so they might as well move in with Roy. No one would put up with Papa's binges for long, and he didn't get much work done when he was drinking.

They'd packed all their belongings in two old trunks, Papa had thrown some well-used tools into the wagon, and off they'd come. Papa said Roy would likely already have most of what they needed anyway. Papa hadn't had a drink since they'd left, and Emma sure hoped he'd left the brew behind for good.

The journey had already become tiresome. Emma hoped the wagon and two mules would make it. The old wagon creaked and groaned with every bump, although Papa took the ruts at a crawl. Emma could have counted every rib on the poor old mules, and she almost cried for them. Mama always said she had a tender heart underneath her tough exterior.

"Do you think we'll have any rain on the way?" Francie asked.

They had a piece of canvas Papa called a "tarp" to throw over them, but the wagon had no top, and it tended to rain more in the spring. Emma listened for Papa's reply.

"We'll see," he mumbled, as if he'd rather not consider the question at all.

The April sun shone brightly, and even with their long sleeves and hats, the girls were turning pinker. At least it wasn't summer yet. Papa said it would be cooler up the mountain.

"I think we're probably almost a third of the way there," Papa said. "It should start getting a bit hillier before long."

"Emma, you and Christie run over to that farm house in the distance there and see what they'll let you have to eat. I doubt the garden's producing much yet, but maybe they'll have some eggs," Papa said. "The rest of us will set up camp."

Papa always sent Emma on the asking errands. He said she had more gumption than either of her sisters. Christie often went with her because she looked adorable with her big blue eyes and honey-colored hair. Christie also seemed little for her age, and if she looked sad, no one could resist giving them some food or helping them out.

Emma and Christie walked at a brisk pace. It felt good to Emma to get out of the wagon and take a walk. The farmhouse lay farther away than it had looked, but they didn't dawdle along the way, and soon Emma found herself knocking on the door.

"Evening, ma'am," Emma said when a heavy-set woman answered the door. "My family's camping down between the road and the creek, and we wondered if you had any extras you could spare for our supper. We've been traveling for days, and we've just about run out of anything to fix."

The lady looked them over with a keen eye. Emma knew she noticed the worn dresses and bare feet. When her gaze fell on Christie, her expression softened.

"Well, come on in." She held the door open wider. "We'll see what we can find."

The girls followed her into the kitchen. "You're in luck," she said. "I just baked bread this morning. I know I can spare a loaf. How many are in your family?"

"Five, ma'am," Emma replied, "our parents and one more sister."

"Well, let's make that two loaves of bread so you'll have one for breakfast. I also have some of last year's blackberry jam in a crock that's started to crack, so you can take that. I'll give you a dozen eggs, a cake of butter, and a hunk of sidemeat. How's that sound?"

"Oh, that sounds just fine. Thank you so much."

"Don't this one say anything?" She nodded at Christie.

"Yes, ma'am, but she's shy. Tell the lady 'thank you,' Christie."

"Thank you ever so much," Christie whispered.

"Well, aren't you just the prettiest little thing?"

The girls walked back with their bounty. Emma carried the eggs and jam, and Christie carried the bread and meat. Mama would thank God for His provision, but Papa didn't go for praying.

Three days later, just as Papa had said, the land had become hilly. When the girls spotted a mountain in the distance, they became excited. No one in the family had ever seen one this size before.

It's so big," Christie said. "Are we going to have to travel up it?"

"I don't think we'll have to go up that one," Papa said, "but I'm sure we'll go up one or two to get to Roy's place."

"How are we going to get another wheel, Papa?" Francie asked. They'd broken a wheel on the rough road. Papa had put on an old extra one he'd brought along, but if another one broke, they'd be stranded.

"Don't you worry, Francie girl. I figure if we stick to the roads, we'll come to a town before long. Almost all towns have a wheelwright. I might even be able to fix the one we broke with some help, but it looks like the rest of it's about to fall apart, so I don't know."

Emma wanted to ask if they had enough money to pay for a wheel, but Papa had been in such a good mood that she didn't want to change it by asking such questions. In the past, they'd never had enough money for much but Papa's liquor, and she didn't even know how he got that.

Mama would say to pray about it. Mama held with praying for everything, but Emma sometimes wondered. She believed there was a God up there somewhere, but she often doubted that he cared much about what went on in this old world. It seemed to her their family had been rather neglected when it came to blessings. Of course, Papa didn't think much about God, and therein might rest the problem. God most likely neglected Papa because Papa neglected Him.

"Mama, do you think if we don't have much to do with God, He doesn't help us?"

"I wouldn't put it that way, Emma. I think God is always close and hoping we'll turn to Him. However, if we don't accept Christ and His sacrifice in our lives, God doesn't force us."

"If we do accept Christ, do things get better?"

"Yes, but maybe not in the way you're thinking. It doesn't mean things get easy or we all at once have everything we think we should have. But, because He's with us, we feel better about everything. We know we belong to Him, and we are never in any situation alone."

Emma understood the words, but she couldn't quite grasp the concept. It all seemed so vague.

"I have my family's Bible, Emma," Mama said. "You should read it. Start with the New Testament. It'll answer a lot of your questions and help you understand."

"Yes, Mama. I will when I have time."

"I hear the winters are pretty rugged and cold where we're going. We'll have to stay inside much of the time then, and you should have plenty of opportunity to read God's Word."

Papa didn't say anything or even look at Mama. That's the way it'd always been when Mama talked of God. Papa tolerated it if he had to, but if he was where he could, he'd just walk away.

When Emma looked at Mama and Papa, she decided she'd rather take after Mama. Maybe she would try to read and understand the Bible. Papa preferred his liquor over anything else. Mama put God and her family first, so maybe knowing God was a good thing.

Somehow, that old wheel held together, and the wagon crawled into the foothills. Papa stopped in a small settlement, but it didn't look like much to Emma. He left the family in the wagon while he went into a small general store. He came back a few minutes later.

"This place is called 'Tucker's Barn,'" Papa said. "I guess the barn's the biggest thing here, but the guy in the store said they had a blacksmith who might take a look at the wheel."

Papa pulled the wagon to the shop, which turned out to be a stable of sorts.

"I broke a wheel on the trip here," Papa told the brawny man who came up, "and I was wondering if it could be fixed or if I need a new one."

"Abel Bush here," the man said as he put out his hand. "Where're you headed?"

"I'm Lester Cagle, and this here's my family." Papa shook the man's hand. "We're going up the mountains to my brother's place near the Linville River."

"Getting up the mountain will be hard," Mr. Bush shook his head. "It'll take a toll on your mules and your wagon. I'd get anything new I could, if I were you. Actually, I'd get a whole new wagon and team." He grinned. "But, I'll look over everything for you and tell you what I think. I won't charge you for the advice."

"I'd appreciate that. Do you have any work I could do to pay for what we need?"

"Well, I don't know about that. Let me see what I think first."

"You all might as well get out and walk about some," Papa told Mama.

"Can we walk over to the barn?" Emma asked.

"If you'll stay with your mama and not try to go off on your own," Papa answered.

"I feel strange going into someone's barn without permission," Mama said.

"It must be sort of important if the place was named 'Tucker's Barn' after it," Emma reasoned.

A boy who looked to be about eleven looked up from playing out front. He stared at Christie.

"You want to see the barn?" he asked.

"Why did the settlement get named after a barn?" Emma asked.

"This ain't no ordinary barn," he said. "Well, I guess it might have been when it was first built, but it became a gathering place for folks around here. The man who came here first built the house and barn in the 1760s. The barn became a meeting place as more folks came to the area. It's been used as a voting place, a muster ground, a store, and for dances and such."

"That's pretty interesting," Emma said, and the boy beamed. They walked through and, although it was spacious and in good shape, the barn didn't look all that special to Emma.

"Well, let's head back and see how long it's going to take before we can get started," Mama said. Emma wondered if she was afraid to let Papa out of her sight for too long. Of course, if Papa wanted a drink, he'd never let Mama stop him.

Papa had busied himself cleaning out the stable when they got back. "Come on and help me girls," he said. "Abel said he'd give me an extra wheel and let us set camp here for the night if I'd muck out the stable for him. I figure that way we can get an early start in the morning. Abel says it will be slow going up the mountain."

"Well, at least we're getting close, aren't we, Papa?" Francie said as she picked up a pitchfork.

"That we are, Francie girl." Papa always seemed to favor Francie.

They left early the next morning before anyone was about. Mama rushed to fix them a little mush from their meager supplies. Emma was still hungry, but she didn't say anything. She knew Mama was doing the best she could.

They started the climb, and the mountain became steeper and steeper. Emma wouldn't have called the faint trail a road. It looked more like a path people traveled on foot. She hoped Papa could tell where to go. It wouldn't be a good thing to get lost in the woods on the mountain. They all got down from the wagon, even Papa, and walked.

"This will save the mules," Papa said. "At least we aren't hauling much, and the wagon's a light one, so they should make it."

The mules might make it, but Emma began to doubt that she would. She wasn't used to such climbing, and she soon became winded. She noticed Francie and Christie were also breathing hard. Mama and Papa seemed to do a little better.

"How long do we have to walk uphill like this, Papa?" Christie asked.

"A long time, pretty girl, a long time."

It did turn out to be a long time, and Emma didn't think she could keep going. Her lungs and her legs both ached and burned. They didn't even stop for lunch. They just got a swallow of water from the jug in the wagon.

Emma couldn't believe the steep inclines, and she hated to think what would happen if someone fell off the edge of one of the cliffs that came up on their left from time to time. The trail also seemed to disappear at times. She could almost be glad not to be swaying in the wagon for fear of tumbling down a cliff.

At last they made it to the top, and the land leveled out. They were all exhausted, even the mules.

"Let's take a break," Papa said.

Mama got out some cornbread fritters she'd fried last night, and they each had one with some water. It wasn't much, but it helped ease the hunger pains in Emma's stomach. She sure hoped Uncle Roy would have supper going when they got there, whenever that would be.

Papa had hoped they'd make Uncle Roy's that day, but dusk fell before they made it much farther. Emma didn't rest well that night. Too many night noises echoed through the dark, and the leaves intensified the sounds. She found herself worrying about bears, panthers, and all kinds of dangerous critters.

They didn't have anything for breakfast the next morning, but Papa had managed to go out in the woods and find a small stream where the mules could get some water and Mama could refill the water jug. That cold water tasted mighty good.

"Well, we'd better get moving if we want to make Roy's before nightfall," Papa told them.

Emma thought the area at the top of the mountain looked prettier than a painting. The trees showed only a hint that it might soon be time to put out their new leaves, and they almost seemed to be stationed there to protect her. At least they kept her from seeing any more huge cliff edges and drop-offs. Her spirit took wing. She almost felt as if she could reach up and touch the sky.

She looked up to see an eagle soaring overhead. Emma could imagine it grow larger, swoop down, scoop her up, and fly her up to have a full view of the whole area. Now wouldn't that be amazing! She'd be like Icarus, except her wings wouldn't melt.

The air had turned much cooler than it had been at home, even a month ago. It also smelled clean and fresh, and it made her feel alive and well.

"You look pleased, Emma," Mama said and smiled at her. Emma smiled back.

"Doesn't anyone live in these parts?" Francie asked.

"It don't look like it, does it?" Papa replied.

"Do you know where to go, Papa?" Emma asked.

"I think so. There's supposed to be another road to the left up here a ways. Roy said it was more of a trail than a road. If we get into the area of Councill's Store, we've gone too far."

"Will we know which trail to take?" Christie asked.

"I think it'll be the second one we see. I don't think there's another one until we get into Councill's Store," Papa laughed. "Roads like we know them don't seem to have made their way over the mountain."

They found the turn just fine. Uncle Roy was right. It sure wasn't much of a road. Papa kept looking at the position of the sun, and Emma guessed he worried about the time. They'd have to make it to Uncle Roy's before they could get anything to eat.

"This trip hasn't been so bad," Francie whispered to Emma.

About that time, one corner of the wagon collapsed to the ground, and the girls tumbled out onto the ground. Emma and Christie landed on top of Francie. They all screamed.

"Whoa," Papa called to the mules.

Mama scrambled down and ran to help the girls up. "Are you all right?" she asked as she pulled them to their feet.

Christie had scrapes all over her face from where she'd slid along the wagon bed. She began to cry. Emma felt bruised, but she didn't appear to be hurt much. Francie, however, had fallen on her arm, and with her sisters hitting against her, her arm looked broken between the wrist and elbow.

Papa got two sticks and set the arm. Francie didn't yell out when Papa pulled the bone in place, but she looked as white as a corpse. Emma didn't know how she stayed quiet, and she hurt for her sister. Mama tied on the splint and made a sling, and Francie grimaced in pain.

When Francie had been taken care of, Papa located the wheel that'd come off. The pin had broken, and so had the wheel. Papa set about trying to put on the wheel Abel Bush had let him have. This used wheel still looked better than any of the others on the old wagon.

All of a sudden, ferocious black clouds began to march across the sky. Emma had never seen such ominous looking clouds develop so fast. The sun had been shining when the wagon wheel broke.

The black clouds rolled and billowed like a mighty army and conquered all the fluffy white soldiers in their wake. They'd already conquered the ruling sun. At least no artillery clash followed, as often happened in the summer thunderstorms back home. Emma stood watching the battle play out.

It started to rain, a cold drenching rain. They pulled out the tarp and huddled under it. Francie lay with her head in Mama's lap, and the other two girls sat around her. Papa hunkered over trying to fix the wheel, but without a way to make it stay on, Emma didn't hold much hope. It had grown dark, as much from the rain as from the time.

"Looks like you could use some help," a voice called out. Emma couldn't see from her position under the tarp, but the man had a friendly voice.

"I sure could. I'm Lester Cagle, and my wife and three girls are under the tarp there."

"Pleased to meet you, Lester. I'm Fredrick Moretz. Just call me Fred. What have we here?"

"The lynch pin to the wheel came in two, and the wheel broke as the wagon fell. My oldest daughter broke her arm in the fall."

"Oh, my. I could help you get that other wheel on, but I don't have a pin or anything to make it hold. Where are you folks headed?"

"We've come to live with my brother up near the Linville River. He has a cabin there."

"Depending on how far back he lives, you may not be able to make it by nightfall, and this is miserable weather to be camping out. Why don't you come home with me? I live up another mountain, but I have a dry cabin, and you'd be welcome. We can get some things to fix your wagon with at my farm and come back in the morning."

"That's mighty kind of you, but will you have room? There's five of us, and my girls are growing up."

"I have four children, but the three boys will enjoy camping in the barn. We can make room."

Say yes, Papa. Please say yes.

"That does sound much better for my family. If you're sure it's not too much trouble."

"Not at all. My wife will be pleased to have some company. She gets lonesome with no female friends close by."

Emma heard Papa and Mr. Moretz moving about for a while. Then, they came back to get the women. Emma saw Mr. Moretz had a covered wagon. The girls crawled into the back with Mr. Moretz's help. Mama and Papa helped Francie, and Mama got in after her. Papa and Mr. Moretz sat up front. They'd hitched the mules up behind Mr. Moretz's horses.

Emma noticed all their things were loaded into the wagon, as well, and so was the good wheel. She guessed it wasn't a good idea to leave them on the side of the road with the broken wagon.

"I took some pigs, chickens, and a calf into Councill's Store to sell today," Emma heard Mr. Moretz say. "Some of the folks come into the settlement on Saturdays to trade and get what they need. I bought some flour, sugar, and coffee from the store, and it all took longer than I expected. I thought I'd be up the mountain before this. I hope the rain setting in doesn't make the mountain slick."

After traveling down the road for a while, Emma felt them turn right and start climbing up the mountain. She moved toward the back of the wagon and looked out but wished she hadn't. These cliffs and ravines looked just as scary as the ones they'd come up yesterday, and her stomach knotted at the sight. She moved back where she couldn't see them. She didn't know what had gotten into her. Papa had always called her the brave one, but she didn't feel so brave now.

Emma felt the back wheels of the wagon slide in the mud. She sure hoped they didn't get stuck in the mud, but at least some rocks dotted the trail. On second thought, getting stuck would be much better than sliding off a cliff.

She prayed silently. *Oh, God, keep us safe. I'll be better and begin to read the Bible the first chance I get if You don't let anything bad happen.*

Was it acceptable to make a bargain with God? Emma wasn't sure, but it didn't exactly feel right. She vowed to read the Bible and see if she could learn more, regardless of what happened. What if they were killed on this mountain? She'd better work on getting right with God soon. She sure didn't want to go to hell when she died, and this place likely contained plenty of dangers.

CHAPTER TWO

Edgar

The rain stopped, and the ground turned drier as they ascended. Maybe God had heard Emma's prayer. Did God answer the prayers of those who weren't saved yet? She'd try to remember to ask Mama about it later. Now wouldn't be a good time, what with Mr. Moretz in hearing distance.

"Sometimes, the rain clouds hang below the tall mountain peaks, and it rains in the valley but not up here," Mr. Moretz told Papa.

It must have been true, because when Emma ventured another look over the side, she saw fog lurking down below. It reminded her of some mystical fairyland, and she could almost imagine a dragon come lumbering out of the forest across the road opposite the cliff. Maybe it would spread its wings and fly off the cliff. Perhaps she could hop on its back and get a different view of the mountains. She almost laughed at herself and her wild imagination. Besides, if in reality she feared even looking at the high drops, how would she ever climb aboard a dragon about to take flight?

When they got up the mountain, the land spread out, almost as if they were on flat land and not a mountain at all. She'd expected to notice the peak and not have this much room. It must be a wide mountain.

Dusk surround them when they emerged from the covered wagon. A woman and three boys came out of the log cabin to meet them.

"I was getting worried, Fred," Mrs. Moretz said. "Afraid you'd end up on the mountain in the dark."

"Well, as you see, I made it just fine, and I brought you some company."

Papa and Mr. Moretz made the introductions, and Emma felt the boys' stares. Mrs. Moretz's name was Eleanor. The boys were Luther, Martin, and Edgar. The younger daughter, Hilda, was still inside.

"Come on in," Mrs. Moretz said. "I have supper cooked, and there's enough stew for everyone."

The huge kitchen table seated eight. They also brought in a smaller table from the sitting area, and Hilda, Christie, and Francie sat there. Edgar hurried to hold out the chair beside her mother for Emma and then sat in the chair across from her. He looked at her with his eyes dancing, and she felt her heart pick up its pace.

Mr. Moretz looked at Edgar and raised his brow. "Well, well. It does seem the boy's learned some manners after all."

"He's just selective when he uses them," Mrs. Moretz said with a grin.

After Mr. Moretz said grace, the adults started talking. Emma tried to listen and gather information.

All the Moretz boys were older than her. Luther turned out to be twenty-one, Martin was twenty, and Edgar was eighteen. Luther and Martin were trying to examine Francie without being obvious.

"Please excuse me," Luther said after a long pause. "I think the young ladies over there need some cheering up, and I'll just take my plate to that extra place." He smiled but didn't look up, as he moved to the small table.

Martin looked at Emma. "How old are you Emmaline?" he asked.

"I'm fourteen," she answered, "but please call me Emma. Emmaline is a mouthful."

"It's a very pretty one, though," Martin said.

Edgar looked at Francie and Christie, then back at Emma. "Just like the girl," he said and gave her a quick wink.

Emma almost laughed out loud. What a tease! She looked over at Christie. If Christie's face hadn't been skinned in their fall, she bet Edgar wouldn't think Emma was the pretty one. Emma knew her brown hair was too dark to be called "blonde," and her eyes were more gray than blue.

Edgar was the most handsome of the three Moretz brothers, however. He had sandy brown hair, sparkling blue eyes, and you could just tell he enjoyed life. She'd better watch herself around this one. Her hand quivered as she reached for her water glass. What was wrong with her? She'd never acted like this before.

"You have so much cooked, it almost looks like you were expecting company," Emma heard Mama say to Mrs. Moretz.

"When I'm cooking something that will keep over, I sometimes do that so I don't have to cook so much the next day," Mrs. Moretz replied. "Our mountain spring stays quite cool, and it keeps things well."

Emma looked at Edgar again. She'd never really had a beau. Mama had been married by the time she was Emma's age, but Emma had never even been courted.

However, Francie had. Several callers had come around at different times, but when they saw Papa's problem, they never came again. Most respectable men also expected a dowry of some kind, and that wasn't about to happen with the Cagle family.

Emma looked over at her older sister. Francie had the pretty, feminine curves, but her face looked rather plain. Emma and Christie were more slender, but Christie had the pretty face.

Where did that leave Emma? Somewhere in the middle, like always. She sighed.

"I'm wondering what's going on in that pretty head of yours," Edgar said to her.

"I'm just thinking about my sisters."

"If they make you sigh like that, I'll trade you a couple of brothers for them, but I'd rather you take me."

Emma felt her face heat up. She looked around, and the adults were all busy with their own conversations. "I'm not sure I could handle you," she said back.

Edgar laughed easily. "Oh, I think you could handle me just fine. You'd have me wrapped around your little finger in no time."

"Edgar, quit your teasing." Mrs. Moretz had heard his last remark. "These are our guests, and they don't know us well enough for that."

"Yes, Mama, but I was just trying to get to know them better."

"Edgar, don't you talk back to your mother," Mr. Moretz told him.

"No, sir. I didn't mean it to sound like I was."

"Enough said, son."

"Yes, sir." Edgar turned back to Emma. "I hope I didn't offend you, Emma. I only tease those I like."

"I hope you'll tease me forever, then," Emma whispered. Edgar raised his eyebrows in surprise and then gave her a huge smile.

The meal was wonderful. The hot stew was full of meat, potatoes, and carrots, and the family passed plenty of bread and butter to go with it. They could have milk, water, or coffee to drink and even apple jacks from dried apples for dessert. It was the best meal Emma had eaten in a long time—maybe ever.

When they'd first entered the cabin, Emma hadn't taken the time to look around. She'd been interested in the people. Now she looked.

The cabin was larger than the shack they'd left behind. It looked sturdy with thick, squared logs. There were two stone fireplaces, one in the kitchen area and one in the sitting area. Only the one in the kitchen burned now. The door toward the back and off the kitchen must be a larder, because Emma had seen Mrs. Moretz go through it to get some staples. The other room, between the larder and the sitting area, must be a bedroom.

Mama, Mrs. Moretz, and Hilda began cleaning up the kitchen and washing dishes. The rest of them went into the sitting room. The boys pulled in extra chairs from the table.

Edgar positioned his chair beside Emma, and Luther sat beside Francie. Martin seemed unhappy, but he went to talk to Francie and Luther. Hilda soon joined Christie.

"If Edgar bothers you or teases you too much, you let me know, Emma," Mr. Moretz said. "We don't get much company up here, and I'm afraid my boys haven't learned many social graces."

"I'm sure Emma can hold her own," Papa said. "She's my outgoing one who'll stand up to anyone."

"Good for her," Mr. Moretz said.

"Is that true, Emma?" Edgar asked. "Are you the brave one?"

"I thought I was, but I wasn't so sure when I looked over the edges of the mountain cliffs today. I think I may have turned into quite the coward."

"You'll get used to it. I was born here, and I don't even notice them. Give yourself time."

"Will where Uncle Roy lives, near the Linville River, be on a mountain?"

"You'll likely be more in the valley, and that's not so far from here either. I don't know how far up he lives, but it might be only seven miles or so."

They talked for a while, before the adults started making sleeping arrangements. The boys were sent to the barn with bedrolls.

"I hate to cause your family an inconvenience," Mama said.

"You're not," Mrs. Moretz replied. "Those boys are always going off hunting or fishing and sleep out all night. They'll be just fine in the barn."

The back end of the cabin was partitioned off by two quilts hanging from the rafters. Behind the quilts were two beds where the boys usually slept. Mama and Papa would have one bed, and the three girls would share the other. Hilda would sleep on a trundle bed in her parents' bedroom.

Francie had a restless night. Her arm must have been hurting something awful. First she tossed in bed, trying to find a comfortable position, and she woke Emma up several times during the night. The last time Emma woke up, she found Francie sitting up in a chair.

"Is it morning?" Emma whispered.

"It's not time to get up yet. Go back to sleep," Francie whispered back.

"Can't you sleep?"

"No, my arm is bothering me too much."

"What did you think of Luther?"

"He seemed very nice. What did you think of Edgar?"

"I don't know if I'd call him 'nice,' but he was interesting and amusing. I think Martin was upset Luther got your attention before he did."

"Luther thought so too, but he said he was the oldest, so it was only fair. I think Martin should've been paired with you, but Edgar wouldn't give."

"I was a little surprised by that, but I think I might like Edgar better, anyway. Martin seemed almost sullen."

"Maybe that's because he didn't have a girl of his own to talk with. Edgar took an instant liking to you. Maybe it was love at first sight. Now go back to sleep."

"All right, but don't tease. Edgar did enough of that already."

Emma awoke to the smell of coffee. She looked over. Papa and Christie were still asleep, but Mama and Francie had slipped out. She got up and realized how cold it had gotten overnight. This was supposed to be spring, wasn't it? Didn't spring make it up the mountain?"

"Good morning," Edgar said as she entered the sitting area. "How did you sleep?"

"Very well, thank you. And you?"

"I slept well, despite Martin's snoring. I began to think we had a sleeping bear in the barn with us."

"I do not snore!" Martin declared.

"Now, don't you two start," Mrs. Moretz called from the kitchen. "Why can't you get along like these girls do?"

"Do you and your sisters always get along?" Edgar asked Emma.

"We do most of the time. We're really pretty close to each other."

"Luther and Martin are like that, but I often get left out," Edgar said.

"That's because you're such a pest," Martin told him.

"I'd better see if I can help." Emma headed for the kitchen.

"Stay and talk with me," Edgar called to her back. "There's plenty of cooks in the kitchen." When she looked back at him, he patted the chair beside his.

"Let me go check with your mother, and if she doesn't need me, I'll come back."

Mrs. Moretz said they had everything going, so Emma returned. Edgar gave her a big smile.

"So, besides fearing you might drop over a cliff, how do you like our mountains so far?"

"I think they're beautiful. I feel closer to heaven, somehow, and the air smells fresh and clean. I think I'm going to like it here."

"That's good to hear." He gave her a big smile.

"When did your family come to this country?" she asked.

"Years ago. My grandfather and his brother came from Germany and settled in Pennsylvania. Grandfather married and later decided to join some of the other settlers and bring his family to North Carolina. His brother stayed in Pennsylvania. Grandfather moved into the Salisbury area first, but the best land there had already been taken, so they moved farther west. He settled in the Meat Camp area."

"What a strange name. We came through Tucker's Barn yesterday, and that was an odd name for a settlement too."

"Meat Camp began as a hunting camp. The men also processed the meat they killed at a cabin there. A settlement has grown up around it. Anyway, my father was the youngest son, and the two oldest divided the property there. Father married Mother and moved here for the available land. He built the cabin with his brothers' help, and all of us children were born here."

"Is Meat Camp close by?"

"Not really. It's a ways out of Councill's Store. If you came through Tucker's Barn, you came in from the south. Meat Camp is in the opposite direction. Where did you live before?"

"Papa was a tenant farmer. We've lived in lots of different places in North Carolina. We needed to move again, so when we got Uncle Roy's letter asking us to come here, we came."

"Well, I'm glad you're here," Edgar smiled again. He made Emma feel comfortable. She felt as if she'd known him for a long time. She liked that, and she liked how his eyes sparkled at her. She decided she liked Edgar Moretz better than any boy she'd ever seen. He seemed different, that's for sure.

"Breakfast is ready!" Mrs. Moretz called. This time Edgar, Emma, Hilda, and Christie sat at the little table, and Luther, Martin, and Francie sat with the others. It made more sense to Emma to put the younger people at the smaller table.

"It's not fair that you don't have a brother for me," Hilda told Emma.

"You're too young to talk to boys," Edgar told her. "You can play with Christine."

"I'm not too young," Hilda pouted. "I'm only three years younger than Emma."

"Yes, but Emma acts like an adult. She doesn't pout like a little girl."

Breakfast consisted of pancakes, bacon, honey or cherry preserves, and coffee, herbal tea, or water. Emma had never eaten as well as she had here.

"You eat a lot for a thin slip of a girl," Edgar told her. "I like that."

"Your mother's a good cook."

After breakfast, Mr. Moretz and his two oldest sons took Papa to show him the crops. Emma tagged along. Truth be told, she often preferred to be outside. When she followed them out, Edgar came also.

"We just have enough cleared now to plant enough to keep us fed through the year," Mrs. Moretz explained, "but someday I'd like to plant some fields to sell."

Their garden plot stretched a long ways, but it looked as if only some onions, potatoes, and early peas had been planted. However, the rest of the ground had already been prepared for more planting.

Edgar must have seen the question in her eyes. "The threat of frost hasn't passed here yet, so we won't plant the rest until sometime in May."

"Are you a mind reader?" Emma asked him.

"Not nearly often enough." He grinned. "But I'd like to be able to always read your mind."

"You'd probably be disappointed."

"Oh, I doubt that."

Personally, Emma didn't want him always reading her mind. That could prove downright embarrassing.

When the men got ready to go fix the wagon, Luther and Martin volunteered to go help with the wheel. Mr. Moretz gave them a proud look.

"Why don't you four ride the horses, Father?" Edgar said. "That'll make it faster going. You can use the horses to pull their wagon back. I'll bring the ladies down in our wagon with their mules and meet you at the bottom of the mountain in a little while. That way, you won't have to come back up here for their things, and the women won't have to go all the way to the broken wagon just to come back."

"How thoughtful of you, Edgar," Mama said with a smile. It looked as if Mama wanted to help Edgar with his attempts to see Emma. Luther and Martin gave Edgar an ugly look.

"How will we get our wagon back home?" Martin asked.

"We'll hitch the horses to it," Edgar told him.

"That'll be fine, son, but you take care. These ladies aren't used to the mountains yet."

"I'll be so cautious, they won't have one concern," Edgar said.

Mrs. Moretz packed the Cagles a sack of food to take for dinner. "If your uncle isn't expecting you today, you might need something, even if you do get there by dinner time," she said. "Please come again soon," she added. "I've enjoyed this so much, and I know the boys have too."

Mama hugged her, and they all said their good-byes and thank-yous. Edgar, true to his word, kept the wagon slowed as they went down the mountain. As much as he could, he drove away from the side that dropped off. At first the fog enveloped them, but it lay thickest in the low spots, and that veiled the steepness of the ledges to some extent.

"It must have been hard to build this road," Emma said.

"We didn't build it. The road follows a trail made by animals and Indians. The settlers in this area helped it out here and there so we could get a wagon up. We're lucky, though. There are cabins strewn around the mountains with no road at all."

"How do they get anything in and out then?"

"They walk or use a sled tied to a horse or mule for hauling."

Emma sat in the wagon seat between Edgar and Mama and smiled the whole time. Francie and Christie were in the back. Never before had Emma felt so important and special.

They got down the mountain before the men brought the Cagles' wagon, so they got off, spread a quilt, and sat beside the wagon.

"Is it okay if Emma and I walk down the road a little ways?" Edgar asked Mama. "We'll stay within sight."

"I think that'll be fine."

Edgar reached out his hand to help Emma up from the quilt. As his hand enclosed hers, Emma's insides turned to watery mush.

"I've really enjoyed meeting and talking with you, Emma," he said when they were far enough away not to be heard.

"I've enjoyed it too."

"There's something different about you, and I can't figure out what it is. Maybe it's a boldness. You don't seem to mind looking me in the eyes, and you don't withdraw when I tease you. In fact, you seem to almost like my teasing, so I can't let you get away. I hope we can see each other again."

"I'd like that." Emma wondered if it could happen. She knew the Moretz family would be busy on their farm with planting, hoeing, and harvesting. Then winter would attack, and the weather would turn bad. She didn't even know what awaited her at Uncle Roy's, but she hoped she'd be able to see Edgar again. The sooner that happened, the better she'd like it.

They hadn't walked far when they saw the wagon and horses coming. They turned around and started walking back.

"Edgar, maybe I need to tell you my father has had a drinking problem, and he can be mean when he's drunk."

Emma thought she'd better tell him that before things progressed. If Papa's drunkenness would make a difference to Edgar, she wanted to know it now and not begin to care for him and end up being hurt the way Francie had.

"He hasn't had anything to drink since we left home, so I'm hoping the move gives him the incentive to quit," she added.

"Has he ever hurt you, Emma?" Edgar's voice turned soft and tender, and his face showed deep concern.

"No, I've always managed to stay out of his way."

He looked relieved, but then his eyes took on a mischievous glint. "Do you get drunk?"

"Of course not!" How preposterous! She laughed at the idea.

"Then I don't see a problem."

Emma started falling in love with Edgar Moretz right then.

"I don't want that Moretz boy coming 'round to see Emma," Emma heard Papa tell Mama from the front of the wagon.

"He seems a nice enough boy," Mama replied. "The whole family seemed nice."

"Regardless, Emma is just too young to be courted yet."

"You married me when I was fourteen."

"That's different, but you were likely also too young. Oh, don't get me wrong. I would marry you all over again if I had the chance. I have no regrets, but we should've waited a spell. You were just too young. I've always thought that's why you lost our first baby, our son."

Mama winced. She hated to think about the baby boy they'd buried not long after his birth.

"So, it's fine if Luther wants to court Francie?" Mama asked after a long pause.

Papa took a deep breath. "I reckon it is, although I hate to see it. I know I can't keep her forever. At least Francie's sixteen, and Luther, being the oldest, will probably inherit their farm. That should put Francie in a good situation, and she won't be moving that far away. I want Emma to wait to be courted until she's sixteen."

"Emma seems as old as Francie most of the time," Mama said. "She's always been mature beyond her years."

"Regardless, I'll not have her sparking yet."

Emma seethed inside. How dare Papa say that and not even listen to Mama! He sure had stuck Emma in the pickle barrel. She hoped she wouldn't have to be the one to tell Edgar he couldn't come to see her.

CHAPTER THREE

Uncle Roy

Edgar had been right. They didn't have to travel all day to get to Uncle Roy's cabin, but if he hadn't sent a detailed map with his letter, they would've never found it. It didn't set close to any trail but stood back in the woods by itself.

If Emma hadn't seen the Moretz's cabin first, maybe she wouldn't have been so disappointed in Uncle Roy's cabin. After all, his cabin certainly didn't look much worse than the places they'd been living.

Whoever built the cabin must have been a novice. It didn't seem at all sturdy and solid. Even some of the chinking appeared to be crumbling away. That could be a problem come winter. The log structure had no glass, but the one window cut in the front had a hastily made shutter that could be opened or closed.

"Well, how-de-e-e," Uncle Roy called. He hurried out of the cabin and was buttoning up his shirt as he came. He must have still been in the bed, although it was late in the day. Uncle Roy hugged them all. He smelled of strong odors from not bathing in a long time. He exclaimed over how big and pretty the girls were as he ushered them into the cabin.

"It ain't in much shape," he told them. "My Maybelle kept it as clean and neat as you please." His sorrow touched Emma's heart.

His comment about the place not being in much shape didn't describe the cabin accurately. Dirt and grime hung everywhere. Dirty dishes could be seen scattered throughout the kitchen area, with some even on the floor. Bugs were helping themselves. Dirty clothes littered the floor, especially near the bed area, and some of them looked as if they could stand on their own from the amount of soil and grease they held.

The small cabin held few furnishings. A slim table and six chairs stood in the kitchen. Shelves and pegs attached to the wall could hold some kitchen wares, but they stood empty, since everything seemed to be dirty. The kitchen had the only fireplace, but it could provide enough heat for the small cabin. No fire burned in it now, however, and the room felt cold and looked dark and foreboding. A soiled, torn curtain hid a group of shelves that had probably been designed to hold supplies. It stood in the back corner.

Two straight chairs had been placed close to the window in the front on the other side of the room. A rickety bed with sheets, which must not have been washed in a year, set to the back. It stood low and didn't have a headboard. Like all the other furniture, it looked rustic, probably made by someone who had never made furniture before. More pegs surrounded the walls around the bed, but they were also empty.

"I know it ain't much to look at. It needs a woman's touch." Uncle Roy grinned. "It'll have plenty of touches, now that y'all are here." He rubbed his jaw. "I don't reckon I've got many fixin's for a meal. I stay up until late at night and usually skip breakfast myself."

"That's okay. We've had a big breakfast. We'll just work a bit and then eat a late dinner." Mama looked as dismayed as Emma felt. "Let's do some cleaning, girls, before we bring our things in. There will be less to move around that way." She glanced at Uncle Roy. Emma knew she was trying not to make him feel she thought the cabin was inadequate. Well, Emma had hoped for more, but she took a deep breath and fell in to help.

Mama had the men carry everything in the cabin out at the start. Emma and Christie washed the caked-up dishes. Uncle Roy must have used them for quite a spell without washing them.

When Christie bent to pick up some of the dishes from the floor, two mice scurried out. She screamed, but Emma caught only a glimpse of streaks as they ran out the opened front door. When Emma tried to move the dirty dishes from the dish pan, another one was inside the pan. She managed to kill it and throw it outside. Disgusting!

Francie wasn't able to do much with her broken arm, but she used one bucket and brought up water from the nearby creek. By the time the dishes were washed, the men had all the furniture and dirty clothes out of the cabin.

They found plenty of homemade soap on the supply shelf. Maybelle must have made it, and it didn't look as if Uncle Roy had used any of it—that was for sure.

The whole place seemed to be crawling with chiches, nasty insects that looked a bit like a tick. They'd also bite and suck the blood out, but hot water would kill them.

The women swept first. Then, they scrubbed down the whole cabin—even the walls—with the soap and scalding water. Papa had started a fire in the fireplace, and Mama had every pot she could find heating water. They poured it in wooden buckets, which made it easier to handle, and splashed it all over. Then, they used a broom to do plenty of scrubbing, but they had to be careful not to get burned. Next, they did the same thing to all the furniture outside, and the men set it back inside the cabin.

When all that was done, they took a break and pulled out the food Mrs. Moretz had sent. The bag held two loaves of bread, ham, bacon strips, boiled eggs, a bag of dried string beans, and a bag of dried apples for Mama to cook.

They ate the meat and bread for dinner. Mama said she would cook the beans and apples for supper, and they could have the boiled eggs for breakfast tomorrow.

"Lester and I can go a-huntin' if you ladies won't be needin' us anymore," Uncle Roy said. "These woods are full of game, and the river is full of fish. That's what I've been living on lately. The garden stuff from last year is all gone."

"The girls and I are going to do some laundry this afternoon," Mama told him. "If you want to bring some meat back for supper, that'll be good."

Do some laundry, they did. Papa and Uncle Roy tied up a rope near the clearing where a garden plot had once been. Then, they made a fire in the clearing and brought out Maybelle's big iron pot and a couple of tubs. After the carrying, the men went hunting.

First the women started water heating in the iron pot and carried up water from the creek for the tubs. Mama took the stuffing out of the mattress and pillows. Maybelle had been able to save enough feathers, but they were teeming with bedbugs, lice, and vermin. Mama burned the ones in the mattress, and boiled and dried the ones from the pillows. She washed the tickings first, and boiled them for a long time in the lye soap solution. Emma carried them down to the creek and rinsed them before hanging them out. Next came the bedding, and last came Uncle Roy's clothes.

"Why didn't you also wash the feathers in the mattress?" Christie asked.

"That would have been too many feathers to work with at one time," Mama said.

When the tickings were dry, they restuffed and restitched them. They gathered dried leaves for the mattress and tore the biggest part of the stems out. It wouldn't be as soft as the feathers, but they could save more of them later and redo the mattress next spring. Living out in the woods like this, leaves lay thick everywhere.

Finally, they changed all the water and washed their dirty things. Emma looked at her two faded, threadbare dresses hanging on the line. The one she had on was in even worse shape. Maybe it was a good thing Edgar wouldn't be coming around for a while, but her heart felt heavy at the thought.

Well, she hadn't been dressed fancy when they'd met, and that didn't seem to hold Edgar back. He'd not only seen her in a ragged dress and liked her anyway, but at that time the dress had been dirty from the travel and camping out as well. The thought made her feel better.

Emma wondered where Mama's Bible had gotten. She might need some comfort in the upcoming days, and it seemed to be a comfort for Mama, especially when Papa had his problem. After all, Emma had sort of promised God and herself she would start reading it.

Even though Papa couldn't read, the three girls could. Mama had seen to that. Emma liked reading and writing better than the others. She would have loved to go to school, but she'd only been able to do so one year. They were living on some land owned by a wealthy farmer then, and his daughter had taken a liking to Emma. She and Francie had been allowed to study with the governess every morning, six days a week. Emma had seized the opportunity, but it had lasted only for about ten months. Then they'd had to move again. Since Mama had already taught her a lot, the tutoring enabled her to expand her education in ways that she never would have been able to do otherwise. She'd marveled at her sudden access to stories and books.

The family had offered to take Emma in as companion to their daughter, but Papa wouldn't hear of that. He was too proud to even consider the idea, but he wasn't too proud to get falling down drunk. People could sure be a mystery sometimes.

At least those months of schooling had opened up new doors for Emma. She'd developed an even better imagination and she'd learned to love words. She could take the words all strung together and ride them to parts unknown and into all kinds of new adventures.

After they completed the laundry, the women were dog-tired. At least the cabin looked much better.

"We all need to get a bath before the men get back," Mama said. "You girls scrub yourselves good with plenty of soap, and don't forget your heads. Some of the vermin have bound to made their way to us. A good bath will probably revive us."

Revive them, it did! The water in the stream felt ice cold, but once she stood in it awhile, Emma's body became numb, and she didn't feel its icy claws so much. They washed and rinsed several times, even their hair.

They waded out, dried off, and donned all clean clothes from the wash. The thin items had dried quickly, and only Maybelle's two quilts were still wet.

"We'll have the men build us a keeping box in the edge of the stream, to keep our food stuff cold, like the Moretz's spring does for them," Mama said.

It would sure keep it cold. Emma still felt frozen, and she involuntarily shivered from her bath.

When the men returned with some squirrels, Mama sent them to take baths and put on clean clothes. Uncle Roy looked like a whole new person. All cleaned up, he looked just about as handsome as Papa. He only needed a shave. Maybe Emma could at least trim his beard in the morning. She felt too tired now, and supper still needed to be cooked.

Despite her exhaustion after supper, Emma borrowed Mama's Bible and pulled a chair close to the fireplace for light to read. She began in Matthew. She promised herself to read a chapter every day, at least by the time she went to bed. She wanted to find out about God and have some of her many questions answered, and she wanted to quit feeling as if she were all alone. True, she had her family, but when Papa went to drinking, or there were things she didn't understand, she still felt terribly alone.

Things eventually fell into a routine at the cabin, and time rode in a smooth carriage with soft springs for a while. Uncle Roy found some seeds Maybelle had saved, and they planted what could be put out early. Uncle Roy said frost could occur up into May here. The women cooked, cleaned, planted, washed, made candles, mended clothes, and such.

Uncle Roy and Papa went hunting or fishing almost every day, but they were all getting tired of just meat with no bread or vegetables. Uncle Roy did manage to scratch up one bag of corn, which he and Papa took to a little grist mill at someone's house in the Linville River area. They brought back enough cornmeal to make cornbread, but it was coarser without a little flour to go in it. Thankfully, there was still some butter left from what Mrs. Moretz had sent to see them through the first of the cornmeal. Mama said she could use some of the grease from the meat to season with.

Uncle Roy had a little money put back, and they all went to Councill's Store one day. Besides the store, Councill's Store was a regular settlement with a few houses and other businesses. It might have been a little bigger than Tucker's Barn had been, but Emma couldn't really tell, since she didn't get to see all of either town.

The store turned out to be bigger than Emma had expected. It had goods of all kinds, truly a sight to behold. If it didn't have a big selection of any one thing, at least it held a variety of items. Emma could've browsed there for hours.

They'd come to town on a Saturday, and the place buzzed with activity. Uncle Roy said most folks out in the country waited until Saturday to come to the store or to take care of any business they might have here. He bought some flour, sugar, and coffee. He offered to buy Mama some fabric for a new dress, but she said she would get some for Francie instead. Emma knew she was thinking Francie might be courted soon by one of the Moretz boys, probably Luther.

If the stares she and Francie were getting from the young men and some not so young were any indication, she might have more to choose from than just Luther. Papa didn't look at all pleased.

"Why are the men here so rude?" he asked Uncle Roy.

"Folks are just beginning to come here to settle in numbers, and there are more men folk than women. Don't be surprised if your girls get offers from men they've never even met. Since people live so scattered out in these parts, there's not much opportunity to court regular-like."

He was right. Francie received three offers before they left the store. Two were from young men who asked to come courting. One appeared shy, but he had a face that resembled a mule. The other looked more handsome with brown, slicked back hair and pale eyes. He had nice manners, so Francie told him where they lived but said she was probably going to be seeing someone else soon.

The last one came from a middle-aged man with a heavy beard, who stood holding the hands of two children, a boy and a girl. He said his wife had died a year ago, he worked at a saw mill, and he needed a wife and mother. He proposed.

"I'm sorry," Francie said kindly, "but I am interested in someone else." He nodded as if he'd expected her to say that and left.

Emma didn't think she would've been so nice, but Francie said she took the offer as a compliment. She felt it an honor just to be asked, and why hurt anyone's feelings. The whole situation seemed so old world and bizarre to Emma.

They loaded the things they'd bought in the wagon, after which they looked at the livestock some of the men had brought into town to sell or trade. Mama really wanted a milk cow, but they couldn't afford one. They did get some baby chicks, which Uncle Roy called *biddies*.

"We'll build a chicken coop close to the house," Uncle Roy said, "or the foxes and such will get them."

As they were looking at the livestock, a young man with a baby in his arms approached Emma. "Miss, I wonder if you'd be interested in marriage or at least let me come a-calling on you," he said. He held the baby out for her to see. "My wife died in childbirth about three months ago, and little Johnny needs a mama. I'd sure appreciate a woman in my life right now too."

The baby was cute, but Emma knew exactly what he was doing. She'd used Christie's looks in the same way to get sympathy and make people more willing to help.

She decided to use Francie's reasoning. "I'm sorry, but I'm interested in someone else."

"Who's the lucky fellow?" This one wasn't going to be put off so easily.

"Edgar Moretz. Do you know him?"

His face held a funny expression, and he stood staring down the street. Emma looked that way and saw Edgar approaching.

Edgar came up to them as soon as he spotted Emma. "Well, hello, Emma. I'm surprised but happy to see you here."

"Sorry to bother you, miss. I wish you all the best." The young man tipped his hat and left.

"What was that all about?" Edgar asked.

"I think he was asking about a mother for his baby and a wife for himself."

"He was asking you to marry him?" Edgar's eyes held no merriment. Apparently he could have a serious side.

"So it seems, and if not that, he wanted to at least come courting."

"What did you tell him?"

"That I was already interested in someone." Emma watched to gather his reaction.

His face relaxed. "I hope that someone is me. Are you interested in me, Emma?" His eyes and voice had grown soft, and she felt caressed.

"I'm more interested in you than anyone I've ever met. I hope that's okay with you."

"Oh, that's more than okay with me. That's fantastic. I like it that you don't try to hide how you feel, and you don't play games with me, Emma. I appreciate your honesty. In fact, I came to town to try to find a job today, but I haven't had any luck. I felt sure at least the saw mill would hire me, but they said to check back with them in a few weeks."

"Do you need a job?"

"I do if I'm going to think about marrying any time soon. Luther will probably inherit the farm, and there's Martin, who's still older than me. The farm might support two families, but never three with my parents also there. I need to start thinking about working for a place of my own, like Father did."

Emma smiled up at him.

"Father is letting me plant a small field on my own, so I can have what my cabbages bring," he continued. "Since I haven't found any jobs open here, I thought I might go over to Meat Camp and see if my uncles need any help in the grist mill. They have a nice size mill they run there."

"That's going to be farther away, isn't it?"

"It is. That's the worst drawback."

"Emmaline! What are you doing?" Papa only called her Emmaline when he grew angry. "I told you that you're not supposed to be seeing boys yet."

Emma hung her head and said nothing. Saying nothing always worked better with Papa's anger.

"I'm sorry, Mr. Cagle, it was my fault. I was so excited to see her unexpectedly like this that I didn't give Emma a chance to explain."

"She's just too young yet, Edgar," Papa's anger was cooling. "I don't want her to start courting until she turns sixteen."

"We're beginning to like each other, sir. Would it be possible to write her along, so we could get to know one another? That wouldn't be like seeing her, would it?"

Papa thought a minute. "I reckon that would be all right."

Emma and Edgar both smiled. Edgar would make a great attorney, Emma decided. He could be quite convincing.

"I'm so glad I ran into you today, Emma," Edgar said. "I'll write you soon."

Emma could tell he didn't want to leave but knew he must with Papa there. "I'll write you back," she told him.

"Good-bye, Mr. Cagle. Thank you for being so understanding and fair in letting us write."

"That's a right nice young man there," Papa said as they walked off. "But I don't want you ever lagging behind like that again. Why, anything could happen."

"Yes, Papa." Emma knew Edgar had climbed a few notches in Papa's estimation. Papa had liked the compliment Edgar had given him, and he also liked it that Edgar hadn't tried to change his mind about the courting.

Edgar had done the right thing. Papa could be very stubborn, and he never let anyone change his mind. However, he might change his own mind when he saw they were honoring his demands. Yes, he just might change his own mind.

"Papa, do you think there's a little money for me to buy some things to write Edgar back with?"

"I don't know, Emma. Why don't you go ask your Uncle Roy? Now, don't you go writing that boy before he writes to you. It's not proper."

"No, Papa. I won't." Emma sure hoped Papa would continue to do what was proper himself. This was the longest she'd ever known him to go without a drink.

CHAPTER FOUR

Letters

"Well, now, I think Maybelle had some writing paper, ink, and such from where she used to try to send a letter to her Mama down in the eastern part of Wilkes," Uncle Roy said when Emma asked him. "Let's just go home and look. I know there's some paper there. If you had to, you could make you some ink from pokeberries, but you might have to wait a bit for the berries to turn. Lester and I also killed a wild turkey last week, and there should be some feathers from it around to make a quill from. I think we can fix you up."

Luther came to see Francie Sunday afternoon. He brought a letter from Edgar. Emma went to their sleeping loft to read it in private. She opened back the little window flap cut in an outside wall and hinged to let in air in the summer. That also allowed more light in. Mama and Christie moved about in the kitchen, and Francie and Luther sat in the two chairs under the window talking.

Emma carefully opened the letter. She didn't want to chance ripping it. Edgar's neat, uniform handwriting called to her.

Dear Emma,

I so wish I were coming to see you, as Luther comes to see Francine. I told him I expected him to give me a full report about how you looked and what your cabin was like. I want to be able to picture you there.

I'm glad your father gave us permission to write. At least I can hear from you, and we'll be able to get to know each other better from our letters. I feel I know you remarkably well now, even though we've met only twice. I may not know all your likes and dislikes, but I know your character and personality, and those are the most important things to me. I also know how pretty you are.

What about you? Do you feel you are getting to know me well enough to like me? I know you said you're interested in me, but there's a difference in being interested and liking someone. I must say, I like and care for you already. I hope our feelings will continue to grow for each other. I'm so excited by the prospect.

Since we're not allowed to see each other yet anyway, I did go to Meat Camp to check on a job. Uncle Fritz said there wouldn't be enough extra work now, but if I would come back at harvest time, he'd probably have work for me until around Christmas. That will be good. For now, I'm concentrating on my cabbage crop, as well as helping around the farm.

When I get back from Meat Camp in the winter, I can also hunt and trap and sell the pelts. The fur on all the animals grows very thick in our cold winter climate, and they usually bring a good price.

My plans are to save all I can and buy us a small farm as soon as I'm able. What do you think? Would you like being a farmer's wife someday? Land is cheap on the mountains, and my brothers would help us build a cabin. I've known people who've even got it free, but I don't want to be pushing west and more into Indian territory than we already are. We'd have to clear the land for planting, and that can be a chore with this lush growth, but I could do it. I guess we'd have to clear things with your father too, wouldn't we?

But, look at me rushing ahead and letting my imagination run wild. I hope I'm not scaring you off. Do I need to slow down? I can if I need to. I'm not always a patient person, but I would do anything I could to make things better for you. I know you may not be developing feelings for me yet, like I am for you.

I hear Luther getting ready to leave, so I'd better close for now. I want him to carry this to you. I eagerly await your reply.

With warm regards,

Edgar

My, oh my! What a wonderful letter. Edgar sounded as gifted with words on paper as he'd been in person. He had the gift of gab, and not a drop of Irish blood in him. If he didn't become an attorney, he could become a writer. His plans also showed he had some business sense. How impressive!

She thought about hurrying to write him a note to send back with Luther, but she decided against it. After the letter Edgar had written, he deserved more.

She pulled out the Bible. Mama had told her to keep it as long as she read it every day. She realized as she read her chapter that, somehow, God felt very close to her. It made her feel warm and comfortable inside, and she'd already found the answers to some of her questions.

She heard Luther getting ready to leave, so she went down. "Would you tell Edgar I really enjoyed his letter, and I plan to start my reply right away?"

"I'll do that, and I plan to come again next Sunday, if that's okay with Francie. You might send your reply back then. I don't mind delivering your mail."

"Thank you," Emma replied.

Luther seemed nice. Her heart leaped with joy for Francie, and she rejoiced things had turned out as they did. She felt she and Francie had the two easy-going Moretz brothers. She didn't quite know what to make of Martin. His seriousness made him seem so dour.

"What about it, Francie?" Luther asked. "Should I come again next week?"

"I'll look forward to your visit next Sunday afternoon," Francie told him. He smiled and bid them good-bye.

"What do you think of Luther?" Emma asked Francie, when they were on their pallets in the loft that night.

"He's very nice, a cut above any other boy who's ever shown an interest in me."

"Are you falling in love with him?"

"Not yet, but I would marry him if he asked me. I'm not as naive as you, Emma. Falling in love isn't the most important thing. Look at Mama. She fell in love with Papa and has had a heap of problems ever since. Living with a drunk is hard for us all, but it must be especially hard to be married to one. No, I plan to marry with my head first, and my heart can follow."

Emma knew surprise and shock must show on her face, but the dark would hide it. She'd never guessed Francie felt like that. She thought every girl wanted to fall in love. Of course, most ended up marrying through arranged marriages or for other reasons, but she assumed they still wanted love. She certainly planned to marry for love. If she didn't love her husband, she thought it would be almost impossible to be a good wife. Yet, what Francie said did make some sense. Emma decided she'd marry with her heart *and* her head. That sounded best.

She thought of Edgar. He seemed to fit the bill for both. Just thinking about marrying him gave her a warm, jittery feeling inside.

Emma wrote to Edgar at different times. She didn't have enough time to think it through and say all she wanted to say at one sitting. She finally finished it Wednesday afternoon.

> *Dear Edgar,*
>
> *I was too impressed with your letter to put it all into words. After you got Papa to let us write, I thought you should be an attorney. When I got your letter, I decided you would make a good writer, but, then I saw the business ventures you were planning. I've concluded you'd be gifted at whatever you set your mind to do.*
>
> *By the way, where did you learn to write so well? Have you attended school somewhere? Do you like to read also? I love to read, but I don't have any books except for Mama's Bible.*
>
> *I would also love it if you could come to visit with Luther. I enjoy watching your eyes dance with merriment when you tease me. Although your letters are wonderful, and I'm so glad we can write, I can't see your face with them.*
>
> *Did Luther give you the full report as you asked him? What did he say? I will correct it, if he's misinformed you. I can tease too, as you can see.*
>
> *Like you, I'm surprised by how well we've gotten to know each other in so short a time. I felt comfortable with you from the very beginning, which is remarkable, considering you are the first suitor I've ever had.*

I'm not exactly sure what my feelings are for you right now. They're too new to me, but I do have feelings. I am interested, I do like you, and I'm beginning to care about you. I think it will take more time to see how deep my feelings for you will grow.

You asked if you were rushing things and scaring me off. My answer is "no, not at all." I'm not ready to marry you at this minute, but the prospect of doing so in the future is not at all unattractive to me. Each time I see you and each letter I receive seems to strengthen my feelings.

I was rather surprised but pleased that you express your feelings so openly in your letter. I like that immensely, and it encourages me to do the same. I think the easy communication we share is a most positive asset.

You asked me if I could ever see myself as a farmer's wife. I could. We've lived on small farms all my life. I can already do all the chores required of a farmer's wife. However, I'm not acquainted with the mountain farms, and there could be some differences. I'll probably learn some of those here at Uncle Roy's cabin, however.

I've been busy here, helping with the cooking, washing, planting, making soap and candles, etc. Papa and Uncle Roy have cleared an extra field and are planting corn there. I guess we will have plenty of cornmeal, grits, and hominy come fall. I see what you were talking about in clearing land for planting. Life is like that too, I think. There are always problems to be cleared so we can plant better things.

If you think of any way I could help out and earn a little money, let me know. I would like that. I can sew, teach (I've taught Christie some), and do the general household tasks. I'm also stronger than I look, and I don't mind hard work.

Well, I guess I have rambled on enough. You're probably tired of my chatter by now. Besides, I want to get this to you as soon as I have an opportunity, so I can get another one from you. Tell me all that's happened with you and all you're thinking.

With deep regards,

Emma

"Emma," Papa told her at breakfast on Thursday, "Roy and I are going by the Moretz place today. He needs to see a man in the area on some business. Do you want me to take that letter you've been working on by their cabin?"

Emma wondered if Papa might open and read the letter. She didn't trust him. "Luther said he could take it Sunday when he comes here," she said.

"Suit yourself, but we'll be going right down their road, if you have it finished."

The fact that Papa didn't get upset or try to convince her to let him take it eased her suspicions. "Okay, thank you. Maybe Edgar will even have time to answer me by Sunday."

"You two almost seem to be getting more involved than Luther and Francie. Don't go too fast, Emma."

"I don't plan to, Papa. I'm not ready to get married yet."

"Good girl."

Edgar did send her a letter with Luther on Sunday. Emma could hardly wait to read it. This time she took it out into the woods. She'd found a downed tree at a pretty spot beside the stream, and she came here often to be by herself. When she could, she read the Bible here. She sat down on the log and opened the letter.

My Dearest Emma,

I hope it is okay to call you that, because that's exactly what you are. I was overwhelmed, in a good way, by your letter. Your vocabulary is amazing. I don't know of another woman in these mountains with as good an education.

You asked me if I had gone to school. No, my mother has taught all of us children. I told her you thought I had formal training, and she was pleased. She said I was always her best student since I enjoyed the lessons, and the other two boys couldn't wait to be through. We only studied through the colder months. You must have been to school, however. It would have been easier to do so in the flatlands than here in the mountains.

I'm glad you think so highly of me. I hope I can live up to your expectations. I am interested in many things, but I love life on a farm. It suits me just fine. I don't think I would like living in a town at all, so practicing law is probably out. Maybe I could be a winter-time writer, but I doubt if that would prove very profitable. No, a farmer will be just fine.

I'm staying busy here. On a farm, there's always loads of work to be done. If things slow down, Father has us out cutting wood. It takes a lot of wood to make it through a winter up here.

Luther reported you looked well and seemed thrilled to get my letter. He said you immediately took it off to read in private. He told me your cabin was adequate and as clean as could be. He said it looked like most of the other cabins in the area. It sits in a forested area, but there's a clearing for a garden patch, and the men seemed to be clearing more. Was the report correct? What more can you add?

You mentioned your uncle and father were planting more corn. I feel I should give you some rumored information, but I fear it may be more gossip than anything, for I have no firsthand knowledge. Other men in the area say your uncle makes corn liquor in the fall and winter and sells it. Many men in the mountains do, because it is often the easiest way to make money. However, since you told me of your father's problem, I felt compelled to mention it to you. I choose never to touch the stuff myself, so I don't know if the rumors are true or not.

I express my feelings to you for two reasons. First, I believe it is important for us to be open and honest with each other. Only then can we really know one another and ascertain if we're right for each other. I also open up to you because it is so easy for me to be myself with you. You accept me for who I am, and that encourages me to show you more of what I think and how I feel. You even like my teasing, and, believe me, that usually causes people to retreat faster than anything.

You said that each letter you receive from me seems to strengthen your feelings. If that be true, expect at least five letters a day from me. If I spent a lifetime of doing nothing else but searching, I don't think I'd ever find someone more suited to me than you. From what you've told me, we will make a great farm couple. I'm pleased you are able to do so much already and don't mind the hard work a farm requires.

Don't even think about helping me earn money for our place. God will help us work things out. We just need to keep our trust in Him.

You mentioned in your letter the only book you had to read was your Mama's Bible. Does that mean you're a Christian? I accepted Christ as my Savior when I was eleven. My journey in faith is an important part of who I am, and I'm hoping that's something else we can share. I would never marry anyone who didn't believe in God. I probably should have told you all this before. I think my feelings for you have developed so fast I've been a bit stunned, but I'm enjoying every second of getting to know you.

Eagerly awaiting your reply.

Love,

Edgar

Love. He signed *"Love, Edgar." Does that mean he loves me?* My, but things were moving fast. She'd seen him twice and received two letters, and he was talking of love and marriage.

Did she love him? She thought she might be beginning to, but she'd thought that the first time she'd met him. And, he chose not to have anything to do with liquor. That was gigantically important to Emma. Yes, she was definitely falling in love with Edgar Moretz.

Emma made her way back to the cabin. Luther would stay for supper this time, and she saw the three men out looking at the crops. Supper would be held a little early so Luther could get back up the mountain before dark.

An afternoon shower hit, and Emma ran for the house. Even in May, the rain felt cold here.

"Luther asked me to marry him, and I said yes," Francie whispered, "so Luther asked Papa for my hand, and Papa said yes. Oh, I'm so excited! I'm finally going to be married."

"Congratulations, but you'd think we considered you a spinster already, and you're just sixteen."

"Yes, but think of all the fellows who ran away from courting me because of Papa. I truly thought I might end up an old maid."

"That's not why you're marrying, is it, Francie? That wouldn't be fair to Luther. Have you told him about Papa?"

"No, ninny. I'm marrying Luther with my head, just like I told you. I wouldn't tell Luther about Papa for all the world and have him run away too."

Emma didn't like how that sounded. It just didn't seem right to keep secrets from the man you planned to marry.

"Do you think you know him well enough already?"

"Yes, I do. You know how nice he his, and we can discover more about each other after we're married."

How different could two sisters be! Emma had told Edgar about Papa's problem on their first visit. She wondered if Edgar had told Luther. She doubted it. Edgar didn't seem the type to talk about other people's problems. For that matter, how different her relationship with Edgar appeared from Francie and Luther's!

"Mama, do you need me to help with anything? If not, since Luther will be staying, I want to write a quick reply to Edgar's letter for him to take with him."

"You go ahead, dear. Francie's arm has healed nicely, and she can help since the guest is her fiancé."

> Dear Edgar,
>
> I'm going to make this letter short, since I want Luther to take it to you right away. I was overjoyed with your last letter. It read like you were right here beside me, talking to me in person. It almost seems too good to be true that you and I have met and are such a perfect match for each other. I cherish the fact that you hold me dear.
>
> What I feel compelled to answer is your question about my faith. I certainly believe in God. My father doesn't seem to have much faith, and refuses to listen, but Mama has taught us from the Bible for as long as I can remember. She has a strong faith.

I read a chapter in the Bible every day now. I want to know who God is. I have never accepted Christ into my life nor been baptized, but I am considering doing so. I just want some of my questions answered before I make that step. I will seek harder so we can also share in this area.

To address another of your questions, I was privileged to have a governess for ten months of instruction. The daughter of a rich farmer became my friend, and Francie and I shared her governess until we had to move. Otherwise, Mama has taught me.

Luther seems to have given you a pretty accurate description of how things are here. The cabin needs some repairs, and everything is pretty rustic, but we women keep it clean, and Mama has made it feel like home. Your house is sturdier and nicer, however.

I have been expecting five letters a day from you, since my feelings do grow with each one. Alas, I have been disappointed in this regard. Can you see my playful smile?

Love,

Emma

P. S.

By now, I'm sure Luther has told you he is engaged to marry Francie. I'm happy for them, but I'm afraid they don't yet have our closeness.

Wednesday, Edgar rode by to give Emma his next letter himself. He went up to Papa in the cornfield first. Emma saw him as she came from the stream carrying a bucket of water. She slipped around the cabin, where she could hear what was said without being so close that Papa might get angry.

Edgar dismounted and held the letter out. "I wanted to bring this by and leave it for Emma. Would you give it to her for me, please?"

Papa looked at Edgar for a few seconds. "This letter writing is getting a little out of hand, don't you think, son?"

"No, sir. I think we've learned a lot about each other from our letters."

"Do you like what you found out?"

"Yes, sir. Very much."

"Well, why don't you give her the letter yourself? She's standing right over there." Papa nodded toward Emma. "Come here, girl."

"Thank you, sir." Edgar started walking toward Emma as Emma approached him.

"You two stand right there where I can see you now," Papa called.

"I wanted to bring this by right away, Emma." Edgar handed her the letter. "I would write you more than five times a day if I could get them to you."

"Maybe we should get carrier pigeons," Emma teased.

"That's a good idea. Now, why didn't I think of that?" Edgar answered with a twinkle in his eyes.

"Will Papa let you stay a while?"

"I don't think so, but he let me see you for a bit, and that's more than I'd hoped. Maybe he'll gradually ease the restrictions. You look wonderful, Emma."

"My dress is faded and patched, and I've been working all morning, so it must be because I'm glowing with happiness from seeing you."

"Things will work out for us. Read the letter, Emma. You'll understand what I mean. I need to leave now before you father gets upset, but I'm having a hard time turning from you."

"We'll surely see each other at Luther and Francie's wedding."

"I love you, Emma," he whispered and turned.

"I love you too, Edgar," she whispered back. He turned and gave her a tremendous smile, as he continued to walk.

Emma watched as he walked back to Papa, shook his hand, and thanked him for allowing Edgar a moment with Emma. He then mounted his horse and waved to Emma as he rode away.

"I do like how that young man handles himself," she heard Papa tell Uncle Roy. She was on her way to her log by the stream to read the letter.

> *My Dearest Emma,*
>
> *Like you, I wanted to address the matter of faith right away. I must admit, at first what you wrote disturbed me, because the Bible says that Christians are not to be unequally yoked. However, as I always do when I have a concern, I prayed about it.*
>
> *God has laid it upon my heart that you are seeking Him, and therefore you will find Him. This is according to his Word in Matthew 7 when Jesus said, "Ask, and it shall be given you; seek, and ye shall find; knock, and it shall be opened unto you: For everyone that asketh receiveth; and he that seeketh findeth; and to him that knocketh it shall be opened." In other words, Emma, because you want to know God, you will; because you are seeking answers, you'll find them; because you are looking for salvation, you will be saved.*
>
> *None of this is complicated. It's all very simple. Because all of us are sinners and do wrong, Jesus came and died on the cross. Now we can stand before a Holy God without sin, not because of what we do but because we've been cleansed by His blood. All we have to do is ask Christ to come into our lives and save us.*
>
> *You don't need to do anything beyond this to start your walk as a Christian. You don't have to be good, or understand the Bible, or do*

anything beyond asking Christ to forgive your sins and accepting Him as your Savior. It's not about what we do, because we could never be good enough or do enough to earn salvation. It's all about what Christ did for us with His sacrifice on the cross.

Wanting to know more of God, and seeking answers to your questions are good things, but open your heart to God, let Him touch you, and ask for forgiveness and salvation in Christ right now. Then, those other things will be easier for you. At the moment you're saved, the Holy Spirit comes and lives inside you, and He becomes your guide in your journey of faith. That makes everything so much easier. We don't have to rely on ourselves.

I also feel it is God's plan for you and me to become husband and wife. I feel sure things will work out for us. We must be patient, although I understand how hard this will be, for me at least. I do want to get us a place first, and we must honor your father's wishes. We can do both of those at the same time.

My love for you is enormous, Emma, but still it grows. It almost scares me at times, but I am so thankful you came into my life. You have been such a blessing to me, and I am sure it will be even truer after we're married. I look forward to that day with great anticipation.

All my love,

Edgar

Tears rolled down Emma's eyes as she read the letter. Edgar had made everything so clear to her. She had confused herself trying to understand God and the Bible all at once. She had read through Matthew, and she remembered the verses Edgar mentioned. She also knew John 3:16. Mama had taught it to her long ago. She understood what Edgar was saying. She stared at the flowing water in the stream, but she didn't really see it.

Edgar's letter had touched her, but so had something else. She knew what she needed to do.

"Dear Christ," she whispered, "I know I'm a sinner. Please forgive me. Come into my life and save me. Thank Thee for Thy sacrifice on the cross. Help me to be the person Thou would have me to be, and help Edgar and me according to Thy will, I pray. Amen,"

The tears still flowed, but she felt a peace and a presence she'd never felt before. She couldn't wait to get out her Bible and read some more.

Luther and Francie wanted to marry before winter. They planned their wedding for September the fifteenth. Because their cabin was bigger and there was more cleared space around it, the wedding would take place at the Moretzes. That only gave them two months, but it wouldn't be a fancy wedding.

Mama and Francie had already made her dress from the lavender cloth Uncle Ray had paid for earlier. Mama had pulled out some pretty white lace she'd been saving for a long time to trim it with, and the dress suited Francie very well.

Martin would be Luther's best man, and Emma would be Francie's maid of honor. There would be no other attendants. Mama was also working over one of her old dresses for Emma. It was a pretty green dress that Mama hadn't worn in years because she considered it too dressy to wear every day, but the cloth was still good and strong. By taking in the seams and hemming it more, it would fit Emma just fine.

Emma had been sewing Papa and Uncle Roy white shirts to wear. They wouldn't have a suit, but the new shirts would look nice.

"Do I get a new dress?" Christie asked.

"Sure you will," Mama said. "We'll cut it out of the dress Francie ripped, because she outgrew it so soon. The fabric is still nice, and the yellow will look pretty on you."

The dress Mama was talking about had been made from homespun, but it was a pretty color, and everything looked good on Christie. Christie would be happy with it and pleased just to get a new dress.

Hopefully the day would be pretty, and they could hold the wedding outside. Mama and Francie went over to make plans with Mrs. Moretz. Emma stayed home with Christie at Papa's request, and therefore she didn't get to see Edgar. Sometimes she found it hard not to resent her father, but she wanted to have a better attitude.

CHAPTER FIVE

The Accident

On September the first, Edgar rode to the cabin and knocked on the door. By the look on his face, something terrible had happened.

"I have some bad news," he said. "Luther is dead."

"Oh, no!" Mama exclaimed. "What happened?"

Francie just sat at the kitchen table with silent tears rolling down her face. She clutched her hands together but didn't move a muscle or say a word.

"Come in and have a seat," Papa told Edgar, "and tell us what happened."

"Luther and Martin went out camping last night, as they've done many times before. They set up camp, got up early, and went out to a ledge they knew. It set over a stream where the deer come to water. They sat there a long time waiting, when a buck came to the stream. Luther stood up to get a better look. His legs must have been numb from sitting on the rock so long. He stumbled and fell before Martin could catch hold of him. It looks like he slammed into the rock, hit his head, and broke his neck. He died before Martin could get down to him."

Emma could tell Edgar was fighting tears himself. Her heart went out to him. "I'm so sorry, Edgar," she told him and took his hand in hers. Papa didn't say anything. Edgar gave her a weak smile.

"I'm sorry for you too, Francie," Edgar looked at Emma's oldest sister. "Luther loved you. He told me he did."

Francie nodded but said nothing.

"Well, I need to get back home. We knew you needed to know, and I was the one in the best shape to come. The funeral will be tomorrow at ten in the morning."

"Instead of a wedding, we'll be going to a funeral," Uncle Roy said. "How sad."

"Papa, may I walk Edgar out to his horse?"

Papa nodded. They held hands on the way out.

"I love you, Emma." His tears broke forth, then. Emma put her arms around him and held him. He hugged her back tightly. Edgar needed her touch right now and, at that moment, she didn't care what Papa would say.

"I love you too, Edgar, so much," she said as they continued to hold each other.

He pulled back, looked her in the eyes, and kissed her on the forehead. "We'll talk at the funeral," he told her as he mounted his horse.

Emma wished she'd been able to tell him she had accepted Christ as her Savior, but she knew this wouldn't be the best time. She should have written him already, but things had been frenzied with the wedding plans, and she had hoped to see him soon and tell him in person. She wasn't sure the talk Edgar wanted to have at the funeral would be the time either. She would pray about all of this and let God be her guide.

For the rest of the day, Emma found herself doing a lot of praying. She prayed for Edgar and the whole Moretz family. If Edgar had been the one in the best shape to come tell them, Emma could only imagine how the others must feel.

She also prayed for Francie. Her sister worried her. She hadn't broken down or cried, but neither had she talked to anyone. It seemed as if she'd pulled inside herself, like a turtle withdrawing into its shell.

Emma didn't think Francie was in love with Luther from what she'd said, but she must have cared something for him. She must be in shock. That would be understandable.

Emma also prayed God would guide her in what to say to Edgar. She wanted to be a help to him, but she didn't know what to say or do.

A group of people stood around the cabin as they pulled up. Emma hadn't expected so many at the funeral. News must have spread quickly. She learned that some of them had been there last night to be with the family and sit with the corpse. The itinerate preacher stood on the front porch and gave the eulogy. He called for anyone not saved to take care of it right away, because we never knew when our time might come. He said Luther had been saved and baptized, so the family had the assurance of knowing he was in a better place.

Emma looked at Papa. She couldn't tell if he listened or not, but she sure hoped he had.

They buried Luther a ways behind the house near a small stand of trees. His was the first grave there. Mrs. Moretz and Hilda sobbed at the gravesite and looked as if they might collapse into the open hole with the wooden coffin. Mr. Moretz had his arm around his wife helping to support her, but silent tears were streaming down his own face. Edgar held on to Hilda with one arm and pulled her close. He stared at the grave but didn't look like he saw a thing.

Martin stood with his family, but he shook back. His fists were clenched at the end of rigid arms, and an angry scowl sliced across his face. Emma said another silent prayer for them all.

When the preacher said the last prayer, everyone moved back toward the cabin. Food weighed down the kitchen table, but Emma didn't feel like eating. She got a cup of apple cider and went outside. She meandered along without a planned destination. Edgar joined her.

"How are you?" she asked, touching his arm to give comfort.

"I'm doing as well as one could expect under these conditions. We'll all miss him so much, but I know he's in a better place, like the preacher said. We've all been saved, except Hilda. How is Francie doing?"

"I don't know. She hasn't broken down, but she hasn't talked to anyone, either. I don't know what she's thinking."

"It's bound to be hard on her. I can't imagine how bad it would be if I lost you."

"I don't think what Francie felt for Luther is the same as I feel for you or you for me." Emma looked at Edgar and saw she had his full attention. "Francie told me she was marrying with her head and not her heart. I made up my mind right then that I'd marry with both. Oh, I'm sure she cared for Luther, and I know she's hurting, but I don't think her feelings had grown as deep as mine have."

"Are your feelings for me deep, Emma?"

"Yes, they are." Her voice softened with the emotion she felt. "They're so deep there's no way to describe what I feel, other than to tell you I love you with all my heart."

"That's enough, darling Emma. My love for you is indescribable too. It knows no bounds."

They had slowly walked to the barn. They realized where they were and sat down on the bench in front, where they could be seen.

"I asked Christ into my life after I read your letter. You made everything so plain to me. I'd confused myself by trying to answer all my questions first. When you explained how simple salvation was, I knew you were right from the reading and studying I'd been doing."

"That's great news, Emma. Thank you for sharing that. I feel good knowing I had some small part."

"I would call it 'some large part.'" She smiled at him.

"Would you like to talk to the preacher about baptizing you? I know he's going to be here another week or so."

"Yes, I'd like that."

"Here comes your father."

"Oh, no." Emma looked up, but Papa didn't look angry.

Papa approached the pair and stopped in front of them. "I watched you two walk toward the barn and sit down here without ever going out of sight. I planned to tell you this after the wedding, but that's not possible now. I've been real proud of the way you both have acted. I've found no fault in either of you. Edgar, you have my permission to come calling whenever you want."

Edgar stood up and extended his hand. "Thank you, sir. I won't betray your trust in me."

Papa nodded his hand. "I believe that, son, indeed I do." He turned and walked back to the house.

"Well, what do you think of that?" Edgar asked, as he sat back down.

"I'm amazed. I'd hoped he'd change his mind, but I hadn't seen any signs he had."

"Didn't I tell you God would take care of things? I knew things would work out for us. Isn't God good?"

"Yes, He is. It won't be so bad to wait on getting a place, if we can see each other as we wait."

"Well, I don't know about that." Edgar's eyes were sparkling. "It could make waiting harder in some ways."

Emma guessed what he was thinking and blushed.

"Don't worry, Emma. I would never hurt or dishonor you. You know I was teasing. I'm just as glad your father changed his mind as you are."

"I know." She smiled.

"What are you two doing courting like this at Luther's funeral?" They hadn't heard Martin come up. "Mama wants you, Edgar."

"We're coming." He got up and took Emma's hand as they started to the house. Martin had quickly walked ahead, as if he wanted to get as far away from them as he could and as quickly as possible.

"Martin's just hurting so much now, he wants to lash out. He and Luther were as close as twins. Don't pay any attention to what he says."

"I won't, but I'll pray for him."

Edgar squeezed her hand and smiled at her before he let it go, since they were nearing the cabin. Emma went into the sitting room and sat down with Mama and Francie, while Edgar went to find his mother."

"When are we going home, Mama?" Francie asked. "I'm getting tired."

"I feel I should stay for a while longer, but I'll see if your father or Uncle Roy will take you home if you want."

"Yes, Mama, please do that. I need to lie down."

"Mama, I think it would be good to let Hilda spend the night with Christie," Emma said. "I think it'll make it easier for her if she gets away tonight."

"That's a good idea. I know Christie would be excited. Would you ask Hilda, and I'll talk to Eleanor."

Roy, Papa, Francie, Christie, and Hilda went to the Cagle cabin. Mama and Emma stayed. When Papa went to say their good-byes, Mrs. Moretz said she would like Mama and Emma to stay the night with her, but if that wasn't possible, Edgar would bring them home later.

"I'd like your company, Kathleen, if it's not too much of an imposition to ask you to stay, but I warn you. We may not get much sleep."

"I would be pleased to stay, if it would help," Mama said.

Gradually the others left. Some of the men had milked and done the nightly chores, and the women had left the kitchen clean and neat.

Emma went to sit with Mama in the front room. The Moretz family sat together around the kitchen table.

"What can I do to help you, Martin?" Emma heard Edgar asked his older brother. "You can't let grief consume you."

"I wish it would," Martin snapped, "but grief isn't merciful enough to kill."

Martin was just making it harder on the rest of his family with his bitterness. Couldn't he see how much his parents were hurting? His mother started crying all over again at his thoughtless remark.

"I wish I could do more to help," Emma whispered to Mama.

"I've seen a difference in you lately." Mama looked at Emma. "I guess it's Edgar's influence, but you seem more satisfied, and you seem to think of others more."

"Thank you, Mama, but it's also that I've accepted Christ as my Savior." Emma hadn't told anyone but Edgar. There had never seemed to be an appropriate time, and she preferred to tell him first.

"Oh, Emma, I am so happy." Mama hugged her. "I've prayed for all of you for so long."

"What's this all about?" Mrs. Moretz asked as she came to the sitting room.

"Emma just told me she's come to Christ."

"That is wonderful. I knew you were a Christian, Kathleen, from our conversation when you were first here, and that's why I wanted your company tonight. I might need a friend to pray me through the night. It's wonderful to know Emma has joined us. Edgar is probably my child with the strongest faith, and I know he's quite smitten with Emma. This is great news indeed."

"What's the good news?" Edgar came in to sit down with them. "We all could use some good news now."

"Emma just told us she's been saved," Mama said.

"That is reason to celebrate," he said with a smile, "even in the midst of this tragedy." He paused before changing the subject. "I'm really worried about Martin. He's not taking Luther's passing well, and his attitude seems to get worse instead of better."

"I think seeing it happen has made it harder on him," Mrs. Moretz said. "He hasn't said anything, but I think he blames himself. He's the one who talked Luther into going that night."

"I tried to tell him Luther is with God, and God would see us through this. Martin said God had allowed this to happen, and he didn't want to hear anything about that kind of god. I think he's blaming God."

"Oh, no!" Mrs. Moretz said. "I knew he was angry, but I didn't know he was angry with God. This isn't good at all."

"How are you doing, Mama?" Edgar asked. "We really haven't had a chance to talk."

"I'll be okay." Mrs. Moretz looked at her son. "I'm hurting terribly. It's so hard to lose a child, but I can feel God's presence. He'll see me through my grief, and I will get through the bulk of it. Of those in our family," she continued, "your father, you, and I are the ones I worry about the least in Luther's death. We rely on God more than Martin or Hilda do. They seem to take things on themselves, instead. I guess they're at different places in their journey of faith. We'll just have to pray for them."

"Mama, thank you for sharing your faith with me through the years. You're a big reason I know God."

"I've shared my faith with all of you the same, Edgar. You just grabbed hold and wanted it more. Sometimes I think your understanding and trust are even greater than mine, but I'm so proud of you."

"And now Emma is on her own journey," Edgar said. He seemed to realize he and his mother had been carrying on their private conversation at the exclusion of their guests.

"Yes, she is." Mrs. Moretz smiled.

"And I think she's already way up the path," Edgar added.

A warm feeling swept over Emma, as if someone really special hugged her. Emma felt blessed.

Mrs. Moretz wanted them to eat supper together as family and friends, so they ate from the bounty of food left by neighbors. After supper, Martin said he needed time by himself to do some thinking and would sleep in the barn. They let him go and prayed he would work through his problems.

Emma and Mama were to sleep in the two beds behind the quilts again. Mama thought one bed would be enough.

"Why don't Fred and Edgar pull one of the beds out here, and Edgar can sleep in it," Mama said. "I'm sure he would be more comfortable in a bed than on the floor, and Emma and I will sleep in the other bed."

Emma agreed with Mama, so that's what they did. They set the bed close to the front window and as far away from the quilt divider as they could.

Emma and Mama washed the dishes and cleaned up. When it got dark, Mr. Moretz went to bed, but Mama and Mrs. Moretz sat in the kitchen talking, and Emma and Edgar went to the sitting room and did the same.

"Having you here is a real treat," Edgar said. "I just wish it had been for the wedding, not a funeral. I'm looking forward to the day when we can be together all the time."

"Does that mean you plan to ask me to marry you?"

"Yes. Haven't I made that clear? It's what I am working for. Will that be fine with you?"

"Oh, yes. It's what I want too."

"I'm guessing your father will not approve of you marrying for a while yet, since he thought you were too young to be courted. I need to earn some money and get us a place, anyway. The difficult time is going to be when I go to Meat Camp to work with Uncle Fritz, and I won't be able to see you for a time."

"We'll make it, Edgar. We weren't allowed to see each other for most of these last four months. We can write if there's a way to get the letters back and forth. Maybe we should write often and give the stack to each other when we can."

"I like the way you think, Emma." He leaned in close. "I hope you didn't mind that I told you about the cornfield and the rumors I heard about the liquor."

"No, of course not. I appreciate the information. There could very well be some truth in the rumors, and I'll be more aware of what may be going on now. I've seen no sign of anything out of the ordinary so far, and I keep praying nothing occurs. Don't ever hesitate to share anything and everything with me, Edgar. I see that as one of our greatest strengths as a couple."

"You're right. Communication and sharing is one of our strong points, but I think we have many."

They talked well into the night. When the clock struck twelve, Mama and Mrs. Moretz started to bed.

"I guess I'd better go too," Emma said. "We should get a little sleep before morning."

"You can eat breakfast with us, and I'll take you home sometime after that. Good night, Emma. I love you." He kissed her on the cheek.

"Good night, Edgar. Sleep well."

Emma felt sleepy and tired, but she still lay awake in the bed for a long time. She could tell Mama had already fallen asleep by her even breathing.

Edgar did seem to be doing well, considering the circumstance. Mrs. Moretz held more grief, but Emma believed she'd be okay.

Martin worried her, as he did Edgar. She sensed something wrong there, but she didn't know what to do about it, other than pray. She said her prayer and asked God to help them all, especially Martin. She thanked God for bringing her and Edgar together, for His love, and for the love she and Edgar shared. She asked for continued guidance so she and Edgar would always serve Him and glorify His name. She finally fell asleep.

"I'm going over and talk to Francie," Martin announced at breakfast. They all looked at him with surprised expressions.

"I'm going to take Emma and Mrs. Cagle home this morning," Edgar told him. "We can all go together."

"Why don't I just take them there?" Martin asked.

"Because I plan to stay with Emma for a while. Her father has given me permission to call."

"I'm not going to stay long," Martin said. "I'll just ride my horse over so I can come back when I get ready."

"If that's what you want," Edgar told him.

Martin left before Edgar and the Cagles. Mrs. Moretz insisted Mama take some of the food people had left, since it wouldn't keep much longer. They loaded it in the wagon, said their goodbyes, and got on their way.

"Please come again soon," Mrs. Moretz said. "The people here are so few and spread out that I don't usually see anyone, unless there's an itinerate preacher holding services, a wedding, or a funeral. I don't really have any close friends. I'm hoping you are my friend, and we can see more of each other."

"I'd really like that," Mama said and hugged Mrs. Moretz.

They met Martin riding home on their way. He certainly hadn't stayed long at all.

When they got to the Cagle cabin, unloaded the wagon, and sat down, Papa looked at Francie. "Are you going to tell them, or am I?" he asked.

Francie looked in her lap and said nothing. Papa sighed and shook his head. "Martin was just here. He wanted to talk with Francie, but he must not have had much to say, for it didn't take long. He asked her to marry him, and they came to me to ask my permission. I questioned them, but they both said this is what they wanted. I gave my permission, but I thought they would wait a while, past the mourning period, at least, but they're planning to marry real soon. I think that's a mistake."

Emma, Edgar, and Mama sat with their mouths open. Emma spoke first.

"Oh, Francie, this is not right. Martin is grieving so hard right now, and he's angry at God and the world. He's in no shape to marry or even to know what he wants." Emma shook her head. "This can't be a good time for you to make such an important decision either. Wait to get married. It's fine to be engaged, but give yourselves time and don't rush into a marriage you could live to regret. You and Martin don't really know each other. You've only seen each other twice, and one of those was at his brother's funeral."

"Emma's right, Francie," Edgar said. "Martin's in a bad state, and he's not capable of making any responsible decisions."

"I echo Emma's feelings, Francie," Mama said. "You're hurting now, and it's the wrong time to make such a life-changing decision."

Francie looked up, but she didn't look at anyone. "Nonetheless," she said with a stern voice, "it's what we plan to do. Martin plans to go to some of his relatives in Pennsylvania, and I'm going with him, as his wife."

Emma had never seen Francie like this. She had withdrawn, and didn't seem to care anymore. How could Emma get through to her?

"Why, Francie? Why are you doing this? You don't have to marry like this. There are plenty of men around here who would marry you. Remember the young man in Councill's Store who asked if he could come calling? You started seeing Luther instead, but I bet he's still interested. And the young man with the baby was desperately looking for a wife. He seemed nice, and I think he would appreciate you. You have other options. Give things some time."

"I have to get away, and that's all there is to it."

"Do you hate it here or dislike us so much that you have to leave?" Mama asked, obviously hurt.

"I don't like it here, but I love you and my sisters, Mama. I'm certain I'll miss you terribly."

Emma noticed Papa had an odd expression of pain. She supposed he would miss Francie if she left. She'd always seemed his favorite.

"Well, I need to go out and help Roy," he said and left.

"I need to get home," Edgar said. "If Martin has told my family the news, they will need me there."

"I'll get Hilda for you," Mama said. "I hear her in the loft playing with Christie."

Emma walked out with them. "I'll be back Sunday," Edgar told her. "We'll talk more then."

"Come and have dinner with us," Emma said.

"Are you sure that'll be all right with you mother?"

"I'm sure."

He kissed her cheek. With a doubly heavy heart, she watched him ride away on the wagon. She hated to see Edgar go, and she was deeply troubled about Francie and Martin.

When she went inside, she didn't see Francie. Something besides Luther's death seemed to be troubling Francie, but for the life of her, Emma couldn't guess what it might be.

"Leave her alone for a while," Mama said. "Give her a chance to think things out. You might try to talk calmly with her tonight when we go to bed, and I'll try it in the morning."

Emma nodded. That made sense. She would give Francie time to think and then talk with her.

CHAPTER SIX

Francie

Emma and Francie said little for the rest of the day. When they did talk, the conversations stuck to the tasks at hand.

That night Emma lay in the dark, wondering how to start and what to say. She prayed and asked for guidance, then rolled to face Francie and said, "Francie, you and I used to be so close. We were best friends as well as sisters. What's happened to us?"

"I guess the Moretzes happened."

"What does that mean?"

"I don't know. Edgar came into your life, and you've become so happy. It's obvious you two are deeply in love, and I'm left out."

"Oh, Francie. Just because I love Edgar, it doesn't mean I love you any less. I've missed our friendship. I'd love to be able to tell you about Edgar and our plans. I can share things with you that I can't share with anyone else."

"There's your religion too. I've seen how you read the Bible every day. I know you pray at times, even silently at the table like the Moretzes do out loud. It seems like I'm not only sharing you with Edgar, I'm sharing you with God too. There's no time left for me."

Francie was jealous? The notion seemed ridiculous to Emma, but that had to be part of the problem.

"I'm giving you time now," Emma told her sister. "Tell me how you feel about Martin. Tell me why you have to leave here."

There was a long pause, and Emma didn't think Francie planned to answer. She tried to think of some way to get Francie talking again.

"It's Papa," Francie finally said.

"Papa?"

"Papa's recently started brushing against me, so he feels me in inappropriate places. He cornered me against an outbuilding once, extended his arms on either side to pen me in, and started to kiss me on the lips, but I ducked under his arms and ran away. He didn't run after me." Francie took a tremulous breath. "I've got to get away, Emma. I can't take the chance of what might happen if I stay."

Emma lay there so stunned she couldn't say a word. Such an occurrence had never entered her mind, and she had a hard time accepting the possibility. This changed so much of how she saw Papa.

"The day he brought me home early from the funeral, I stayed close to Christie and Hilda until Papa left and went to help Uncle Roy out in the woods. I'm so glad Hilda came along, or I don't know what might have happened that night, because Uncle Roy is such a sound sleeper. When I asked to be taken home that day, I didn't know you and Mama were going to stay overnight."

Emma didn't know what to say. She'd never even considered the possibility of this.

"You don't believe me, do you." It was a statement rather than a question. "He's never bothered you, because you're not as developed as I am, and I'm the oldest."

"I would've expected this more if Papa was drinking again, but he's been sober since we've come here."

"Is that what you think?" Francie raised up and leaned on one elbow. "That might have been true when we first got here, but ever since the corn crop's been ready, he's been drinking. He hasn't gone on binges or got rolling down drunk like he used to, but he drinks some all during the day. He doesn't get as mean, but it still changes him. You haven't been close enough to smell his breath, have you? I almost wish he were drinking more than he is. At least then he'd be too intoxicated to harm me in that way."

Emma hadn't been close enough to Papa to smell his breath. If Edgar hadn't told her about the rumors, she might not have believed Francie. She didn't want to believe her now, but something deep inside her recognized it as truth.

"I am so sorry, Francie. I didn't have any idea. He hasn't already dishonored you, has he?"

"No, but I'm scared it's going to happen if I don't get away. I thought marrying Luther would fix it, but according to some things Papa has whispered recently, I'm thinking I'd better get as far away as possible."

"When did this start? Was he doing this before we came here?"

"No, it's just been for a few weeks. I'm guessing he was stepping out on Mama with other women before we left. Then we came here, and it was impossible for him to find any other women. I think that's why he's behaving this way. I'm available."

"Considering all this, I'm surprised Papa would allow you to marry."

"I was too, at first, but I think a part of him wants to do better, and that part wants me away so he won't hurt me. I think Papa is confused and battling himself."

"It does seem he has his demons, and he wants to drown them in alcohol. Does Martin know about this?"

"I didn't tell him all of it, but I told him Papa was drinking again, and I was afraid of him. He probably thinks Papa hits me like he's hit Mama. I feared if I told Martin everything, he'd think I'd already been spoiled and not want to marry me."

"Why did he say he wanted to marry you? He could go to Pennsylvania by himself. In fact, it might be easier to do so."

"He said he wanted to take care of me since I was Luther's fiancée. Luther had told Martin he really cared for me. Martin says the Bible says something about a man should marry his brother's widow, so he thinks that applies to me, to us."

"I don't think that applies to us today. At least, it's not done today. Romans 10:4 says, 'For Christ is the end of the law for righteousness to everyone that believeth.' Because Martin feels obligated certainly doesn't sound like a good reason to get married to me, and your running away isn't much better."

"Emma, that's because you know what love for a man is. I don't. I admit I cared more for Luther. He was nicer, friendlier, and easier to get to know than Martin is, especially now. I still hadn't begun to love Luther, though, not like a woman should love her husband, but I think I would have. I'm hoping things will get better with Martin once we're away from here. I don't see this as any different than an arranged marriage, which is really the way it's usually done, especially among the wealthy. I can't stay here and avoid Papa much longer. This is the best choice for me. I know it is. And, who knows? Maybe Martin and I will grow to love each other."

"I hope so, Francie. I really hope so." Emma scooted over to Francie's pallet. She pulled her sister into her arms and hugged her. Then, Francie's tears broke loose. She sobbed on Emma's shoulder, and Emma just held her.

"Thank you for listening to me and believing the things I told you," Francie said, when her tears were all cried out. "I wasn't sure you would. I do feel better now that I've told someone."

"Good." Emma released her and went back to her pallet. "You know God is waiting for you to come to Him too, Francie. I didn't know it, but He'd been waiting for me all the time."

"I've got too much on my mind right now. I'm not ready for that."

"God will help you sort out everything."

"I'll think about it. Christie has been asleep the whole time, hasn't she?"

"Yes, she has." Emma could tell Francie was just putting her off about God, but she hoped her sister would think about it soon.

"Good night."

"Good night, Francie. I'll be praying for you and Martin."

Francie and Christie were still asleep when Emma climbed from the sleeping loft the next morning. Uncle Roy had already rolled up his pallet, and he and Papa were out. She found Mama in the kitchen.

"You girls slept later than usual this morning, but I thought Francie, especially, probably needed her sleep. The rest of us have already had breakfast, so you can fix whatever you'd like."

"Francie and I stayed up talking last night. Is Papa drinking again? I know you've smelled him if he is."

Mama looked surprised. "Just a little. It's not as bad this time, not like it used to be. He's controlling himself better."

"Are he and Uncle Roy making and selling it?"

Mama frowned. "I don't know. I haven't asked. Why would you think so?"

"Edgar's heard rumors that Uncle Roy had been making it before we came."

"Oh, I see. Did you find out why Francie is marrying Martin right away? She's not expecting, is she?"

"No, Mama. Francie's still a virgin, but I understand why she's marrying Martin. I don't like it, but I understand, and her mind is made up."

"What's her reason?"

Emma bit her lip. "Don't ask me to answer that, Mama. Francie told me in secret, sister to sister. I can't break her confidence. She and Martin have talked, and they both want this. I really think Francie has a better reason than Martin, but he's twenty, and she's sixteen. They're old enough to choose for themselves."

"Do you really think it'll be okay?"

"I'm certainly going to pray that it will be."

"I'm still going to try to talk with Francie myself, but I'll pray too."

"And, when we pray, Mama, we need to trust God and leave it to Him."

"So, now my daughter is giving me advice about my faith?" But Mama said it with a pleased smile.

Emma kept a watch-out for Francie when Papa was around. It wasn't hard, because Papa spent more and more time out in the woods.

Sunday rolled around quicker than she expected. She woke up and immediately jumped out of bed to dress. Edgar would be here soon, and she couldn't wait.

She went down to help with breakfast. Then, she would help start dinner so that she would be free to sit with Edgar when he arrived.

Edgar came about ten o'clock. He brought Emma a basket of apples.

"I thought you might not have apple trees here, and our trees had plenty this year."

Emma gratefully accepted the basket. "Thank you. We have some walnuts and persimmons, but we don't have apples. We'll enjoy these." She sat them on the kitchen table. "Mama, I want to show Edgar a special place near the stream. May I take the Bible so we can have our Bible study together down there?"

Emma could tell Mama didn't know how to answer. It wasn't at all proper for her to be down in the woods with Edgar without a chaperone. She hoped Mama didn't suggest taking Christie, because she wanted to talk to Edgar about Francie and Martin. "It'll give you and Francie some special time together," she added.

"Why don't you take Christie with you, then?" Mama suggested.

"Christie went back to bed," Emma said. "She's not feeling well."

"You and Edgar go on then," Mama said, giving up. "I'll go up and check on Christie, and then Francie, and she and I can talk while we finish the chores."

Emma picked up her Bible, took Edgar's hand, and led him into the woods before Mama could change her mind. She noticed she'd worn a trail where she'd gone to her special place so often.

"Now, who's the crafty one?" Edgar asked.

She laughed. "I want to show you my favorite place here, and I do want to have our own worship time. But I need to talk to you in secret."

"I'm intrigued, to say the least."

It wasn't far to the log. They sat down and just rested in silence for a moment. The leaves were gorgeous. The fall colors were so much brighter here than below the mountains.

"This is pretty," Edgar said. "I like it here. It is so peaceful. Now, when we're apart, I can imagine you here. The first item from your day's agenda can be checked off. Which item is next?"

"Let's have our time of devotion." Emma read from where she'd left off in her Bible, and they discussed it when she'd finished. Edgar's clear understanding amazed her, and he explained his thoughts so well. She wished they could do this together more often.

"Let's sing a hymn," he suggested.

"I'm not very good at singing," Emma told him.

"You don't have to be. The Bible says to make a joyful noise to the Lord. Just sing along with me, and we'll make a joyful noise."

They sang, "All Hail the Power of Jesus' Name!" and "Come, Thou Almighty King." Edgar had a good voice and carried the tunes very well. He made it easier for Emma to follow his lead.

After the songs, Edgar led them in prayer. "I enjoyed this worship time," he said. "Maybe we can do this next Sunday."

"I'd like that," Emma said, "and I'd like to stay in the house sometimes. Mama would be glad to join us, and it would be a good way to witness to the rest of the family."

"I do love you so, Emma. I want to kiss you so badly right now, but I don't think it would be a good idea—not out here alone in the woods like this."

"I understand." She saw a look of disbelief on his face. "I really do. I'm not sure I'd trust myself either, and it's better not to give temptation a foothold."

He smiled in understanding. He seemed rather pleased she desired him enough to be tempted too.

"What's this secret you wanted to discuss with me?" he asked.

"First of all, I wanted to tell you why Martin asked Francie to marry him," and Emma proceeded to tell him that part of what Francie had told her.

"Martin's thinking is all warped," Edgar said. "He's become obsessed with Luther and trying to take care of the things he thinks Luther intended. If he doesn't have feelings for her, marrying his brother's fiancée because he thinks it's required of him seems a poor reason to get married. I don't think Martin has any feelings right now except for his grief and hurt, which consumes him."

"I told Francie it wasn't a good reason, but she wouldn't listen."

"Martin told Father and Mother he was leaving because he couldn't stand it around here with Luther dead. He said he'd even thought of killing himself in the same place where Luther died, and if he didn't get away, he was going to go mad. With him talking like that, they could hardly argue against his leaving."

"There's more," Emma said quietly. "Francie and I had a long talk last night. She confided in me why she wants to get married right away and go to Pennsylvania with Martin. Because she told me in confidence, and it's very private, I need to ask you first to promise not to tell anyone, not even Martin or your parents."

Edgar drew back with a frown. "Is this necessary, Emma? Don't you trust me?"

"I trust you, Edgar, and if it were my secret, I'd tell you right away. But this is Francie's secret. When I tell you what it is, I think you'll understand. Without promising, you might feel compelled to tell Martin."

"Is it something Martin should know?"

"He would probably like to know it, but I don't think it would alter the situation, and I think Francie should be the one to tell him."

"All right, then, I promise."

Emma told him all Francie had told her. At first Edgar's anger flared, and then he became worried.

"Are you sure she hasn't been molested?"

"I'm sure, but she's afraid it will happen if she doesn't leave soon."

"I can see why she'd want to get away, but what about you and Christie? You might not be safe either after Francie leaves."

"From what Francie said, I think Papa is drawn to her more. So far, Christie and I are slender. I don't think he'll bother us, but I'll still be cautious. If there is the least indication of inappropriate behavior, I'll come to you. If you're not at home, I'll go to your mother." Emma placed a hand on Edgar's arm. "I don't think we have anything to worry about. I speak up and take action more than Francie does. Papa knows that."

"You promise me this, Emma. You'll not wait, but you'll come immediately, if you become the least bit uncomfortable about the way he's acting."

"I promise. I'll take a mule and come immediately."

They went back to the house to find they were late for dinner. They'd stayed out longer than Emma had realized.

"The others have already eaten, but I waited for you," Mama said as they took their seats at the table.

"Was Papa upset we weren't here?" Emma asked, fearing he might take back his permission to court.

Mama shook her head as she placed bowls of stew on the table. "I don't think he noticed. Christie stayed in the loft since she's still not feeling well, and I think he assumed you were with her. I think he must have forgotten Edgar was coming, or else he didn't know it was Sunday."

Emma lowered her voice. "Is he having problems again, Mama?"

"More so than he has since we've been here." Mama's drawn face revealed her disappointment.

"Do you need help with anything, Mrs. Cagle? Is there anything I can do?"

"No, thank you, Edgar. Everything is fine."

"Well, please come to Mama or me if you ever do need any help."

"Thank you, I will."

"This is excellent rabbit stew, by the way," Edgar said, "and the cornbread is delicious."

"Emma fixed the cornbread and started the stew this morning. All I've done is stir it occasionally and finish everything."

Edgar leaned back with raised eyebrows. "I'm impressed. She's a great cook."

"Yes, she is, and she'll make someone a wonderful wife." Mama looked at Edgar and smiled.

Martin and Francie married on Sunday, just two weeks later. Everything had been readied for her marriage to Luther, so most of the preparations had already been made.

Since the Moretzes were in mourning, only the two families attended. The same pastor who'd held the funeral conducted the marriage. He'd made arrangements to hold his Sunday services later than usual. Emma got the feeling he thought Francie was already pregnant, which made sense, considering the rush.

The ceremony took little time. Afterwards, the couple put their few possessions in a covered farm wagon and left with a team of four horses. The wagon and horses were a wedding gift from Martin's family. Mr. and Mrs. Moretz had also given him enough money to see them to Pennsylvania. They planned to spend the night at an inn in Wilkesborough.

Mrs. Moretz didn't try to hide her tears as she hugged Martin and kissed him good-bye. Emma had heard her tell Mama she seemed to be losing her second son now.

Mama hugged Francie as if she wouldn't let her go. Francie had never told her the real reason she was leaving. She let Mama believe she didn't want to let a Moretz get away.

Emma tried to hide her tears, but they came anyway. "Write to me, Francie," she begged as she hugged her sister. "Please write and let me know how you are, and when I become an aunt. I'm going to miss you so much."

Emma feared Francie and Martin wouldn't be happy. Martin had never appeared overly happy, but now he seemed miserable all the time, even on his wedding day. She knew she needed to take her own advice and leave it with God. That was easier said than done, however, and she would need to work on it.

They all stood waving as the wagon pulled away. Edgar came up and put his arm around Emma's shoulders and led her away from the others.

"Emma, you are so beautiful, especially in that emerald dress. Coming home Sunday, I realized I'd never told you that. I wouldn't change a thing about you. I like it that you're slender."

Emma looked around. All the others had gone into the house for refreshments. "Kiss me, Edgar," she whispered.

He gently took her in his arms and began to kiss her just as gently. The kiss became much more as both their passions erupted. Emma held onto his upper arms to keep her legs from giving way. He automatically pulled her closer until they were almost molded together in one form. Emma didn't know if they would have ever separated, but the sound of a slamming door forced them to part. Breathless, Emma turned as Christie approached.

"Mama sent me to get you," Christie said. Emma nodded. "I had to slam the door to get you to notice," she added with a mischievous grin.

"Thank you, Christie," Edgar said.

Christie ran back toward the house but looked back to see if they were coming. She still looked rather pale and unhealthy.

"I needed your comfort," Emma told Edgar. "I feel alone, almost abandoned, since Francie left, but I had no idea kissing you would be so intense."

"Neither did I," he said with his eyes dancing. "I'm more certain than ever that you're the one for me."

They went back inside the cabin and ate some of the food that had been set out for the wedding. Then Papa announced they should be leaving.

"Let's all have a family prayer for Martin and Francine," Mrs. Moretz suggested.

"Roy and I will go hitch up the wagon," Papa said and left with his brother.

"Dear Heavenly Father," Mr. Moretz prayed, "we ask Thy protection for Martin and Francine as they travel to Pennsylvania. May their journey be easy and their way be smooth. Bless their marriage, we pray. They are beginning it with a heavy burden from our loved one's death. Grant that they may find love and happiness with each other and peace and comfort in Thee. Help each one here who loves them, to put them in Thy hands and trust in Thy care. We pray this in Jesus' name. Amen."

"Amen," the others said.

As Mama stayed a minute to say good-bye, and Christie remained with her, Edgar walked Emma out. They moved slowly, in no hurry to get to the wagon.

"Thank you for the kiss, Emma," Edgar whispered.

"I might not have invited it if I'd known how passionate it would become, but I enjoyed it," she whispered back.

"You're so special to me, Emma. I love you so."

Emma didn't get a chance to answer, because her family suddenly stood close by.

CHAPTER SEVEN

Papa

Monday seemed strange without Francie. They all missed her.

Emma found herself also worried about Christie. She didn't eat enough to keep a gnat alive, and her color had turned pallid. She said she felt fine. She did seem to have enough energy, but Emma couldn't help being concerned.

Papa and Roy left around mid-morning and didn't return for dinner or supper. Emma hoped they returned soon. Papa only stayed out late at night when he'd drunk too much liquor. Emma could tell Mama had similar thoughts, and she looked worried.

Papa didn't come home until late Wednesday. Even then, Uncle Roy had to drag him into the cabin.

"Les'er jes' can't hol' his liquor," Roy said, stumbling across the threshold. "Course, as much as he drunk, don't guess mosta us could." He laughed as if he thought he'd told the funniest joke.

Emma recoiled. They both reeked of alcohol, urine, and sweat. Roy and Mama put Papa on the bed. He lay there passed out.

"Guess I need ta git my pally, don' I, purty woman," Roy said to Mama. He wasn't as drunk as Papa, but he looked plenty drunk all the same.

"Why don't you just lay down beside Lester? I'll sleep in the loft with the girls tonight," Mama told him.

"Dat's right nice a ya. Dat's swat ya are. Ye're a nice woman."

"What are we going to do, Mama?" Emma asked. "We can't keep going through this again and again. You know Papa will be mean in the morning with his hangover, and you know the drinking will only get worse."

"I don't know what to do, Emma." Mama sounded so tired and defeated. "I'm going to pray about it. That's what I'm going to do."

"Me too, Mama." They shared a hug.

The next morning, Mama, Emma, and Christie tiptoed around, trying to delay Papa's waking as long as possible. They ate bread and preserves for breakfast and drank water to keep from making much noise. After breakfast, they went outside to gather walnuts and persimmons.

They had worked for a good while when they heard Papa bellow. He cursed profusely and hollered for Mama.

"Don't pay his foul language any mind," she told them. "Just filter the words out like he didn't even say them. Take Christie and stay away for a time," she told Emma.

"But you shouldn't be in there with him alone."

"There's nothing you can do to help, Emma. He's going to do what he's going to do. You go on now so I won't have to worry about him hurting you and Christie."

"I'll be praying for you, Mama," Emma said as she clutched at her shawl, grabbed Christie's hand, and ran to the woods.

"Get in here, woman, and get me some coffee made, and make it quick!" she heard Papa yell. "You are totally worthless or you'd already have it made. You good for nothing . . ."

The voices were finally out of range, and the girls were out of sight. They stopped running and began to walk slowly.

"Where are we going?" Christie asked.

"I don't know, but we're going to have a fun day in the woods. Here, hold your shawl around you. It's cool today, especially here in the shade."

Emma set out to entertain Christie. She found a mossy area, and they built a little playhouse interior using the moss and sticks. They made chairs, beds, and tables. They found twigs and broke them to look like stick figures, dressed them in a leaf, and played for a long time. Emma felt too old to be playing like this, but it provided a good diversion, and Christie certainly enjoyed it.

"Can we come back here and play with the moss house again sometime?" Christie asked.

"Sure, we can."

They found a sunny spot and sat on huge rocks. Emma told stories of kings, queens, princes, princesses, and knights who fought dragons, saved kingdoms, married the one of their dreams, and lived happily ever after.

"Is that what's going to happen to Francie?" Christie asked.

"Of course it is," Emma answered because that's what Christie wanted to hear, and they both knew this was a day for make-believe.

They found a persimmon tree and scared an ugly possum away. They ate persimmons from the ground for dinner. They were sweet and juicy from the early frost.

Emma taught Christie to skip rocks across the widest part of the stream. She showed her how to hold a blade of grass taut against the base of her hands and blow to make a shrill whistle. They cut sassafras twigs and chewed them for their flavor.

"Winter will be here soon, and we'll start your lessons again," Emma reminded her sister.

"Will you teach me?"

"Would you prefer Mama or me?"

"I like you because you make the lessons fun."

"Then that's how it'll be."

They walked around observing the trees and wildlife, and Emma shared what information she could think of about what they saw. When Emma judged it to be about four o'clock from the position of the sun, they started home.

"Thank you for today," Christie said, "I did have fun."

"I had fun too, Christie. When we get home, if Papa is upset, you go directly up to the sleeping loft. Say you're tired or not feeling well, whichever is true. I'll bring you up some supper as soon as I can."

"Okay."

"Les and Roy went out again," Mama said as soon as she saw them. "I feared you might run into them." Mama was keeping the left side of her face turned away from her daughters.

"We didn't. Did he hit you again, Mama?"

"I guess it was silly of me to try to hide it." She turned and faced them. Her eye and cheek had already turned a deep purple. They looked black and so swollen Emma felt sure she couldn't see out of that eye. It would likely be completely closed by morning.

"Mama, we've got to do something. I'm afraid he's going to hurt you bad or even kill you sometime. Did he hurt you any other way?"

Mama looked down.

"Mama!"

"He tore my dress almost off," she said, barely above a whisper. "That's when Roy told him they needed to check the still and took him out."

"If they went there, he'll be worse when he gets back. You know he gets worse with each successive drunk spell he pulls. We've got to get out of here."

"There's nowhere to go."

"We'll go to the Moretz's place."

"No, I can't let them know about this. What would they think of us?"

"They'll think we're smart not to stay here, and they'll show us loving kindness."

"I can't let them know how bad things are."

Emma's frustration broke through. "Mama, Edgar already knows. I told him the first time I met him, when it appeared he might be interested in me. He's made me promise to come to him if things ever got bad, and I'm going to keep that promise. I'm going to take a mule and go to the Moretz's."

"Soon it's going to be too dark to ride up the mountain."

"Okay, then. I'll leave at daybreak, before Uncle Roy and Papa return. Will you come?"

"No. I'd better stay here."

"Are you coming with me or staying here, Christie?"

"Leave her," Mama said. "She can stay in the loft if need be."

Emma could tell Christie felt torn. "I guess I'll stay here," she finally said. "I'm afraid of riding up that mountain on a mule."

Christie hung her head. Emma thought she saw her tremble, so she just nodded. They ate supper and went to bed early.

Emma didn't sleep well at all. She must have awakened twenty times or more.

She finally turned over and realized the cabin had begun to lighten just a little. She picked up the shoes Uncle Roy had bought her for Francie's wedding before she eased down the ladder. The mornings and evenings were already too cold to go barefooted. She just hated the thought that corn liquor must have paid for the shoes.

She didn't feel hungry, so she skipped breakfast. She would have loved to have something hot to drink, but she didn't want to take the time to make it.

She put on her shoes and took two shawls from the peg. It felt cold this morning. A light frost sprinkled across the darkening multicolored leaves on the trees and lay like sugar sprinkled across the brown ones on the ground.

Emma took the least stubborn mule and put the bridle Roy had fashioned on it. They didn't have a saddle, so she would've liked a blanket to sit on, but she felt sure it would slide off and her with it, especially on the steepest part of the mountain.

She mounted the animal. She couldn't get in a comfortable position, but she could manage. She kicked the animal lightly, and it took off at a good pace.

On the steep part of the mountain, sitting on the mule did become too uncomfortable, and Emma felt like she might slide off. When the mule's breathing became heavier, she got off and walked. After she led the mule over the crest, she stopped to rest and let them both catch their breaths.

The sun still hung behind the clouds, but it wasn't foggy, and Emma had an incredible view of the valley below with the fall colors. The hues were beginning to dull, but the scene still took her breath away. Strange how God seemed so close at such moments.

She crawled up on the mule again and continued her ride. When she rode up to the cabin, Edgar came running, and she slid off the mule.

"Your father?" he asked.

She nodded.

"Did he hurt you?"

"No, I'm fine. He just passed out drunk, and when he came to, he hit Mama and ripped her dress. I'd taken Christie into the woods to keep away from him. He's gone back out now and won't be home for a while, but I wanted to get away while I had the chance. Mama wouldn't come with me. He's going to be even meaner when he gets back this time."

"Come on. Let's go tell my folks and decide what to do."

When Emma explained to Edgar's parents what had happened and answered their questions, they prayed about what to do. Emma liked the way they asked God for guidance for all their problems.

"We need to get Kathleen and Christie to come stay with us," Mrs. Moretz said.

"What will we do if she won't come?" Mr. Moretz asked. "After all, she wouldn't leave with Emma."

"Could we stay there to protect her?" Edgar asked.

"I'm not sure it would look right for us to stay there with Mrs. Cagle if her husband's out," Mr. Moretz said, "not unless your mama comes."

"When Papa comes home, it will be late in the day, and he'll be so drunk he can't stand up. He'll sleep it off until sometime up in the morning. When he wakes up, he will be mean and terrorize everyone around him."

"What are you saying, Emma?" Edgar asked.

"There's no use to go today. He won't be a problem until late tomorrow morning at the earliest. More than likely, he won't be home until tomorrow night, and we could wait until the morning after that to go. Of course, he could be gone three days, but it's never been longer than that."

"You're saying *we*," Edgar said to Emma, "but I don't want you to go back with us. If there's trouble, I don't want you there."

"If you're there when he wakes up," Emma said, "there will very likely be trouble. He'll be in a foul mood, so maybe I shouldn't have come here at all. It would be my fault if one of you got hurt."

"No it wouldn't," Mr. Moretz said. "It would be Lester's fault. You did the right thing by coming here. It's too dangerous for you to stay. Now, we've got to figure out the best way to get your mother and sister out. Will Roy be a problem?"

"I don't know. He isn't mean like Papa when he gets drunk, but he might try to help Papa out."

"How many guns do they have?" Mr. Moretz asked.

"Two, and also hunting knives."

"What are the rest of you thinking?" Mr. Moretz looked at his wife and son.

"Based on what Emma told us, I'd say wait until tomorrow to go," Edgar said.

"What if he isn't home then?" Emma asked.

"We'll wait until he comes," Mr. Moretz said.

"We could be stuck there, then," Edgar said. "It would be too dark to come back up the mountain."

"Will your mama be concerned if we stay there overnight?" Mr. Moretz asked Emma.

"No, sir. I'm sure she trusts you and Edgar, but wouldn't it be better if I also went? I've lived through many of Papa's drunks. I know how to keep out of his way and what to say. Christie, Mama, and I will sleep up in the loft. We'll be out of the way. In the morning, we can go outside and leave you to watch until Papa wakes up."

"That does make sense, Edgar. After all, we'll be there."

"I sure do wish Luther and Martin were here to help us out," Edgar said.

"I do too, son, but surely we will be able to handle two drunk men."

"I think I may have a better idea," Mrs. Moretz said. "Why don't we all go right now? I'll talk to Kathleen privately. I think I can get her to come back here with us. That would make everything easier, wouldn't it?"

"Yes, it would," Mr. Moretz said, "but are you sure you can convince her to come?"

"I think so, but if I can't, you can bring us back today and go back to your original plan of taking Emma and going back later."

"It sounds like it's worth a try," Edgar said. "I think Mama can do this. At least this way, we won't be around here worrying about it all day."

Edgar and his father went out to hitch up the wagon. Mrs. Moretz threw some food in a bag in case they needed it for dinner. They were in the wagon and ready to go in less than thirty minutes.

"We don't have a covered wagon anymore, but this will do," Mr. Moretz said. "We are short on horses, but this pair will be fine, since we won't be hauling much. We'll tie your mule to the back."

The wagon looked much newer and nicer than the one Papa had driven up the mountain. Emma knew Martin and Francie had taken the covered wagon and four of the horses with them.

"I had hoped to wait and buy more horses in the spring when the grass is in." Mr. Moretz added. "That way, we won't have to feed them over the winter."

Nothing happened to impede the trip down the mountain. Hilda and Edgar's parents sat up front. Emma and Edgar sat on the quilt in the back, and the mule walked along behind.

"I'm proud you came right away when you saw there'd been trouble," Edgar told her.

"I feel as if Papa might kill Mama if he doesn't stop this cycle. Coming to you was the best thing I could think to do."

"I hope you'll always come to me with your problems, Emma, whether they are little or big."

"I think I've done a pretty good job of that so far. I tell you everything. You've become my best friend and my only one since Francie left."

"You're my best friend too. I'll be glad when we're married so we can be best friends *and* husband and wife."

"What are you saying back there?" Mr. Moretz asked Edgar. "Are you teasing Emma again? It's hard to hear over the noise from the wagon. I don't see how you put up with him, Emma. He's always been the pest in the family."

"He wasn't teasing me this time. I think he was serious."

"I was indeed," Edgar said.

"Were you thinking about the kiss?" Emma whispered.

"Yes, I think about it all the time. I can't get it off my mind. I wish I could kiss you again right now."

"If it's anything like the first one, your parents might have a hard time getting us apart."

"If we wouldn't be in such big trouble, that sounds wonderful."

"I'll admit, you've had a positive effect on our boy, Emma," Mr. Moretz said. "He's not nearly the prankster or tease he used to be. He finally seems to be settling down."

"I rather like his teasing."

Mr. Moretz laughed. "No wonder you two get along so well, then."

They stopped and ate dinner after they got down the mountain. Mrs. Moretz had even packed some cherry cider. They ate quickly and were soon on the way again.

"I'll go in and tell Mama you're here," Emma told Mrs. Moretz. "That way I can make sure Papa's not here, but I don't think he will be."

"Don't tarry," Edgar said as he helped her out of the wagon, "or we'll get worried there's trouble and come in after you."

Only Mama and Christie were there. When Emma told Mama about the Moretzes, she could tell her mother had mixed feelings.

"Oh, Emma, I wish you hadn't brought them here. You know I didn't want to face them."

"Mama, you've done nothing to be ashamed of. They just want to help."

"I appreciate their concern, but it puts me in an embarrassing situation. Go ahead and tell Eleanor to come on in, I guess. What else can we do?"

Emma hurried back to the others and took Christie with her. "Mama said to come on in, Mrs. Moretz."

Mr. Moretz got out of the wagon and helped his wife and Hilda down. Mrs. Moretz quickly went inside.

"Why don't you go show Hilda our chickens and see if there are any eggs today?" Emma told her sister.

The adults followed along slowly to stretch their legs and give the two mothers the chance to talk in private. They took the mule back to the barn, and Emma noticed the day had turned warm for October.

"Is that all the wood your uncle and father have cut for winter?" Edgar asked as he looked at the stack of wood against the back of the house.

"That's it," Emma said. It looked like a large amount to her. "They haven't cut much since they harvested the corn."

"That won't last long when the cold weather hits," Mr. Moretz said. Emma saw him also looking at the crumbling chinking between the logs, but he didn't say anything about it. "Does the roof leak?" he did ask.

"No, sir." Emma realized they were concerned the cabin wasn't prepared for winter. She guessed that was true, since it seemed Uncle Roy had let things go before they arrived, and no repairs had been made over the summer. She didn't know what the winters were like here, but from the way everyone talked, they must be really harsh.

"Do you see many bears, mountain lions, or wildcats living in the woods like this?" Mr. Moretz asked.

"More wildcats than anything else. I saw a bear one day back in early summer, but it wasn't close, and it left in the other direction.

I've heard some mountain lions at night, but I've never seen one. I try to be careful and watchful when I'm out."

"Can you shoot?" Edgar asked.

"No. None of us girls can. Papa and Uncle Roy usually carry the guns anyway."

"I'll teach you. You need to learn to shoot because this land can be pretty wild and untamed."

Mrs. Moretz stayed in the cabin for about thirty minutes. Emma began to think her mother must be refusing to leave again, but she came out with Mrs. Moretz, and she carried a flour sack with their clothes in it.

"We didn't leave a note," Mrs. Moretz said. "Kathleen said neither man could read, anyway."

Edgar recoiled when he saw Mama's face. He put his arm around Emma's shoulders and gave her a quick squeeze.

They all climbed into the wagon again and headed back toward the road up the mountain and to the Moretz's place. It was time to start supper when they got back.

Emma and Mama had them pull out one of the beds for Edgar again. The three of them could sleep in the one bed fine.

That night Emma couldn't get her mind off Edgar sleeping just yards away. He must have had similar thoughts, because she heard him tossing and turning until she went to sleep. At last fatigue had pulled her into a sleep disturbed by dreams of rants, ravings, and beatings.

Their days fell into a routine quickly. Emma and Mrs. Moretz cooked breakfast, and Mama and Christie would wash the dishes afterward. The men would work outside all morning, while the women did household chores and cooked dinner. After they ate, the men would work outside again, and the women would continue with their morning work, or else they would mend, sew, or do some extra chores. After supper, they held a family devotion and prayer. In the evening they sewed, read, played checkers, or talked.

When Emma found the Moretzes had a few books, and she hadn't read any of them, she couldn't contain her excitement. Only on a few occasions had she ever been able to borrow a book to read after her few months of tutoring. Edgar remembered them all, and they often discussed parts as Emma read.

A week after the Cagle women had come, Papa and Uncle Roy showed up, and they looked sober.

"Don't agree to go back right away," Emma told Mama before she went out. "Don't make it so easy for him. Tell him he has to stay sober for a while, but let him come by here some so you can tell if he is."

Mama hesitated but nodded. Emma knew from experience that Papa would try to cajole Mama into doing whatever he wanted. He would act as if he were so sorry about the way he had acted and promise he'd never do such a thing again. Then, in a few days, he would repeat the drinking and abuse.

Emma went out to stand in the yard where she could hear what they said, but she stood back so she wouldn't be part of the conversation. Papa would want this to be just between him and Mama.

The swelling in Mama's face had gone down a lot, but it was still pretty discolored with a rainbow of colors, especially purple, green, and yellow. Roy flinched and looked away. He stayed in the wagon seat, while Papa jumped down to stand beside Mama.

"I am so sorry, Kathleen." He tenderly touched the side of her face where it wasn't bruised so much. "I didn't know what I was doing."

Mama didn't say anything right away. Emma knew she was gauging how long Papa had been sober, and how much she could say.

"You shouldn't drink, if it makes you unaware of what you're doing and makes you do hurtful things."

"I know. That's why I'm never going to touch the stuff ever again. I was worried to death when I came back and found you gone. You've never left me before. Roy and I thought and thought where you might be, but with the wagon and mules still there, we figured you must have had help, and the Moretzes came to mind. Are you ready to come home, sweetheart? I miss you so much. Please come back to me."

Papa was doing a good job of being convincing. He always did.

Mama hesitated again. She looked back at Emma, and Emma didn't change her scowl. She knew if she smiled, Mama would take that as a sign to say "yes."

"I need you to prove to me you've changed," Mama told him. "You need to stay sober a month before I'll come back."

"Did Emma tell you not to come back? That girl's got too much backbone for her own good sometimes. Come here, girl."

"No, Emma didn't tell me to never come back," Mama said, as Emma went to them.

Papa didn't seem to notice the slight change in wording. He relaxed a little and smiled at Emma.

"It's good to see you, Emma."

Emma smiled back, but she didn't say anything. She wasn't particularly glad to see him right now.

"I've already been sober almost a week," Papa said. Emma doubted that. A couple of days at most would be her guess.

"Then, you stay sober another three weeks," Mama said. "You come by every Wednesday and Saturday and let me see you so I'll know how you're doing."

Good for Mama. She stood straight and tall, as if she refused to bend on this. Since Saturdays were Papa's big bingeing days, Mama's request had also been smart.

"Can Roy and I come for dinner? Meals are pretty scant affairs without my women."

"Run ask Mrs. Moretz if that will be okay, Emma."

Emma did, and Mrs. Moretz agreed—as long as Papa wasn't drinking. Emma breathed a prayer of thanks, surprised by how well things were working out. God surely did answer prayers.

"You and Roy go hunting and bring us some game you kill to help out." Mama said. "I would also like you to chink the cabin and cut more wood for winter. You should see how much wood the Moretzes have cut. There's a woodshed full. It's piled against the outside walls, and it's stacked high against the back of the cabin."

"It would've been better if we had chinked the cabin before cool weather set in, but you're right. Both need doing, and we'll get right on it. It'll keep us busy for the three weeks, that's for sure. But, I want you back, Kathleen. I'd do just about anything to get you back. I know I really messed up. Will you forgive me?"

Mama smiled at him for the first time. "Of course, I'll forgive you, Les, but we'll see if I can come back or not by the way you behave."

Emma felt so proud of Mama! She turned to see Edgar and Mr. Moretz standing near the back corner of the cabin, watching. Mrs. Moretz had also been looking out the front window. They'd all been nearby in case they were needed.

"Well, I'll see you Wednesday for supper," Papa said. "You tell Christie I'll see her then." Papa reached out, pulled Mama to himself, and kissed her tenderly. Emma realized he might actually convince himself he was going to do better each time, until the desire for liquor overpowered him again. What a sad way to live.

CHAPTER EIGHT

Surprises

When Papa came on Wednesday afternoon, he brought Mama a little bag of candy. He acted almost as if he thought he should court her again. Emma hid her smile.

"I'd have rather brought you flowers," he told Mama, "but there was none to be had at this time of year. Roy and I also cut a cord of wood and chinked two walls of the cabin. We'll get to the rest of it this coming week." In addition, he brought Mrs. Moretz six squirrels he and Roy had shot and cleaned that day.

Papa remained on his best behavior at supper. Emma could almost understand what Mama had seen in him in the first place. Of course, she hadn't known then how mean he got when he was coming out of a drunk spell or what a problem his drinking would become.

She looked over at Edgar and knew even he could change. No one knew what might happen in the future. That was the problem with people. You never knew when something might happen to change them. It could be for the worse or for the better. That's why everything should be turned over to God. Only God remained constant and would never change. Why didn't more people realize that?

Papa and Uncle Roy stayed a spell after the meal. They left early in the afternoon, however, so they could make it down the mountain and home before dark.

It had begun getting dark earlier now, and the nights were already cold. There'd been several heavy frosts, and cold winds had blown most of the leaves off the trees.

"That went well, didn't it?" Mama said to Emma. Emma could tell she was pleased with how things were going, and that Papa had actually courted her. It made Mama feel valued for a change.

Things continued to run on the same smooth road through the next weeks. Papa and Roy came every Wednesday and Saturday. Papa would bring Mama some little gift, maybe a length of ribbon or a special treat. He'd also bring some meat he'd hunted for Mrs. Moretz and report on what he and Roy had accomplished around the cabin.

Uncle Roy usually came with Papa, and Emma felt sure it had a lot to do with the meal they ate. Mrs. Moretz did set a good table.

Emma helped Mrs. Moretz with the chores, but she and Edgar also spent as much time together as they could. They would take strolls around the farm, always staying within sight of anyone who might care to look. They played checkers, discussed the book Emma was reading, and talked, laughed, and teased.

"Emma seems more like Edgar than Hilda does," Mrs. Moretz laughed one Sunday. "I've never seen two strangers more natured like each other."

"Are you saying they act like brother and sister?" Mr. Moretz asked.

"I guess they do."

Emma and Edgar looked at each other, remembered the kiss, and burst out laughing.

"I take it you two don't agree?" Mr. Moretz asked. They were laughing so hard all they could do was shake their heads.

The days passed too quickly for Emma. Near the end of October, Papa would come to get them. She toyed with the idea of staying with the Moretzes, but it didn't seem like the right thing to do, although she would have loved to continue to see Edgar every day. Besides, she couldn't see Papa allowing it, but she felt blessed to have had this special time with Edgar. God had used a bad situation for some good.

Edgar took Emma, Christie, and Hilda on a picnic the Sunday before Emma left. She knew he was doing it so the two of them could spend some special time together and still not be alone and unchaperoned.

Christie and Hilda had become even better friends over the last three weeks. Emma felt glad, because Christie needed to have a good friend nearer her own age. Emma noticed that her sister seemed to be feeling better, but she still hadn't regained her full strength.

The Sunday began cold and frosty, but the sun came out early, and by mid-morning Emma could tell it was going to warm up nicely for the time of year.

Edgar drove the wagon, and they took quilts, just in case it became colder. They packed a basket of food and a jug of cherry cider. They also took their Bibles so they could do their Sunday Bible study before they ate.

Edgar went part of the way up a taller mountain. He stopped in a clear spot, and they spread the quilt. As they usually did during their Sunday worship time, Emma read the Bible verses, they discussed them, sang some hymns, and Edgar closed in prayer. Christie and Hilda listened, asked a couple of questions during the discussion, and sang along on the songs they knew.

They ate dinner and sat for a while afterwards just talking. No one mentioned Emma and Christie leaving, but it lay heavy on everyone's mind.

Edgar helped them into the wagon, and they went to the top of the mountain. Emma shivered from the change in temperature and the brisk wind.

Edgar put his arm around Emma and pulled her close to help keep her warm. The view was spectacular, but the cold bit so hard they didn't stay long.

They started back down slowly, not wanting the day to end. Christie and Hilda got into the back of the wagon, wrapped themselves in quilts, and laughed and giggled for a while but soon fell asleep. Emma pulled out a quilt as well and wrapped it around her and Edgar. He pulled her close, and she put her head on his shoulder.

"I wish we didn't have to be apart again," she told him.

"So do I, but I also need to go to Meat Camp. I should have left along the first of September, but I wanted to wait until after the wedding. Then, you came, and I decided to stay home longer."

"When are you leaving?"

"Tomorrow, after you do."

"So I won't even get to see you on Sundays for a while." Emma said.

Edgar looked down at her tenderly. "I'm planning on seeing you this Sunday, anyway. The mill runs only half a day on Saturday morning. I'm going to come home afterwards. I can come to see you Sunday morning, leave right after dinner, and go back to be at work on Monday. I'm not going to be able to do that every week, but I'll see what it's like and decide how often."

"Thank you for that, Edgar. At least I can look forward to this Sunday. I think I'll miss you even more this week, after seeing you every day lately."

"I'll miss you just as much."

"I doubt that. You'll be busy working."

"Don't forget, I'll be working for us."

Edgar stopped the wagon just before they came in sight of the cabin. They stayed on the wagon seat, huddled in the quilt.

"Emma, I'm going to ask you to be my wife now." He looked at her intently. "It will be our secret until you tell me I can approach your father and ask him for your hand. Will you promise to marry me, darling Emma?"

"Oh, yes. I'll promise to marry you just as soon as we're able."

He turned to face her and took her in his arms. He kissed her so thoroughly, time ceased to exist. She felt her body go weak and melt into him. When he finally pulled his lips away, she realized she had an ache for him deep within her core, and it radiated out into every inch of her.

"My, oh my," he whispered. He sat for a few minutes, just holding her hand beneath the quilt and staring out in front of him. He almost seemed to be fighting a battle within himself. "I never imagined the need for you could be so strong," he finally said. He looked at her again. "These kisses make waiting much too difficult." He smiled at her, and she knew he had conquered whatever forces had been at play.

"I love you so much," she told him.

"I love you too, Emma. Indeed I do."

They went back to the house and helped Christie and Hilda down from the wagon. The girls carried the food basket and jug into the house.

"Come to the barn and help me unhitch the horses," Edgar said to Emma. She went willingly. He took care of the horses while she folded the quilts from the wagon. He took the quilts from her to carry them back to the house.

"Would you let me do more than just kiss you, Emma?" he whispered to her as they walked toward the cabin.

Emma wanted to ask exactly what he meant by "more," but she was afraid of what his answer might be. Was he asking her to do things God wanted them to save for marriage? She stopped, looked into his eyes, and saw nothing but love and caring. She trusted this man, so she answered him as truthfully as she knew how.

"I don't think so, but I'm not completely sure. I wouldn't now, but in the middle of kissing you, I'm not so sure. I seem to lose myself and turn into mush."

He smiled then and kissed her forehead. "Our kisses affect me until I lose my head. I'm thinking we'd better save our kisses until the day we get married. But, I'm glad you have such passion for me, Emma. We're going to have a spectacular marriage."

Monday morning Papa came earlier than Emma had hoped. He must have left at first light. It didn't take them long to put their few things in the wagon.

They said their thank-yous and good-byes. Edgar hugged Emma and kissed her on the cheek. Emma felt Papa's stare, but he said nothing.

"I'm sure glad to be taking you home," he told Mama.

"I'm glad, myself," she said, and he smiled.

The repairs on the cabin looked good. Roy was waiting for them inside.

"Welcome home," he said. "Lester doesn't cook much better than I do. Without Wednesday and Saturday meals, I think we would have wasted away." He laughed. "I got you a welcome-home surprise. I bought us a milk cow. I got her at a good price since winter's setting in and she'll have to be fed, but we still have some corn fodder and such."

"Oh, thank you!" Mama said. "Milk and butter will be a big help. The grease I've been using for seasoning just doesn't taste as good in everything."

The men had killed a deer. They had its hide stretched and had salted down much of the meat. Mama started a venison stew for supper. Mrs. Moretz had sent chicken and dumplings for dinner.

The week dragged by for Emma. She missed Edgar with a longing that felt like an illness. The fact she knew he had gone to Meat Camp made the missing worse, although she didn't really understand it. If Edgar had been home, they still wouldn't have seen each other until Sunday.

Finally, Sunday arrived. Edgar arrived earlier than she'd imagined. She ran out to meet him as he got off his horse. He took her in his arms and twirled her around.

"Oh, Emma, my Emma. How I've missed you. I left a little before dawn when I saw there was a full moon, and the sky was clear."

"You have a new horse."

"Yes, I needed one to come to and from Meat Camp. Father got this mare for a good price. I think I'm going to like her."

They went inside, and she poured him a cup of coffee and fixed him some eggs for breakfast. The others had already eaten.

"How is the job?"

"It's different, and I stay very busy. I'm glad to have the job, but I must say I prefer farming to milling."

They sat around the kitchen table and had their worship. Mama and Christie joined them. Papa and Roy were out hunting and planned to stay out until dinnertime.

Edgar asked her about the book she was reading. She had brought one of his back with her. They discussed it, and Edgar sat at the kitchen table while she finished cooking dinner.

Emma had planned a special dinner. She'd soaked some venison strips in apple cider vinegar and water to get out the gamey taste, tenderized the meat by beating it, and slowly simmered it in a pan until tender. Then, she took it up, made gravy, and put it back in the gravy. She stewed potatoes and carrots together, added butter, and made biscuits. For dessert, she'd made an apple cobbler.

When they sat down to eat, Edgar asked for permission to say grace. Mama gave it, since Papa didn't say anything.

"This is an excellent meal," Edgar said as they began to eat. "I don't think I've ever tasted better venison."

"I don't know about that," Emma said. "Your mama's an excellent cook."

"This is scrumptious," Uncle Roy agreed. "You outdid yourself, girl. I don't know what you did to this deer meat, but it's mouth-watering good."

"Well, thank you, all." Emma beamed with pleasure.

After dinner, it was time for Edgar to head back to Meat Camp. The time had seemed so short Emma felt like crying.

"I'll come again in two weeks," he said, "if the weather holds. I'm afraid November and December may get too cold or snowy. If I get held there anytime, I'll write, if I think I can get the letter to you before I can come again."

She walked him to his horse. He took her in his arms and just held her for a long time. She stood savoring the feel of him. He brushed his lips quickly across hers before he mounted. He reached down from the horse, took her hand in his, and squeezed it before he released it and rode away. They didn't need to say "I love you." They knew.

Things passed in the same vein for the next weeks. Emma felt half herself from missing Edgar. She did her chores, read her Bible, prayed, and knew God was with her, but she didn't feel truly happy until she had Edgar near her.

He came every other Sunday. There'd been cold rains, some light snow, and even some sleet, but never on their Sunday. Every other Sunday had always been clear, even if it had sometimes been cold and windy. That changed on December third.

It started snowing Saturday morning. Soon the howling wind turned it into a blizzard. Everyone huddled in the cabin, but even with the repairs, the house felt drafty, and the fireplace couldn't warm them unless they sat directly in front of it.

Emma and Christie brought their pallets downstairs and placed them on the other side of the table. Emma planned to get up through the night to add logs to the fire.

Uncle Roy had his pallet on the other side of the cabin. Emma didn't worry about him as she did Papa. Papa had never tried to bother her or ever looked at her oddly, but she knew what he'd been like with Francie, so she tried to be cautious.

Emma prayed Edgar had not tried to come home. She knew he tended to be as desperate to see her as she was to see him, and she feared for his safety.

Sunday, everything outside had heavy layers of white. It looked like a different place, a whole new, frosty world. When Papa went out to bring in some wood, he said everything had frozen solid, and the snow clung so thick and slick he had to stomp his feet for an indention to help him walk. At least the wind had died down, but he thought the temperature must be close to zero and maybe below.

Uncle Roy chiseled out some icy hunks from the frozen snow and carried them inside in buckets to melt for water. It had become too difficult to get to the creek, and the water there might be frozen anyway.

"I'd like to go out and play in the snow," Christie said.

"No, darling," Mama told her. "This snow is too frozen to play in, and the weather's too cold to get out."

Edgar didn't come, and Emma prayed he had remained in Meat Camp. Had time ever moved this slowly? She read some from her Bible and the book she had borrowed. She and Mama mended some clothes and made a stew, but the day still crept by slower than a snail's pace. Why didn't time move this slowly when Edgar visited?

It snowed again Monday, but this snow was light and fluffy, and no wind pushed behind it to form a blizzard. The flakes were huge, though. By Tuesday morning, the snow piled so high that Papa and Uncle Roy had to work to get the door opened enough to get out, even with the porch there. Emma guessed the snow had drifted in the night, because she had heard some wind then. The men finally worked the door open so they could get more wood, milk the cow, and feed the two mules and chickens.

It stayed cold through Wednesday, and Emma feared Edgar wouldn't get to come this Sunday, either. Thursday turned warmer, however, and some of the snow began to melt around noon. Everything froze back overnight, but Friday was even warmer, and Emma began to have hope.

Sure enough, the warmer days melted much of the snow, leaving only patches here and there along with the mud. Edgar came about ten o'clock, and his smile stretched from ear to ear. They wouldn't have much time, but he'd come. Emma had never been so glad to see anyone.

"The next time I come home, I'll be staying," he said. "Uncle Fritz won't need any more help this year. It's seemed like a long time, although I've worked only a little over two months."

He held her hand and wouldn't let it go for the longest time. Like her, he was just happy they were finally together.

"I'm determined we'll be married before the next winter sets in," he whispered to her when no one could hear.

Mama didn't want her to help with dinner, so she and Edgar talked. When dinner was almost ready, Edgar mysteriously went to his horse and came back with a package, which he didn't explain.

They went to the table, and Emma saw her favorite foods. Suddenly it dawned on her. It was her birthday! With her concern about Edgar coming or not, she'd completely forgotten, and, besides, they usually did no more than wish someone a happy birthday in her family.

The whole family and Edgar sang happy birthday to her, and Edgar handed her the package. She opened it to find a Bible.

"I thought you needed one of your own," Edgar told her. "Now your mother will be able to use hers more."

Emma was speechless as she ran her hand over the leather cover. "Thank you ever so much," she finally managed to get out.

"We never do much to celebrate birthdays," Papa told Edgar. He looked at Emma. "This was Edgar's idea. He and your mama cooked it up the last time he was here." Papa sounded as if he disagreed with the celebration.

"I have another surprise," Edgar said. "I asked for tomorrow off to travel back. I can stay later today, just so I get home before dark."

That was the best gift of all. Then, in two weeks he would be back for good, just in time for Christmas.

Wednesday, December the twenty-first, Mr. Moretz came to the cabin. He knocked on the door and came inside when Emma opened it.

Emma's heart felt like lead. His unexpected appearance reminded her of when Luther had died and Edgar had come unexpectedly to tell them. Had something happened to Edgar, and his father had come with the dreadful news? Emma felt as if her blood had drained from her body.

Mr. Moretz gazed soberly at the Cagles. "I came for two reasons," he said. "I took the family into Councill's Store to do some Christmas shopping, and I heard that some of the Cherokee have been raiding settlers' places. I wanted to give you folks word and tell you to be careful. You're welcome to come stay with us if anything looks dangerous. Also, Edgar is due home sometime Friday. The missus wants to give him a welcome-home Christmas party on Saturday, it being Christmas Eve and all. You're the only others we're inviting."

"I don't know," Papa said thoughtfully. "Maybe we ought to stay here to protect our place if the Cherokee are prowling around."

"The weather's also too unpredictable this time of year," Uncle Roy added.

"The women are welcome to go, though," Papa said.

Was Papa wanting a chance to do some partying of his own? The holidays were always the times he seemed to want his drink in the worst way.

"The girls can go," Mama said, "but I'd rather stay here."

Mama must be thinking along the same lines as Emma. Emma wanted to attend the party in the worst way. She should be at Edgar's welcome-home party, but she'd worry about Mama.

"I can come get them," Mr. Moretz offered.

"I don't want you to have to come again so soon, just to turn around and go back," Emma told him. "I can drive Christie and me in the wagon."

"I don't think that would be safe."

"I'll bring them up and come back and get them," Uncle Roy said, and Emma could have hugged his neck. Apparently the unpredictability of the weather must have just been an excuse.

"Unless you have special plans for Christmas, why don't you let them stay through Christmas, and Edgar or I will bring them back Monday?" Mr. Moretz asked.

"No special plans," Papa said. "It's just another day to me."

Papa almost sounded angry. Emma could see he didn't like the way things were working out.

"Well, it's settled then," Mr. Moretz took control, probably for Emma's sake. "Roy, you can bring them up anytime Saturday, and we'll get them home Monday." He looked at Mama. "You know we'll take good care of them, so don't worry."

"Thank you," Emma whispered to him, as she opened the door to let him out.

After Emma's birthday surprise, she guessed Edgar would get her something for Christmas. She had racked her brain, trying to figure out what she could get him. She had no money to buy anything. She would have made him a shirt, but she had no cloth. Mama suggested she bake him something, but that didn't seem like enough. Finally, Uncle Roy came to her rescue.

"Take some of those pelts or hides out there and make him a vest or a jacket," her uncle told her.

"Oh, thank you, Uncle Roy. That will be perfect."

Now, if she could just get it made. She'd always been a good seamstress, but she'd never worked with leather. Mama helped her with the pattern. Uncle Roy helped her cut it out and showed her how to put it together. She spent hours and hours working on it. She even lined it with some brown silk Mama had saved from the skirt of a dress she'd had long ago and never worn much.

"I always thought I would make one of you girls a dress from it," Mama said, "but none of us have ever needed anything but work clothes, and I didn't think dark brown was a good color to wear to Francie's wedding."

Working with leather turned out to be much slower and more tedious than cloth, but Emma felt pleased with the finished coat. She just hoped Edgar would be pleased.

"Here, take this and give it to Christie for Christmas," Mama whispered. She secretly pushed her bag of candy into Emma's hand. "Christie will enjoy it more than I will."

Emma baked some cookies to take the others. She feared it would be hard to get them to turn out right in the fireplace without the oven slot to the side, but she improvised by constructing a makeshift rack and letting the fire burn down to hot embers, and they turned out just fine.

Emma and Christie left Saturday right after an early dinner. That way, Emma could help Mrs. Moretz cook for the celebration, and Uncle Roy could get home before late. Edgar ran out the door by the time Uncle Roy stopped the wagon, and he swung Emma down into his arms.

"This is the best Christmas present I could ever have," he said.

"I'm not sure I like the idea of being someone's possession," she teased.

"Oh, you'll love being mine because I realize how precious you are, and I'll be so good to you."

They went inside and the scent of evergreen greeted them at the door. The most beautiful Christmas tree stood in the front corner.

"What's that?" Christie asked.

"We've never had a Christmas tree before," Emma explained.

"Well, being German, we've always had one," Mr. Moretz said.

"What type of tree is it?" Emma asked. "It's lovely."

"It's a fir," Edgar told her.

"I made many of the decorations," Hilda said to Christie. "Come I'll show you."

Emma placed her presents under the tree with the others. She'd put Edgar's coat in a white flour sack and tied it with a red ribbon. Christie's candy was in the little cloth bag it'd come in, and the cookies were tied in a square of hemmed homespun, which could be used for a kitchen towel.

"Can I help with anything?" Emma asked Mrs. Moretz.

"No dear, I did all my baking yesterday. You just sit and visit. Since you and Christie will be spending the night, we'll wait to open presents in the morning. I wish your parents and uncle would have come. It's not going to be as much of a celebration with so few of us."

"As long as Emma is here, that's all I need," Edgar said.

"I guess we know where we stand with our son, then," Mr. Moretz said to his wife.

"Now, look who's teasing," Edgar told his father.

The rest of the afternoon went on in much the same vein, with conversations, teasing, and laughter. Emma thought the ham, potatoes, cabbage, carrots, and cornbread at supper delicious, as well as the apple betty for dessert.

Edgar and Emma played checkers. She won the first game, and he won the second.

"You should play again to break the tie," Hilda said.

"Not on your life," Edgar told her. "I know to quit when I'm ahead."

"But you're not ahead," Hilda said, not understanding her brother's teasing.

They all laughed.

"I'm as ahead as I'll probably get," he told her, and Emma playfully elbowed him.

Mr. Moretz and Edgar pulled one of the beds out from behind the quilts again.

"I'll be glad when Emma and I can marry, and we can quit rearranging the furniture," Edgar said.

His declaration in front of his parents surprised Emma. She thought they were keeping it a secret. Perhaps the secret was just for Papa or the fact that he'd already asked her.

"When do you think that'll be?" Mrs. Moretz asked.

"As soon as her father will give permission. He wants her to wait until she's older. He let Francie marry at sixteen, so that will be another year if he expects the same of Emma. At least he's letting us court now, so I am thankful for that."

Emma lay awake that night, thinking about the possibly of being married to Edgar by this time next year. She smiled in the dark. She lay on one side of Christie, and Hilda slept on the other side of her sister. She couldn't hear Edgar at all on the other side of the room and quilt.

They got up at daylight on Christmas Day. Hilda and Christie had been awake for a while, but none of the adults wanted to get up until the day lightened.

"We're going to eat breakfast first," Mrs. Moretz told the younger girls when they wanted to open presents right away.

When they'd finished eating and the dishes had been washed, everyone gathered in the sitting room.

"You're our guest, Emma. Would you like to hand out your presents first?" Mr. Moretz said.

She did, and Christie opened hers first. She couldn't contain her excitement because she'd never had a Christmas present before. Papa hadn't allowed it, but seeing Christie now, Emma almost wished she'd secretly made something for Christie anyway.

"Candy!" she exclaimed. "Thank you, Emma!"

Mrs. Moretz opened Emma's gift for her, her husband, and Hilda. "Oh, look, cookies! We'll certainly enjoy these. I haven't baked any Christmas cookies yet this year."

"Thank you," they all said together, taking one each.

Edgar opened his last. "What can this be?" he said. "It's big and heavy. Is it a horse?" The younger girls cackled with laughter. "Oh, my!" he exclaimed as he took the coat out of the bag. He rubbed his hand down the leather. "This is gorgeous! You made this, Emma?"

She nodded, and he put it on. It fit perfectly. Everyone had nothing but compliments, and Emma found it hard to contain her joy.

Edgar handed his out next. Hilda had a cup and ball game, where a wooden cup was attached to a spindle handle with a cord and wooden ball. The player tried to toss the ball up and catch it in the cup in one motion. The thick string made the tossing easier and kept the ball from falling to the floor. Hilda loved it.

"A man in Meat Camp makes them to sell," Edgar told them.

His father had a pocket knife, which he needed, because he had broken his. Edgar gave his mother a pretty bottle of perfume, and she smiled brightly.

He handed Emma a larger package. She opened it to find yards of a pretty blue fabric to make a dress, but that wasn't all. There was also enough navy wool material to make herself a winter cloak. Under all the material and matching thread lay an elegant gold filigree brooch.

"Oh, Edgar, this is too much. Either one would have been fantastic, but together, it's just too much. You must have spent most of the money you earned."

"Not at all. I had my cabbage money, the money from working in Meat Camp, and I'm starting to hunt and trap for the furs now. Besides, nothing is too much for you, Emma. I wish I could give you more."

"Now it's our turn," Mr. Moretz said. He handed Hilda hers first. It was a new dress Mrs. Moretz had made of bright green cloth. It looked like Christmas, and Hilda loved it. Christie got a small rag doll Mrs. Moretz had also made. Emma opened hers and gasped. Inside was a lovely dress of soft peach colored silk with an ecru lace insert in the bodice and lace trimming on the sleeves and neckline.

"Where did you get something so lovely?" she asked.

"It was my wedding dress," Mrs. Moretz said. "I wore it the one time and have carefully saved it. I thought you could take it up for your wedding dress. When you were here, I noticed how well you sew."

"Thank you so much. I love it!"

She looked at Edgar and saw his smile. "You'll be the most beautiful bride ever."

"And now, for Edgar." Mr. Moretz handed Edgar a packet. "I think this may be a surprise, son," he said and grinned. Edgar opened it. He looked at the papers and then at his parents.

"Is this what I think it is?"

"It's the deed to this farm. We knew you wanted one and were working to buy one for you and Emma. The way things worked out, you're our only son left at home. By giving this to you now, we know there'll be no question about who gets the farm."

"This is great—it's more than great! You're the best parents a man could have! Thank you, thank you so much!"

"Do you get the feeling he's excited?" Mr. Moretz said with a wink to his wife.

"Emma, do you think your Papa will agree to us getting married soon, since I now own my own farm?"

"You can ask him. If he says we have to wait until a certain time, at least we'll know."

Mr. Moretz read the story of Jesus' birth from the Bible. It had special meaning to Emma this year since she knew Him personally as her Savior.

CHAPTER NINE

Christie

Christmas dinner tasted as delicious as last night's supper had. This time they ate a huge turkey Mr. Moretz had shot, which Mrs. Moretz had slow-roasted on a spit in the fireplace. The aroma alone had been enough to whet everyone's appetite.

Christie and Hilda played all afternoon. Emma borrowed Mrs. Moretz's heavy cloak, and she and Edgar walked outside.

"Can you believe all this is ours?"

"It is hard to fathom, but your parents gave it to you, Edgar. I wasn't included, especially not until we're married."

"Well, I'm including you. What's mine is yours, Emma."

Emma smiled at him. "Thank you. This has been the best day. Do you know this is the first time Christie or I have ever even gotten a Christmas present? Papa doesn't like such things."

"Well, I'm really glad I gave you the three things, then. I may do that every year to make up for what you've missed."

"You're so good to me, Edgar, but I don't need presents. I just need you."

"I want to kiss you so badly, but I'm not going to. The last two times have shown me my emotions are intensifying each time, and I don't think I'm strong enough to stop with just kissing you. Like I said before, the next time I passionately kiss you is going to be after we're pronounced man and wife."

"I hope that's soon," she said, and he agreed.

Edgar took them home Monday right after dinner. "I'll have to drop you off and get back home," he said. "It's getting dark so early now."

"Just wait until I make sure everything's okay," she told him. "In the past, Papa has often started drinking over Christmas."

"I will, and I'll come earlier next Sunday and ask your father for your hand."

"That will be January the first, won't it?"

"Yes, it will. If he says we can marry in the spring, we'll be starting the year off right."

She wondered why wait until spring, and he must have seen the question on her face because he answered, "No itinerate preachers come into the mountains during the winter."

Edgar stayed on the wagon and waited for her to go inside. Neither Papa nor Uncle Roy was there.

"He's okay," Mama said. "If he had anything to drink yesterday, it wasn't much. They're in the barn now."

"Are you sure?"

"I'm sure."

She ran back to the wagon. "Mama assures me nothing is amiss. Thank you for a wonderful Christmas. I love you."

"I love you too. I'll see you Sunday."

Mama had been right. Papa wasn't drunk, but he wasn't happy, either. Something seemed to be simmering just below the surface. It was a good thing Edgar hadn't stayed to ask for her hand today. If he had, Emma felt sure Papa would have said, "No, never."

Christie eagerly showed Mother her doll and candy. Mama was impressed, and Emma saw tears in the older woman's face.

They would have no doubt had other Christmas presents if Mama could have had her way.

Emma started making her cloak first. It would take less sewing than the dress, and she needed it right away. Their shawls were just not enough for winters up here. This was the first time Emma had ever had new store-bought cloth to make herself something to wear. They'd usually had to remake hand-me-downs.

Tuesday, Christie went to the creek to get Mama some water. Emma busied herself with the cooking and had her hands in flour from rolling out crusts for an apple cobbler. Christie came back with the water, but she was dripping wet and muddy. She'd fallen in the creek.

It must have been close to freezing out, and ice still clung to the shady edges of the stream. Christie's teeth chattered like the clinking of iron chains.

Mama hurried to help her change into dry clothes, but Emma felt worry grip her like a steel trap. Christie had seemed rather sickly for a good while. She prayed her sister wouldn't get worse.

Wednesday, Christie said she felt tired. Emma touched her forehead, and she didn't seem to be hot. Still, her sister stayed in bed much of the day. Papa hadn't come home yet since going out with Uncle Roy the night before.

Thursday, they woke up to find Christie hot to the touch. Her eyes were weak, and she wouldn't eat, but Emma got her to drink a little water. She'd make a clear broth with dinner and had her drink some of it.

Christie didn't get any better through the day. Emma spent much of her time trying to nurse her.

Roy brought Papa home Friday. "He passed out near Councill's Store, and I had a terrible time trying to find us somewhere to stay. The night felt too cold to stay outside and looked too dark to haul him home. It took all my money from what we'd just sold to get us a room. He's in the barn now, putting up the wagon."

"Was he drunk?" Emma asked. She knew the answer.

"I never thought he'd be so bad. I have my drink now and then, but I don't get rolling down drunk, and I don't get so mean. I think he's over the worst of his meanness now, although he hasn't been in a good mood for a spell."

Papa came in and didn't look at anyone. His face was drawn and his jaws clenched.

"Supper's almost ready," Mama said.

"Good" was all Papa said.

Edgar came Sunday, but Emma whispered for him not to ask Papa anything. Papa still slinked around moody and distant. Edgar and she had their Bible study together and prayed, especially for Christie. Edgar didn't stay as long as he did sometimes. Christie needed Emma's care.

"Is there anything I can do to help?" Edgar asked her when she walked him to his horse. She wore her new navy winter cloak.

She shook her head. She looked up into his tender eyes and leaned into him for a hug. His very presence comforted her. Despite his teasing ways, Edgar Moretz had a strength and steadiness.

"We'll all be praying for her," he told Emma.

Christie's health continued to decline. Emma sat beside her and applied a cold damp cloth to her forehead to help bring the fever down. She had to keep rinsing it out in the cold water because, as soon as she wiped Christie's forehead, the cloth became warm again.

Christie slept most of the time. She also talked incoherently in her sleep in a hoarse voice. Mama and Emma prayed and prayed. Instead of getting better, her little sister kept getting worse.

"Is there a doctor in Councill's Store?" Mama asked Papa.

"I don't know, but we couldn't pay one if there was, and it would be hard to get someone out this far in the cold."

"Most doctors will take barter or even nothing if the case is urgent," Mama said.

Papa didn't say anything, but he didn't go to see if he could find a doctor. He seemed mad at the world.

When Emma woke up Friday morning, she panicked when she realized she couldn't hear or see Christie breathing. Trembling, she moved her hand under Christie's nose. The air remained still, and she couldn't feel a thing. She sat beside her pallet on the floor and stared at her for the longest time. Still, the reality wouldn't sink in. Pretty little Christie couldn't be dead.

Emma took her cloak from the peg and slipped out the door. She didn't plan to stay out long, but she needed some quiet time by herself before she woke Mama. Papa and Uncle Roy had already got up and had probably gone to the barn.

Emma walked to her favorite spot. She sat on the log despite the bitter cold. The coldness almost felt good blowing over her, as if it were waking her up and forcing her to face facts.

Why hadn't God answered Emma's prayers? Why had he taken Christie, the most innocent of them all? She sat staring into the creek.

Christie had been so easy to please and appreciated any time Emma spent with her. Emma would miss their times together. Although she'd often had to repeat a lesson several times, she would miss teaching Christie. Her little sister had been so pleasant to be around.

She opened her heart to God and let him bring her comfort. Perhaps He had answered her prayers. Christie had perfect health now and would be at peace. Their awful family situation would never affect her again. She wouldn't have to hide in the sleeping loft from Papa anymore. Maybe God needed Christie now, or maybe this was His way of protecting her. Emma wished she understood God's ways.

Tears washed down Emma's face and felt like icicles. Grief was such a personal hurt, Emma realized, an almost selfish one. She would miss her little sister, but Christie was in a better place. Emma grieved for herself and her missing Christie.

Emma returned to the cabin to find Mama had discovered Christie's body and had sent Roy to fetch Mrs. Moretz. Papa had wanted to bury Christie themselves, but Mama had told him she wasn't up to that, and she needed some help to prepare the body.

Mrs. Moretz came as soon as she could get there, and she brought Oralee Blankenship with her. Oralee was a young woman, a little older than Emma, who lived a ways out from the Moretzes with her husband. They hadn't been married long.

"Oralee doesn't mind preparing a body," Mrs. Moretz said, "and she does a good job. I thought a lot of Christie, so I couldn't be sure I'd feel up to it. Fred and Edgar are making a coffin as we speak."

True to what Mrs. Moretz said, Oralee gently washed Christie's body and dressed her in clean clothes. She would be buried in her best dress, the one she'd worn to Francie's wedding. Emma helped Oralee lift the body around, and Christie was cool to her touch.

Not long after Oralee had finished with everything, Edgar brought the coffin, a simple, rectangular pine box with a lid that would be nailed down. It looked smaller than a regular casket, but Christie would fit just fine.

Mama laid a folded sheet in the bottom and rolled down the top length for a pillow. It was the one Christie had used at night. Oralee lifted the deceased girl easily and laid her in the box. Emma tucked the rag doll in beside her.

"If we bury her soon, I think the ground is thawed enough to dig the grave," Edgar said. "Sometimes we have to wait until it softens up some."

"Where do you want her buried?" Mrs. Moretz asked. "I'd be proud if you wanted her grave in the family plot we just started. With Francie married to Martin and Emma and Edgar headed that way, we're family, you know."

"Thank you," Mama said. "I'd like that, but I need to ask Les. He's out right now."

"I'll see if he's in the barn," Emma said.

Papa stood just inside the barn, leaning against the wall. He stared out at something in the distance and didn't look at Emma at first.

"Mama wants to know if it's okay to bury Christie in the Moretz's burial plot."

He didn't look at Emma. "It's fine with me. I don't want no reminders around here." Papa seemed to be turning into a hard man.

When Emma started back, she saw Edgar had come out to watch over her. Bless his protective heart.

When Edgar nailed the lid on the coffin, Mama burst out crying. Emma and Mrs. Moretz tried to comfort her, but tears also streamed down her own face.

Uncle Roy came to the cabin, and Emma told him they were going to have a graveside funeral immediately at the Moretz's.

"That's probably best," he said. "The ground will probably freeze again overnight, and you never know how long it may stay that way."

Roy helped Edgar load the coffin in the back of the wagon. There wasn't enough room for all of them on the wagon seat, so Mama and Mrs. Moretz stayed behind to come later. Edgar, Emma, and Oralee took the coffin with the body up the mountain.

Mr. Moretz, Edgar, and Mr. Blankenship started digging the grave right away.

Emma and Oralee went into the house to be with Hilda. Mrs. Moretz had begun cooking the meat to prepare a stew for dinner, and Hilda had been watching it. Emma and Oralee went in the kitchen to help. Emma saw the vegetables from the root cellar laid out, so she peeled and cut them and added them to the pot.

What was taking the others so long? She hoped nothing was wrong. Her parents, uncle, and Mrs. Moretz should have followed right along.

Roy drove them up over thirty minutes later. Papa had refused to come.

"I'm glad I stayed behind," Mrs. Moretz whispered. "I don't think he would've let your mama come if I hadn't."

They all sat in the sitting room. Mama kept staring at Hilda as big tears drenched her face. At least the loud sobs had subsided. Emma slid her chair over to talk with her. It might not help, but she needed to try.

"Mama, Christie's better off now," she said softly. "She won't ever have to hide again when Papa gets drunk, and she'll never have any more sickness or hurt. We'll see her again someday, you know. The Bible promises us that."

Mama gave her a weak smile, nodded her head, and patted Emma's hand. Mama would be all right. Eventually. Papa was a whole different story, however. He needed to get right with the Lord before things would change and be right with him.

The men came back to the house and washed up. Edgar and Mr. Moretz went into the bedroom and changed their dirty clothes, but Mr. Blankenship had nothing to change into.

They all sat down to eat dinner. This seemed strange to Emma at first, but then she realized it would probably be better to eat now than after the burial. Mr. Moretz said grace and asked for

God's comfort and mercy. No one ate much, but everyone ate some, even Mama.

"Who would you like to say the words at the gravesite?" Mr. Moretz asked.

Mama was silent, so Emma answered. "Either you or Edgar will be fine."

"Edgar, why don't you handle that," Mr. Moretz said, and his son nodded.

Edgar finished his stew and went into the sitting room with his Bible. Emma watched as he bowed his head and prayed before he started thumbing through the book to find the right verses to use.

Emma silently thanked God for giving her such a good man. She felt the best she'd felt since discovering Christie's body that morning. She realized grief had less sting under a thankful heart.

The men had already placed the coffin in the ground. Emma felt relieved. That would be one less traumatic part to the day.

Edgar stood beside Emma and read the verses he'd selected from Mark 10:14–15. "Jesus is speaking here," he said. "Listen to what he says. 'Suffer the little children to come unto me, and forbid them not: for of such is the kingdom of God. Verily I say unto you, Whosoever shall not receive the kingdom of God as a little child, he shall not enter therein.' This tells us Christie is in heaven today and that we should all be more like her. We must come to Christ with the humility of a child."

Emma had told herself she would be strong, but the tears came anyway. She couldn't stop them. It didn't help that Mama sobbed loud enough to be heard. Mrs. Moretz stood beside her since Papa wasn't here, and Uncle Roy tried to comfort her from the other side, but he seemed to feel awkward. Emma thought he must also be remembering burying his wife and son. She wondered where their graves were, because she'd never seen them. She'd never thought about it before.

Edgar gently put one arm around Emma as he held his Bible in his other hand and continued. Emma listened to what he was saying.

"I know Christie Cagle is in heaven," Edgar said, "because she was one of the little children. She was also such a sweet girl. I never saw her upset, arguing, or disobedient. We should all be more like Christie. That's what Jesus tells us here. We are to come before God as little children.

"Find your comfort in the arms of Jesus today," he continued. "If you don't know Him as your Savior, ask Him to become that. He's waiting to come into your life, and I guarantee He will make you feel better than you ever have."

Uncle Roy shifted uncomfortably from where he stood. Emma wished Papa could have heard this.

She looked up at Edgar and smiled. She felt so proud of him.

"Father, will you close us with prayer?"

"Dear Heavenly Father, we are burying one of Thy precious children today, but we know her sweet spirit is not in this pine box. We know she's already in Thy arms. Comfort us just the same, because we grieve at not seeing her again for a time. I pray that each one here and all those who care for Christie will take Thy words to heart. Give us the peace that comes only from knowing Thee. Bless us, each and every one, and put a special touch on the one who is not here today. Soften his heart and restore him to be a godly husband and father, we pray in Thy holy name. Amen."

"That was a beautiful service, Edgar," Emma said.

He smiled at her with eyes that spoke of love. He kept his arm around her as they slowly made their way back to the house.

"You did such a good job," Edgar," Mama said. "Thank you." She had stopped sobbing now, but tears still wet her face.

"I'm glad I could do something to help," Edgar said.

"You've done a lot to help," Emma told him, and he pulled her a bit closer.

"We'd better be getting back before dark," Roy said, and Mama nodded.

"You want me to come sit with you tonight, like you did for me when Luther passed?" Mrs. Moretz asked.

"No, but thank you. I need to see to Les, and I have Emma."

"Is there anything else I can do, Emma?" Edgar asked.

"Would you write to your relatives in Pennsylvania and try to get Francie word about Christie? I know she would want to know."

"I certainly will. I think Father will know an address."

Papa wasn't home when they got back. They readied supper and waited for him, but when he didn't come, the three of them asked the blessing and ate anyway.

"I guess I'd better go looking for him," Uncle Roy said, as he picked up his musket beside the door. "A man could freeze to death out in the woods in this cold."

"Is there a shack or something out there?" Emma asked.

"A little one, and the still has a fire pit that'll heat things up. He'll be all right; don't you two worry. He's probably too mean to die." Roy gave a sad laugh.

Emma slept with Mama that night. They needed each other's warmth and nearness. Emma would have missed Christie even more without Mama beside her.

Roy brought Papa back in the morning. He was drunk, but he could still walk with help.

"Don't know why a man can't go off and mourn by hisself," he fumed. "I lost my Francie and now my Christie. Li'l Christie wus purtier than Francie. She wus goin' be a beauty one day."

Mama didn't take any notice of his comments, but Emma did. She felt like lashing out, taking a frying pan to his skull or something.

"Only Emmie's left of my girls, and she's built like a beanpole."

"You try to touch me, Papa, and you'll live to regret it," she said through almost clenched jaws. "You've always said I have too much gumption. You'd better not try the least thing with me, for I won't stand for it. I'll show you what 'gumption' is. You bother me, and I'll stab you in your sleep." Emma didn't think she'd be able to stab anyone, but Papa didn't know that. The words she spit through a stiff jaw even sounded convincing to her ears.

"I know that, Emmie. You'd stand up to a wildcat and never bat an eye. I know better than to try to tease you." He glanced at Mama.

"Is that what you call your bothering?"

Mama looked at Papa with a puzzled expression, like some stranger sat before her. Or, maybe, she was trying to figure out what they were talking about.

"Sh-h-h-h-h." He put his shaky finger to his lips and rolled his eyes toward Mama.

"You're pathetic," Emma said and started climbing the ladder to the sleeping loft.

"You oughtna talk to your ol' pappy like that," Emma heard him say before she crawled out of his sight.

"She oughtna talk to me like that." He was probably talking to Mama. "What's that *thetic* word mean?"

"It means you need to get better," Emma heard Mama say.

"I guess I do. I think I'll just go to bed and sleep me a spell. I'm not feeling so good."

At least Uncle Roy had brought him home before he reached the mean spell this time. In this mood, he'd feel sorry for himself. If he continued drinking, which he usually did, he would soon be in the mean and nasty mood. At least, he would when he gained consciousness.

CHAPTER TEN

Captured

Papa woke up as Emma put dinner on the table the next day. He ate a good meal, but Emma saw his hands shaking, even though he tried to hide it.

"I need to sell some stuff in Councill's Store," he said after he'd eaten.

"No, you don't, Lester," Uncle Roy said. "It'll wait."

"Well, it's what I'm going to do," Papa said.

Emma knew there'd be no use arguing with him when he got like this. She wondered if he wanted to go into the settlement to sell some of their whiskey, or if he had some other reason for going there.

"I guess I'd better go with you, then," Uncle Roy said. They picked up their guns, hitched up the mules, and left in the wagon.

Sunday morning, Emma woke up to the whistling and moaning of the wind, and the cabin felt extremely cold. It had to be around zero outside, and the wind made it feel even colder. Emma didn't think Edgar would be able to come, but he came anyway. He had a scarf wrapped around his face, head, and neck, he wore his hat tied on, and he wore knit gloves under leather ones. Besides his coat, he had a quilt wrapped around his shoulders.

"I'm so glad to see you, but you should've stayed home where it's warm."

"I'm okay. I have a nice, warm coat," he smiled.

"I just couldn't stand to see you come down with something now," Emma said. "Losing Christie was bad enough."

"I know, sweetheart, but I'm fine. Not even a sniffle. Where's your father?"

She guessed Edgar planned to ask Papa if they could get married come spring. Well, that wasn't going to happen today.

"He went into Councill's Store, and Uncle Roy went with him."

"Was he drinking?"

"Not here, but he had been, and I imagine he's planning to again once he gets away from the house."

Edgar didn't want to leave his horse standing in the icy temperature, so he tied it in the barn. Emma went with him, but even with her shawl and wool cloak, the wind cut right through her.

"Is there anything I can do for you?" Edgar asked Mama when they went in. "Are there any outside chores?"

"No, thank you, Edgar. Emma takes care of most of them. I'm sorry the way Les is behaving. He's trying to forget losing Christie, and he just doesn't handle the hard times well."

"You don't need to apologize for him. I just wish I could get you and Emma out of this mess. Why don't you come home with me? Staying there last time got him to sober up for a time."

"I can't keep running away, Edgar. Besides, the three of us would have a hard time riding your horse up the mountain."

"If you'll leave right now, you and Emma can ride the horse, and I'll walk and lead her. I can easily walk five miles or so. I've gone farther than that out hunting."

"We'll be fine," Mama told him, but she sounded like she might be trying to convince herself.

Mama had just heated up the stew left from supper for dinner, but there would be enough for Edgar. After they ate, they did their Bible study at the kitchen table. Mama sat down and joined them.

"I think I'll just lie down for a little while," Mama said.

Emma didn't know if Mama was really tired or if she decided to let Emma and Edgar have more time without her watching. She sure hoped Mama wasn't getting sick.

She and Edgar talked and even laughed together. Then, Edgar said, "I guess I'd better get started back. It's cloudy out today, so it'll probably get dark earlier."

"It's too cold to be out late anyway," Emma said, but she wished he didn't have to go.

It had already grown pretty dark in the cabin with the shutters closed and latched. The fireplace did give a little light.

He put on his warm outer clothing, kissed Emma on the cheek, and opened the door. The snow fell so hard and the wind blew it so fast that Emma couldn't see past the doorframe. A gust of snow hit them in the face like a hundred stinging bees. It peppered down so hard that they couldn't even see the trees in front of the cabin. Edgar shut the door and looked at Emma.

"You'll stay here," she said. "You can't go out in that. You'd never make it home."

"It's not proper, Emma, and my parents will be worried sick."

"It'll be okay. After all, Mama is here, and your parents would be more upset if you never made it home. Think of me, Edgar. What would I do without you?"

"You're right. I can't try to go home in these conditions, but I sure didn't expect this."

"Mama and I will sleep in the bed, and I'll make you a pallet over here on the other side of the fireplace where Christie and I used to sleep. I know Papa and Uncle Roy won't be coming home in this."

"Since I've got my coat and scarf on, I'll go out, feed and water my horse, milk the cow, and bring in enough firewood to do us through the night."

"Uncle Roy put a rope up to the barn. Use it to find your way, and the wood is against the back of the house."

Edgar made several trips with wood, and Emma got the door for him each time. By the look of things, the snow had already accumulated about a foot high. Mama heard the door open and shut and got up.

"Well, I declare. This snowstorm sure came up fast, didn't it?"

Emma explained their plans, and Mama agreed. She thought it would be foolish for Edgar to attempt to go home in the blizzard.

"In fact, I feel better with you staying here," she told Edgar. "I don't like it when the men are gone and Emma and I are here all alone through the night."

"I agree," Edgar said. "I don't like the thoughts of that either."

"Before you get your things off, would you go to the smokehouse and bring back some meat for supper? It doesn't matter what kind. Just get whatever you come to."

Edgar came back with a sack full of frozen meat and a bucket of snow. He was terribly cold from tracking in and out so much, and Emma began to worry again about him getting sick.

"We can hang what you don't need of the meat right now on the wall outside, and it'll be easier to get to tomorrow. I think even the animals will hole up somewhere from this storm. I don't think anything will bother it tonight. It doesn't look like it's going to let up anytime soon. At least, with the direction the wind is blowing, I don't think it'll drift over the door, so we should be able to get out. We'll let snow melt for our water, since it would be hard to get to the creek."

They were using the sleeping loft as a larder and root cellar during the cold weather so they would have food close at hand.

Mama and Emma cooked supper while Edgar sat at the table and talked with them. It took longer to get the frozen meat thawed and cooked, and they ate late.

The three of them sat and talked for a time after supper, but then they decided to go to bed. Mama went behind the quilt to get ready for bed, and Emma made Edgar a pallet on the floor.

"Now, if I get up and start walking in my sleep," Emma told Edgar, "I may think this is where I'm still sleeping. So, if I come and crawl in beside you, just push me out and tell me to go back to the bed."

She'd managed to keep a straight face and sound sincere, and the alarm on his face showed he was completely taken aback. She rolled with laughter.

"You, you, oh you," Edgar stammered.

He couldn't think of anything to call her. He seemed practically speechless. That made it even funnier. He tried to be angry with her, but he couldn't. He joined her laughter.

"You think you're funny, don't you?" he asked.

"No, I think you're funny. You should have seen the look on your face."

"You're a cruel woman, Emma Cagle. I wasn't sure, if you came and crawled in my bed, that I'd be able to push you out. I know I sure wouldn't want to."

"Now you two just hush." Mama tried to sound stern, but her lips began to curl up despite all her efforts.

"You're right. I shouldn't have said what I did. I know how hard you've been trying to do what's right. I shouldn't have teased you like that. I'm sorry. Will you forgive me?"

He looked into her eyes to determine if she was serious or if she was still teasing.

"I forgive you, but *do* you walk in your sleep?"

"No." She couldn't help but laugh again. "I don't walk in my sleep."

She looked into his eyes and gently kissed his cheek. He reached out and pulled her into his arms and held her for a moment.

"I truly am sorry, Edgar. I don't ever want to come close to being cruel to you, even in teasing. I love you too much."

"Maybe I need to taper off some on my teasing. I see how it can feel. Good night, darling."

"Good night, Edgar."

Emma crawled in the bed beside her mother. The bed already felt warm, and she hoped sleep would come quickly. It felt good having Edgar in the cabin tonight. It seemed different than when she stayed at his place. He felt closer to her here, more like he was truly hers.

Edgar did a good job of keeping the fire burning through the night. Emma heard him putting a log on several times, but she went right back to sleep.

She got up just before light. The fire burned brightly, and Edgar sat at the table. He looked up at her and smiled.

"Good morning," he said.

"Good morning. You must not have slept well. I heard you up throughout the night."

"I got up to put wood on the fire, but I'm sorry I disturbed you. I slept some."

"I went back to sleep each time, so you didn't bother me." She busied herself making coffee. "Was something bothering you?"

"No. Sleeping this close to where you are sleeping just makes me wish we could start making plans for our wedding. If we could set a date, I would feel better."

"I'll talk to Papa when he gets back. I'll pick a time when he's more approachable and tell him you've been trying to ask his permission. I can ask him to be here on a Sunday when you're here."

"That sounds like a good plan. I had begun to think I might just have to run off with you."

"And when did you say you were going to cut back on teasing?"

He laughed. "Cut back, darling, not cut it out."

The hens had almost quit laying during the cold, so Emma fixed some Irish oats for breakfast. Uncle Roy was partial to them in the winter, so he would buy some occasionally. Emma liked them better than cornmeal mush.

"That tasted great on a cold, winter morning," Edgar said. "Now, I'd better get out and feed and milk."

"I hate you to have to go out there," Mama said.

"I'd be going out in it if I were home, so think nothing of it."

When Edgar went out, the snow must have been close to two feet high. He had a hard time walking in it. He brought the milk to the door and handed it to Emma. Then he went back and got wood, which he placed on the floor by the entrance, while Emma worked the door. This way he wouldn't track snow all over the cabin but one time, and they could move the wood when he came in. He brought in buckets of snow last. It took a lot of snow to get a little water.

At least it had quit snowing, so Edgar would have no trouble seeing, but it still felt bitterly cold, although the wind had slacked. It would have to warm up some before the snow would even begin to melt.

Emma had started making a dress from the fabric Edgar had given her for Christmas. She had it cut out, sewn all the darts and tucks in, and she was stitching on the seams now. She sat and sewed as she talked and laughed with Edgar. She marveled that they never ran out of things to say.

She put her sewing down, and they had a Bible study. She enjoyed discussing concepts with Edgar. He had a good grasp of the Word. If Christie's funeral had been any indication, he would make a good preacher.

Mama cooked dinner, Edgar asked the blessing, and they ate. Meals were easier and more relaxed without Papa's bad moods, but Mama looked worried. She felt the same way, if the truth be told, and she didn't want anything bad to happen to Papa. She just wanted him to start doing better.

The snow didn't clear enough for Edgar to leave until Thursday. Emma thought there was still too much snow, and she worried about Edgar riding up the mountain, but he assured her his horse would make it fine.

"I've enjoyed being snowed in with you, Emma, even if it came unexpectedly."

"You didn't get bored?"

He laughed. "With you? Never. One thing you are not, Emma, is boring. I'll come back and check on you Sunday. Maybe your father will be here then, and I can ask for your hand, but if he isn't, I still want to check on you."

Emma felt a thrill course through her. She had assumed he wouldn't come this Sunday since he'd been with her over four days in a row this week.

Papa came back Friday. He and Roy rushed in and begin carrying things to the wagon.

"Get your things together quick!" he yelled. "We're leaving."

"Leaving? Where are we going?" Mama asked after a moment of stunned silence.

"What does it matter? We're going west, to the territories or something. Come on. Get a move on!" Papa said all this while he was throwing things together.

Roy quickly packed also. He said nothing, but he looked worried.

"What's going on?" Emma whispered to her uncle.

"Lester got drunk and picked a bad fight. I had to get involved to keep him from getting hurt bad. We think a couple of men were killed, and we'll be blamed."

"It wasn't self-defense?"

"No, Lester started it, and the men were shot in the back."

"I'm not going," Emma said when Papa came back in. "I'm not going to leave Edgar."

Papa balled up his fist, and Emma feared he would hit her, but he relaxed and pulled Mama's clothes into a quilt and rolled it up. He pushed Mama in front of him toward the door. Mama picked up her Bible on the way.

"It don't make me no matter what you do, girl," he said. "You can stay here or go. You've got too big for your breeches anyway, and you're way too much trouble most of the time. Your only saving grace is that you're a good worker, but so is your mama, and she's coming with me."

"Let her stay, Papa. This weather is way too bad to go dragging her across the country in the winter. Let her stay with me."

"She ain't staying, and I've got no time to argue about it. They might be coming for us now."

"Mama, don't go!"

"I have to go." She pulled away from Papa and hugged Emma tightly. "He'd kill us if I tried to stay," she whispered in Emma's ear. "I'll be okay," she said as Papa pulled her toward the wagon, "and you'll be fine. You'll marry Edgar, and he'll take good care of you." Tears streamed down Mama's face as the wagon pulled away. "Be happy, Emma!" she called out as she waved. "I love you!"

"I love you too, Mama!"

Emma realized the tears ran down her cheeks. She ran in the cabin and threw herself on the bed. She cried until the tears ceased to come. Then, she just lay there stunned and exhausted.

Finally, she sat up. Could she walk up that mountain and go to the Moretz place? She didn't know, but she feared the unpredictable weather.

Edgar would be here Sunday. She would go back to his place with him then. All she had to do was make it until Sunday, just two days away.

She got up and straightened the cabin from the mess Papa had made. He hadn't taken nearly all the pots or things and only about half the bedding.

Roy had gotten a lot of the food, but there would be plenty left for her to cook for two days, and she and Edgar could take the rest with them. They'd probably have to go back for the wagon, but they could take the good of what had been left behind.

Emma milked the cow before she fixed her supper. She didn't feel all that hungry anyway.

She fed the chickens and found two eggs. She scrambled those for her supper and split and fried some leftover biscuits in butter to go with them. She latched the door and sat close to the fireplace and read her Bible.

She remade the disheveled bed and lay down, but she couldn't go to sleep. Emma had never spent a night by herself in all her fifteen years. It felt strange. She heard sounds she would have never noticed had she not been alone.

She got up to put another log on the fire, and she hadn't been to sleep yet. "Where's your gumption, now, Emma?" she asked herself and laughed. She felt silly and childish in a lot of ways.

She went back to bed. The fire burned down, and she added more wood. This time, she finally fell asleep.

Emma woke up to a cold house. She had finally slept and hadn't gotten up again to keep the fire going, but she stirred up enough embers to use some kindling and get it started again. She peeped outside and saw that the sun was shining brightly. It felt like it might warm up later today.

She ate breakfast and did all the morning chores. Even the cow and chickens were better company than none.

She wished she had a dog. It would've helped guard the place, but Papa had always said they didn't need another mouth to feed, unless it could provide some food.

"You could use it for hunting," she'd once told him.

"It'd be more trouble than good," he'd said. "I sure couldn't take it deer hunting, and that's what I like to hunt the best."

She sewed on her dress until dinnertime. All she needed to do now was hem it.

She cooked some stew for dinner, and there would be enough for her supper. After breakfast in the morning, she wouldn't be cooking another meal here.

The air still felt crisp, but the day had warmed more than it had in weeks. Maybe Edgar would have a pretty day to come tomorrow. Of course, she'd already learned the weather changed rapidly here. Just because it was pretty one day, didn't mean it would be the next.

She decided to put on her cloak and take her Bible to the log beside the creek to read and pray. She couldn't shake off her concern about Mama, but she could do little, except pray. At least prayer worked.

She wished she had a gun, but Papa and Roy had taken theirs. Well, the bear would be hibernating, and most of the snakes would be in their holes. She took the butcher knife and laughed at herself. She doubted it would do much good against a mountain lion or a wildcat, but she felt more vulnerable now, and somehow the knife made her feel safer.

Her favorite spot soothed her, even in its winter starkness. She liked to watch the stream flow over the rocks and hear its song. It seemed almost constant and reminded her of God. The water would eventually wear away some of those hard, sharp places, which made its flow more difficult. Is that what God did for His people? Did He wear down the things that hampered their walk with Him?

She read her Scripture and then sat a long time. By this time tomorrow, she'd be at the Moretz cabin. She thanked God for this last peaceful moment of being in her place one more time.

With Papa gone, Emma realized she and Edgar could get married as soon as a circuit rider came to the area. She'd get Mrs. Moretz to help her mark the seams to take up the peach wedding dress to fit her.

She got up to go back to the cabin. She'd become cold regardless of the fact the day had turned warmer, but she'd been out a good while.

She'd only gone a short distance, when she sensed a presence. She looked behind her to see Cherokee braves in the distance. They stared at her and then headed in her direction. She turned and ran with her heart racing much faster than her feet. One of the men caught her before she got halfway to the cabin.

She clutched the knife and slashed out as he grabbed her. She felt it pull through flesh. He grunted but held onto her firmly with one arm.

He held her back firmly against his chest, and she couldn't get to anything more vital, so she stomped his foot with the heel of her shoe as hard as she could. She twisted her body at the same time and got loose, but two others had arrived by that time. They grabbed her arms and held her between them. She knew there would be no escape now.

She realized the futility of trying to get away at all. Where would she have gone? They could easily break through the cabin. The shuttered window and handmade door would have offered little resistance to such strong men, and she had no gun to protect herself.

She looked across at the one who'd caught her first. Blood flowed from the slit in his upper arm. She had cut him deeply.

He looked at his arm and back at her. He lifted his good hand to strike her while the other two still held her, but a fourth Indian came up and restrained the raised hand. He said something sternly in their language, and the first Indian snorted and stomped away.

The two who held her jerked her arms behind her back and tied her wrists together with a strip of leather. They pulled her between them and set off in the opposite direction of the cabin. They headed west.

It all happened so fast that Emma had little time to do more than just react. Now, as they forced her away from the cabin, she realized she might never see Edgar again. And she couldn't even imagine what these strange men might do to her. *Lord, please have mercy on me. Help me.*

They walked at a brisk pace, and Emma had to almost run to keep up. They stopped just long enough to tie a leather rope around her neck with a slip knot, and if she didn't keep up or fell, it cut into her neck. The first brave held the other end, and he jerked her around. No doubt he was upset about the cut she had put in his arm.

They'd wrapped his arm, but some blood still seeped from it. She hoped he would weaken some, so he wouldn't lead her with such cruel force.

They moved until the sun hung low in the sky. Then, they turned south and stopped beside a stream. They tied her neck rope to a low tree branch. The one with the sliced arm and the one who had kept him from hitting her stayed in camp. The other two left.

Sliced Arm made a fire, and the other one brought her water. She hadn't had any since they'd left, and the fast pace had made her very thirsty. He patiently waited until she'd had her fill.

"Thank you," she said and nodded at him. He might not understand the words, but hopefully he would recognize what she meant by the tone of her voice and the gesture. He nodded back, and she sensed perhaps he was her best hope of making it without being harmed. Right now, she would cling to whatever hope she could find.

The other two braves came back with five rabbits, which they began to clean. They skewered them on sticks and put them over the fire on forked posts cut from small limbs. They smelled good, and it surprised Emma that she felt hungry. But then, it'd been a long time since breakfast.

The two hunters seemed to look to the other two braves for directions. The pleasant one gave more orders than Sliced Arm did.

One of the hunters had a deep scar across one cheek. Emma decided to call him "Scarface." The other one had a flat forehead, small chin, and a wide lower part of his face, which made his face look almost square. She would call him "Square Head." She couldn't decide what to call the fourth one, so she would just think of him as the leader.

The leader looked better than any of the other three. He stood taller with broad shoulders, and he looked muscular and fit. His high cheekbones and the way he carried himself gave him a regal appearance. His best feature, however, was his eyes. Although almost coal black, they held a warmth that reminded her slightly of Edgar.

Edgar. She almost cried when she thought of him. He would come tomorrow and find no one there. Would he figure out what had happened to her, or would he think she'd just left with the others? He would be distraught, either way.

The leader said something, and Scarface untied her and handed her a rabbit, still on the stick. They left her leash tied, however.

She ate, but as hungry as she was, she couldn't finish the rabbit. She ate a little over half and handed it out toward the leader. Sliced Arm grabbed it from her hands and began to eat it too.

After he finished eating, Sliced Arm bound her hands again. He tied them much tighter than they had been. He started to walk away, but turned and came back. He threw her on the ground and pulled up her skirts as he moved on top of her. She screamed and bit his arm, his good one. She tasted blood and spit it out.

By that time, the leader and Scarface were pulling Sliced Arm off her. The leader spoke in anger for the first time. He raved at Sliced Arm for at least a minute. Then he gave some command, and Sliced Arm walked away with an angry scowl on his face. He went down to the creek and washed his new wound.

Scarface and Square Head gathered more wood for the fire. Soon they appeared to be making preparations to bed down for the night.

The night had grown extremely cold, and the braves lay down close to the fire. They each had a blanket they pulled from something like a knapsack, but there wasn't one for Emma. At least she had her cloak.

She had room to lie down, but with her hands behind her, she had to lie on her side. The leash wasn't long enough to allow her to get closer to the fire. She lay in the uncomfortable position and couldn't get to sleep.

She prayed and thanked God she hadn't been harmed. She knew what Sliced Arm had intended to do to her. She thanked God for the leader's kindness. He'd now saved her from Sliced Arm twice. She intended to stay as close to him as possible.

She rolled from one side to the other during the night. The shoulder against the ground went to sleep easily, and she rolled to the other side to get her circulation back. Her wrists were also aching from the tight cords cutting into her skin.

Soon her teeth began to chatter. The leader got up and moved toward her. Emma watched him warily. He untied the leash and pointed for her to move closer to the fire on his side. When she sat down, she turned to show him her bound hands. He bent down to examine them and grunted. He took the cords off. It felt wonderful to put her arms in front of her. She rubbed her wrists and saw they were raw and bloody in several places.

The leader started to put her hands behind her again. She quickly pointed out to the woods and shook her head no. She hoped he would understand she was promising not to try to escape. He stared at her and finally gave a nod of his head.

He tied a knot that wouldn't slip in the cord around her neck, put some more wood on the fire, tied the end of her leash around his own wrist, and lay down facing her.

She wondered if she could work the knot undone when the leader fell asleep but decided it wouldn't be a good idea. First of all, the leader would probably feel her moving the leather cord. Then, if she did escape, where would she go? No stars or moon lit the cloudy night sky, and these Indians knew the area much better than she did.

At least the leash reached far enough that she didn't have to be right beside the leader. She felt the heat from the fire warm her cold back and soon fell asleep.

She awoke in the morning to the leader jerking lightly on her leash to wake her. Each brave had a small leather bag from which to eat. The leader showed her he wanted her to hold out her hands, which she did. He poured about a third of a cup of some dried mixture into her hands. She tasted it and ate.

It seemed to contain mainly nuts, dried berries, and dried persimmons. It also had some type of grain Emma didn't recognize. When she finished, the leader offered her some water, and she drank.

Scarface also offered her some of the mixture from his pouch and poured about the same amount into her hand. She ate it, and accepted more water from the leader. They collected water from the stream, packed up their few things, and left camp. Emma noticed that they left no sign that anyone had camped there.

They walked all day at a brisk pace, but not as hurried as yesterday. They stopped twice for water before they made camp again, but they ate nothing for a midday meal. The leader kept her leash tied to his wrist, but with the fixed knot, it didn't cut into her neck. Of course, he didn't jerk her around the way Sliced Arm had, either.

Sliced Arm still watched her, and he still scowled at the leader, but neither said anything to the other. Square Head seemed to stay with Sliced Arm, while Scarface appeared to favor the leader.

They stayed in the forest, sometimes on trails, and sometimes where no path could be seen. They usually walked west, but sometimes they would swing southwest and other times northwest. They never traveled east, which Emma guessed would have been toward the cabin and Edgar.

When the sun stood directly overhead, Emma felt sure Edgar would be at the cabin by now. Would he know she would never leave him of her own choosing? Would he find any signs of what had happened? These Indians were good at covering all signs.

CHAPTER ELEVEN

Missing

Edgar rode up to the cabin about ten-thirty Sunday morning. After spending days with Emma in the snowstorm, he'd missed her all the more when he got back home. She had become such a vital part of him that he missed her more and more all the time.

He dismounted and tied his horse. Emma didn't come running out to greet him as usual.

He went up and knocked on the door, but no one answered. He called out but heard no movement from within the cabin.

He tried the door, and it opened. The cabin appeared as neat as usual, but no fire burned in the fireplace. The cabin stood empty. He felt the ashes in the fireplace. They were cold. No one had built a fire there last night or this morning. Yet, someone had left a stew in the pot.

He glanced around. He wasn't sure, but some things seemed to be missing. If his memory served him correct, there'd been more items here than this. A sinking feeling came over him. Something had to be dreadfully wrong.

He checked the barn. The cow hadn't been milked this morning and probably not last night either, as full as her udder looked.

The wagon and mules were gone. Had the whole family left without telling anyone? That's what it looked like.

No! Emma wouldn't do that. He knew she wouldn't. Maybe they gave her no choice. He believed her father capable of violence and brutality. He felt the life drain out of him, and he grew so weak he leaned against the barn wall.

"Dear God," he whispered, "show me what's happened. Tell me what to do. Please don't let Emma be gone from me."

Maybe they'd gone into Councill's Store for something and forgot he was coming. No, Emma wouldn't have forgotten. She and her mother would have stayed for him.

He knew he was futilely trying to come up with something to mean she wasn't really gone. Yet, something must have happened. He didn't know what, but he could sense it.

He looked into the forest toward the creek. The creek! Emma's favorite spot. He knew she probably wouldn't have gone to the creek until after he arrived, but he clutched at the idea because he didn't know what else to do. He quickly walked toward the log at the creek. On the way, he saw her Bible thrown haphazardly on the ground. He reached over and picked it up. Emma would never have left her Bible out like this. He hurried to the log, but he saw no signs out of the ordinary.

He retraced his path to where he'd found the Bible, and walked slowly toward the house, looking for any clue he might find. He found the butcher knife from the kitchen, and saw it had blood stains on the blade. There appeared to be more dried blood on the ground close to where he'd found the knife. Was it Emma's blood? Had she been injured?

He continued toward the cabin, carrying the knife and Bible. He saw nothing else.

He sat down on the bench in front of the cabin and tried to collect his thoughts. Had someone attacked Emma? If so, where was the rest of her family?

His best guess would have been the Cherokee, but if they'd raided, they would have burned the cabin. Besides, although they may have taken the women prisoners, they would've killed the men for sure, and Edgar would have found their bodies.

Well, he hadn't found Emma's body either, so he would assume she was alive, and if she had any way to come to him, she would. He would not think the worst yet.

Edgar gave the chickens some cracked corn to hold them for a few days. They would just have to stay penned in the coop until he could get back. He milked the cow to get her out of her misery, put a long lead on her, and led her to his horse. He would take her back to his farm for now. If the Cagles turned up, he would bring her back.

He returned home with a heavy heart. He decided to ride to Councill's Store tomorrow to see if he could discover any news.

Edgar's parents seemed as stunned with his report as he'd been at the cabin. His father suggested Edgar go by the Cagles' place before he went to Councill's Store. Maybe they would've returned home by then.

Edgar hoped his father was right, but he doubted it. The tossed Bible and bloody knife didn't bode well for such an easy resolution. There'd been trouble of some kind. He felt it in his gut.

Edgar rode down the mountain early the next morning. The cold stung, but he paid no attention to it.

He went by the Cagles' cabin, but nothing had changed. No one was there. He gave the chickens some water, checked their food, and left.

He did find some news at Councill's Store. Lester Cagle had been drinking heavily, picked a fight with some of the sawmill workers, and shot two of them in the back. Both of them were alive, but one barely hung on, unconscious and not likely to wake up.

Roy had helped Lester get away from the other men. Rumor had it they'd left the state by traveling west. The fight had taken place sometime late in the night on Thursday.

Had her father tried to force Emma to go with them, and she stabbed him? If so, he must have taken her by force. Would her uncle have helped his brother with such a deed? And what of Emma's mother? Edgar couldn't see her allowing such a thing, but maybe she'd had no choice.

Edgar went back home and told them what he'd learned. They were all puzzled.

"Could I get all of you to go back to the cabin with me tomorrow? Maybe you'll see something I didn't. I want to take the wagon and pack up everything I think Emma would want. We'll store them in the barn for her." He started to add "in case she returns," but he refused to think she might not.

"Sure," his mother said. "We'll be glad to go."

They started off after breakfast. Father drove Mama and Hilda in the wagon, and Edgar rode his horse. The silence at the Cagle place screamed to Edgar.

Something had been in the chicken house and left some feathers behind, but a few chickens still scratched about. Edgar would put them in the crates he'd brought and let them out with their chickens for now.

They packed up all the pots, pans, and dishes that were left and all the bedding. He didn't plan to take any of the furniture.

Edgar carefully folded Emma's dresses and clothing. Mama offered to do it, but Edgar wanted to handle her things himself.

He found the dress she'd been making from the fabric he had given her. It looked finished—all but the hem. He closed his eyes and prayed she'd soon be back to wear it. When he found the dress his parents had given Emma for Christmas, he couldn't hold back his tears any longer. This was to be her wedding dress. He pulled the dress to his chest and stood with his back to his family as the silent tears flowed.

This was the end of January, he tried to reassure himself. Surely he'd have Emma back by spring, when the preachers would start coming again. He would grasp this hope and hold on to it for a lifeline.

"It looks like Kathleen's dresses are missing," Mama said.

"How can you tell which ones belong to Emma and which are her mother's?" Father asked.

"Emma has a smaller frame," Mama answered.

Edgar had a hard time hiding his tears then. How he wished Emma's small frame stood before him now. He gritted his teeth and took a load of things to the wagon. He kept his head down until he got outside so his family couldn't see his face. He didn't know whether to look at the fact that Emma had left all her dresses, except the one she wore, as a good or bad sign. He knew from the bottom of his heart that she hadn't gone anywhere willingly.

His father got the tools from the barn and sacked up the salted meat from the smoke house. "No use to leave food for the wild critters," he said.

Hilda bagged up the few potatoes, carrots, and dried beans from the sleeping loft. There didn't seem to be anything else they should take.

The days dragged by roughly for Edgar. It almost seemed as if they were pulling him behind them. He did what he needed to do and helped his father cut more wood on the warmer days, but he felt he lived in a nightmare.

Every time he milked Emma's cow, he felt tears well up in his eyes. She had touched these teats many times. How he wished she could do the milking now! How he wished she could touch him!

He prayed the same prayers over and over again, but other than finding the Bible and knife, nothing helpful turned up.

He had hoped news would come from Councill's Store. Some of the men had promised him they would send him word if they heard any more information, but no one came. He decided to ride down again Saturday. More people came to the town on Saturdays, and maybe someone knew something.

He stayed around Councill's Store for several hours Saturday. No one had any new information. One of the injured men had died, but the other one would recover. Edgar was thinking about heading home when two men came into the store.

"Well, howdy," Mr. Councill said. "How's the Brewer brothers doing today?"

"Oh, we're fair to middlin'. Needed some supplies, and thought we'd jest take 'vantage of this warm spell."

"Well, that's good. This here's Edgar Moretz. He's been looking for some news of the Cagle family who lives near the Linville River. They seem to have left in a hurry. You're out west of there. Have you heard anything?"

"I jest might have, at that. This wagon pulled by two purty sorry lookin' mules came up the road thar 'bout a week ago, I guess it wuz. We didn't know 'em, but thar's a woman and two men. Had some stuff throwed in back of the wagon and looked to be in sort of a hurry."

"Stopped and axed us if we knowed whar they could git some liquor," the other brother continued. "We didn't tell 'em nothin', since we didn't know 'em or nothin'."

"You think that was them?" Mr. Council asked Edgar.

"It sounds like it," Edgar answered. He turned to the Brewers. "Did you ask their names?"

"No, and they didn't offer it. Heard the woman call the driver 'Les,' though, iffin that helps."

"It does. Was there a female about fifteen with them?"

"No. Didn't see nobody 'ceptin' the three middle-aged ones."

"Thank you so much." He shook all three men's hands and left for home.

"It sounds like the Cagles left without Emma, doesn't it?" Father said after Edgar shared what the Brewers had said.

"That makes sense to me," Edgar said. "I know Emma would have fought leaving. Maybe she ran off to the woods to escape."

"With her Bible and a knife?" Mama asked.

"No, I guess not, but apparently she did stay behind."

"Do you know a reason she might've gone into the woods carrying her Bible?" Mama asked.

"Well, yes. There's a spot by the creek she liked. She took me there to have our Sunday worship sometimes."

"Then, maybe that was what she was doing," Father added. "Maybe she took the knife for protection, especially if the men had taken the guns, which seems likely to me."

"But, what would have happened to her?" Mama asked. "She wasn't killed or dragged off by a wild animal, or there would have been signs."

"It must have been a two-legged animal," Edgar said, "but who?"

"The Cherokee have been seen in the area," Father said.

"But, if it had been a raiding party, wouldn't they have burned the cabin?" Edgar asked.

"Probably, especially if they were out to cause trouble. However, if they'd come by for some other reason, or if there were just a couple of braves, they might have taken Emma and left."

"Is that what you think happened, Father?"

"I don't really know, but it makes more sense than anything else we've come up with, given what we now know."

"What can we do?"

"I don't know. We'd never catch up with them before they got back to their main group now. There's Cherokee villages all around west of us, so we wouldn't even know where to go, and we'd never be able to take a village without a lot of men, either. I don't know what we can do, son."

"We can't just give up." Tears were gathering in Edgar's eyes. He felt so frustrated. "This is the woman I love we're talking about—my Emma. I'm not about to give up. It'll be a week tomorrow since I discovered her gone."

"We can pray and leave it in God's hands," his mother said.

"Where were God's hands when Emma was taken?"

As he said it, he felt cold inside. Was this how Martin had felt when Luther had died? He'd thought his brother had been so wrong to blame God. Was Edgar about to do the same thing?

"You could go down to Wilkesborough and see if the sheriff can raise some men to look for her," Father said, "but I think it would be like looking for a needle in a haystack. Picking up a trail would be impossible, and there would be no way to tell what village she's been taken to. Besides, the Cherokee might not even have her. We're just guessing about that."

Edgar felt defeated before he even started, but his father was right. How could he ask the sheriff to raise a posse based on conjecture? It would be too hard to get men to go under such circumstances, and it would be useless if they did. They would have no idea where to search.

He needed to come to terms with his thoughts concerning God. It wasn't God's fault, whatever had happened. But, God had allowed it to happen, hadn't He? Could Edgar hold on to the promise that some good would come from this? He sure hoped so, but what could be good without Emma?

He got his Bible and went to the window to read. "I'm going to take this to God," he told his parents, and they nodded, apparently pleased.

He read some verses in Psalms, but he found no answers to his questions and little comfort for his troubling thoughts. He bowed his head and prayed. First he prayed for Emma's safety and her return. Then, he prayed for guidance and direction. He begged God to show him how to help Emma, how to get her back. He also prayed God would show him what to think about all this. He felt his attitude had soured toward God, but he wasn't sure of what was wrong. He prayed God would reveal it to him.

The patient in spirit is better than the proud spirit.

Edgar wasn't sure where that verse had come from, but he guessed he needed to be patient. There seemed little else he could do but be patient and pray. Patience right now, however, would be a tall order.

The nights were even harder than the days for Edgar. At least he managed to stay busy most days, but the nights were agony. He lay in his bed thinking of all the possibilities. Whomever took her had likely already harmed her. Emma was an attractive young woman. She had a beauty that was hard to describe. Part of it had to do with her love of life and an inner glow of warmth. What had she been made to endure? He was terrified by the likely answer.

He felt certain of one thing. If Emma got a chance to escape, she would take it. She would come back to him if she could. But how far had she been taken? Would it be possible for her to find her way back?

Whomever had taken her would likely have his hands full. It seemed she may have very well injured someone, unless that was

Emma's blood on the knife. It was her knife, however, so, knowing her, he guessed she'd tried to protect herself. Would that make it harder on her in the end? So many questions and no answers.

"Mama, if I wanted to read some Bible passages about patience. Where should I start?" Edgar asked at the breakfast table Sunday. He wouldn't be working today, and he needed something to keep his mind from frightening places.

"The Bible has such verses scattered throughout, but if you want the epitome of patience, read Job."

Edgar had always skimmed over Job. He thought the book depressing with all the bad things Job endured. It also bothered him God had allowed Satan to torture such a good man. It hardly seemed fair, but he could agree with Mama. Job had certainly been patient. He got out his Bible and turned to Job.

CHAPTER TWELVE

The Village

Emma had lost track of the days. She wished she had been more aware of time, but the days had all run together in sameness.

They walked constantly during the days and stopped only in the late afternoon. The braves seemed to know the area, where to find water, and where to hunt. Whenever they turned in a direction other than due west, it seemed to be for a reason. They'd eaten all the dried mix for breakfast. Now the men tried to hunt enough for supper to have some left for breakfast.

Emma had stayed tied to the leader for the first few days. When she needed to relieve herself, she would point to a bush and go behind it. The leader would stand in front of it with his back to her until she finished, but he kept the leather rope in his hand. If he needed a private moment, he would hand her leash to Scarface and take it back again when he came out.

Finally, one morning Emma pulled at the cord around her neck, pointed into the woods to the east, and shook her head. The leader seemed pretty adept at understanding her gestures. Emma felt sure he'd know she was asking him to take the leash off her and saying she would not try to escape.

He looked at her and at Sliced Arm. Sliced Arm said something in a contrary tone. The leader looked back at her. His eyes bored into hers as if he were reading her mind. He removed the cord.

She still tried to stay as close to the leader as she could, for she didn't trust the others, especially Sliced Arm. She noticed if she fell behind, either the leader or Scarface soon moved near her, and she appreciated their care.

It amazed her how much freer she felt without the leash. She remained their prisoner, but she didn't feel as degraded.

When they made camp that afternoon, all the men went hunting. She couldn't believe it. Did they trust her that much? Then, she realized if she did run, she'd never make it back on her own. If the sky stayed clear, she might be able to use the sun to go east, but how would she eat? She had no way to hunt and no way to protect herself against animals or even bad weather. To stay safe, she'd best stay with the leader.

While they were gone, she walked around close to the camp and gathered firewood. She could at least do that much. She had gathered an armload and turned to go back to camp, when she saw someone duck his head back behind a tree. She pretended to walk toward the camp, then suddenly turned around and ran to the tree. There was Scarface trying to get out of sight.

They hadn't left her alone at all. It had been a test to see if she would try to escape. The leader came out from where he'd been hiding. A grin broke out across his face as he said something to Scarface. He looked at Emma, still smiling. Apparently he was teasing Scarface about being caught.

This Indian leader reminded her of Edgar, not in looks, but in actions. He put his hand out, indicating she should go first. This also surprised her because they usually expected her to follow them, and she'd assumed this is what Indian women did. As she walked back, she picked up the firewood she had dropped and put it beside the fire pit.

She turned to find the leader standing right behind her. She almost ran into him. He put the back of his hand gently against the top of her cheek and ran it down to her chin. He said something she didn't understand in almost a whisper.

She felt unsure of him for the first time. What was he doing? Surely he wouldn't turn against her too. She would have no one to protect her if he did.

He looked at her face and backed off, as if he knew he'd frightened her but hadn't meant to. He stood staring at her for a moment before he turned and left. He said something to Scarface over his shoulder and disappeared.

Sliced Arm and Square Head brought squirrels to camp. They looked around and noticed the leader had left. Sliced Arm stared at Emma as if he were undressing her, and Scarface came over to stand close to her.

Square Head started the meat roasting. Sliced Arm said something to Scarface, and the brave stood with his hand on his hunting knife. Suddenly the leader appeared, and Scarface relaxed.

The leader carried a big slab of wood with its bark still attached. It looked almost like a wooden dough trough. Honey dripped from the slab. He bent over and presented the slab to Emma. He smelled of smoke, and Emma noticed he had a few bee stings on his exposed skin.

Emma wasn't sure what he expected her to do. She took the offering, set it on the ground in front of her, put in two fingers, and stuck the honey in her mouth. It tasted sweet and good. After nothing but meat for the last few days, she welcomed the thoughtfulness. She looked up at the leader, and he smiled.

She patted the ground beside her for him to sit down, and he did. He seemed very pleased. She held the slab and offered him some honey, which he accepted.

The thought passed Emma's mind that he might read more into this than she'd meant. She knew nothing of Cherokee ways. She looked at Scarface, who stood near. She motioned for him to sit on the other side of her and handed him some honey. The leader watched, but he neither frowned nor smiled that she'd included Scarface in their honey feast.

The three of them shared the honey until Emma had had enough. After all, she had no bread or butter to cut the sweet, rich taste. She got up, walking around the fire away from Sliced Arm, and handed the trough to Square Head. When he took it, she walked back and sat down between the leader and Scarface.

Square Head ate a little of the honey and then looked to her and pointed to Sliced Arm. Apparently the honey belonged to her, and she could say who got a share. She looked at Sliced Arm and nodded. He definitely needed some sweetening up. Besides, she hoped he wouldn't continue to hate her so much. The meat had cooked enough not long afterward, and they finished off their meal. Emma smiled that they'd eaten their dessert first.

When they turned in for the night, Emma lay down between the fire and the leader, as usual. He spread out his blanket, lay down, and patted it for her to come. Her heart skipped a beat. So, this was what the honey had been about. She shook her head. He got up and came to her. He reached down and took her hand and pulled her gently. She sat up but shook her head firmly and pulled back.

"No!" she said even more firmly and shook her head again. He might not understand the word, but he could her hear her firmness. He dropped her hand, lay down, and turned his back to her. At least he didn't plan to force her.

She almost felt sorry for him. He had protected her, been kind to her, treated her with respect, and raided a beehive for her; and she had rejected him in front of his men.

He turned over and looked at her with questions on his face. She sat up, and he watched. She put both hands on her heart then pointed east. This one would be harder for him. Would he understand her heart belonged to another?

He stared at her for a few seconds, looked around at the other men, and then to the East. She nodded to say her man was in the East. He nodded and closed his eyes. She lay back down.

If she didn't know Edgar, she thought she might have fallen for this Cherokee brave. He had traits that reminded her of the man she loved. But she did know Edgar, so why settle for second best, once she had found the man for her? Besides, she wanted a husband who would share her faith.

She would trust God to get her back to Edgar. He had kept her safe so far, even amid horrible dangers. He had brought Daniel from the lion's den unharmed and the men from the fiery furnace unburned, and He would guide and keep her. She would trust in Him.

The leader didn't seem upset with Emma the next day. He treated her no differently than he had before. He had to be young, perhaps even younger than Edgar, but he had a maturity and integrity that Emma admired.

Sliced Arm said something mockingly to him and laughed. The leader looked at Emma, then looked up and replied. Whatever he said, Scarface nodded slightly. Sliced Arm gave no indication how he felt, but he said no more.

Emma noticed that with all the walking, her figure seemed to be getting more curves. She had begun to fill out as she never had before, and her dress felt tighter. Her muscles were toned, and she could walk fast with less effort and not get winded.

The afternoon of the next day came, and they didn't stop to make camp. They continued to walk, even as the light began to wane. It had stayed cloudy all day, and snow began to fall.

Emma worried they would be caught in a snowstorm. She remembered the time Edgar had been snowed in with her and

Mama at the cabin. She didn't want to be snowed in—or snowed out—with these Indians.

Suddenly, she saw huts appear ahead. A village! They were coming to a Cherokee village. The mud-covered huts looked similar to the chinking material at Emma's cabin, but they had bark roofs. She saw there were also a few houses that looked more like small log cabins. She guessed the way of life had begun to change for the Cherokee.

Children, women, and men, in that order, came out to greet the men and stare at Emma. They walked between a throng of people.

The leader took Emma's hand to lead her without losing her among the others. He led her to a log hut and pulled her inside. An older woman came up and hugged him. By their looks, Emma guessed her to be his mother.

He presented Emma, and she smiled at the woman, but the woman didn't seem very happy to see her. The two Indians broke into a serious discussion. Finally, the woman must have agreed, and the leader left.

The woman turned, put her hand out toward a brightly colored rug, and said, "Sit."

Emma was stunned. She hadn't heard a word she understood in well over a week.

"You speak English?" she asked, but the woman only gave some kind of grunt.

Emma sat down and looked at the woman. "What's your name?" she asked. She intended to see how much English the woman knew.

"You call 'Lily,'" she replied.

The woman went outside, and Emma looked around. The cabin had a dirt floor, and a fire burned in a center pit. Most of the smoke escaped through a small opening overhead. The dwelling had no windows.

Brightly colored woven rugs and a type of cane seats fashioned from tree bark made up the main furnishings. There seemed to be bedding rolls against the wall, and the most beautiful baskets Emma had ever seen were placed about. Many of them seemed to hold necessities. There were some clay pots and jugs close to the fire, and a large, smooth stone that must be used in cooking.

The woman came back and offered her a bowl of food. "Eat," she said.

The bowl held some kind of soup or stew. Emma didn't see any meat in it, but it smelled good, and she welcomed the change from nothing but meat.

"What is this?" Emma asked.

"Ga-ni-tsi."

Emma didn't know any more than she did before she asked, but she tasted it. She decided the flavors were different together, but she liked it. The woman handed her a flat piece of a corn bread to go with it. She hungrily ate it all and drank some water.

"More?" Lily asked.

"No, thank you," Emma said. She also shook her head from habit. At least she could have all the food she wanted.

"Sleep," Lily pointed down.

Emma lay down on the rug, and Lily brought a blanket similar to the ones the braves had used, only larger. Emma didn't think she would sleep, but she felt more comfortable than she had since she'd left home, and she fell asleep quickly.

She woke up sometime in the night. It took her a second to realize where she was.

Someone had kept the small fire going in the center of the hut, and Emma felt really warm for a change. She sat up and pulled off her cloak.

She saw the leader lying across the fire from her, and he watched. She must have awakened him with her movement.

She noticed Lily lay perpendicular between them, near their heads. She still slept. Emma put her cloak to the side, and lay back down. The leader gave her a tender smile. She turned over with her back to him and went back to sleep.

Emma woke up as Lily stirred about the hut. The leader had already left. The fire burned high, and the hut had become smokier.

"I need to go out," Emma told Lily.

"Go," Lily said.

Emma picked up her cloak but didn't move. She wasn't sure where she should go. Lily came, took her wrist, and pulled her outside into the snow. She rounded the hut and pointed toward the woods.

"Go," she said again.

Emma understood and walked out of sight. She saw no one. She came back to the hut to find the leader eating his breakfast. Lily handed her some food, and she sat down on her rug to eat. She looked at Lily and pointed to the leader.

"What's his name?" she asked.

Lily snorted and said something to the leader. He smiled and said something in Cherokee.

"You call 'Hawk,'" Lily told her.

Emma guessed they were shortening and Anglicizing their Cherokee names for her to pronounce. Hawk suited him, however.

"Hawk," she repeated, and his grin widened.

"How do you speak English?" Emma asked Lily.

"Daughter marry white man."

"Hawk doesn't speak it?"

Lily shook her head. When she looked at her son, her eyes softened. She seemed very proud of Hawk and, from what Emma had seen so far, she had a right to be.

"You like Hawk?" Lily asked.

Emma wondered what Hawk had told her. "I like him, but I don't love him."

Lily nodded and said something to Hawk. He looked at Emma, but she couldn't read his expression. He said something else to Lily and left.

"Hawk like you," Lily told her.

Emma hung her head. She didn't know how to answer.

"All Cherokee go to stream every morning," Lily told her, changing the subject. "Cherokee way. Emma stay here."

Emma had a hard time figuring out how she fit into life in the village. She didn't know if she was supposed to be a slave or not, but no one mistreated her. Lily did expect her to work, but Emma didn't mind that. She worked no harder than she had at home. In fact, life here seemed to be a little easier.

Lily didn't like to talk, not in English anyway, so their conversations were limited. They managed, however.

The snow that lay on the ground finally melted away after several days. The winter cold still spread over the mountain region, but being outside on the way here had hardened Emma, and she didn't notice the cold as much.

She worked hard at whatever task Lily gave her. Lily also worked, but they both had times of leisure as well.

Emma missed her Bible. She wished she had held onto it as she tried to run from Sliced Arm. She tried to remember verses she'd read, but she could only recall a few from memory, and most of those were ones her mother had taught her long ago.

Lily showed Emma how to finger weave. They made strips of cloth for belts and sashes and put them together to make blankets and rugs. Emma caught on quickly, and Lily seemed pleased with her.

Hawk rarely stayed around the hut during the day, but he normally came in at night and sometimes at meal times. During those times, he usually watched Emma closely, but it didn't make her feel uncomfortable. After the way he had taken care of her on the journey, she trusted him.

"Where does Hawk usually go during the day?" Emma asked.

"Sometimes hunt with men. Sometimes to house with heat to talk with men and tell Cherokee stories to children."

One morning a distraught mother brought a baby for Lily to see. The baby looked to be a couple of months old and wailed until it almost lost its breath.

Lily took the baby, looked at Emma, and said, "Sick."

She pulled what looked like dried apples with the peel still on them from a pouch, added something else to it, handed them to Emma, and said, "Make tea."

Emma followed instructions and made about a cup of tea. Lily cooled the drink and began giving it to the infant. She chanted to the baby while she gave it the tea. In about ten minutes, the infant had quieted.

She handed the baby back to the mother. The grateful woman said something, and Lily replied. Lily gave the woman some of the tea ingredients, and she left with them and her baby.

"You can help the sick?" Emma asked.

"Sometimes. Father used to be medicine man. I help small problems. Medicine man do more."

"Will you teach me?"

"Why?"

"I had a younger sister, who died with a high fever and tightness in her chest. I wished I'd known how to help her."

Lily stared at her, much as Hawk did when it seemed he was reading her very thoughts. "I teach," Lily finally said.

That began her instruction. Lily showed Emma her medicines and explained their uses in her chopped speech. She said the names of the things in English, if she knew them, and in Cherokee if she didn't. The Cherokee sounds were difficult for Emma to make, so she did like she had with the names of people, and made up a name of her own.

"Show more in spring," Lily said. "Collect plants then."

Emma's heart fell. She wanted to be home in the spring. She had planned to be married then. Well, there was little she could do about it now. She would just pray and learn all she could from Lily in the meanwhile.

Emma guessed it was the end of February, but it could be later than that. She had no way of knowing.

Lily had sent her to the woods to gather wood, but the fierce wind tore at her clothing and sent chills all the way to her bones. She bundled the firewood with a leather strap and started back. Suddenly, Sliced Arm blocked her path, and her blood froze even more. She tried to walk around him, but he pushed her against a tree, his gaze raking her with an evil leer.

She jerked away and swung the bundle of firewood at his face. His hands flew to his face, and she ran. She ran right into a hard chest. Hawk.

He caught her in his arms to keep her from falling. She looked up and saw Hawk glare at Sliced Arm as the injured brave staggered toward them. Sliced Arm's face oozed blood from where the ends of the firewood had hit him. He'd come awfully close to losing an eye.

Hawk stepped in front of Emma and said something to Sliced Arm. His voice hung cold and hard. He didn't even sound like the Hawk she knew. She peeped around Hawk to see what would happen.

At first Sliced Arm glared fiercely at Hawk, but as Hawk continued to talk, Sliced Arm looked down at the ground. Hawk said something in a demanding voice, and Sliced Arm walked away, back to the village.

Hawk turned and smiled tenderly at Emma. He put his hand on her back and started her toward the village. She stopped and ran back to retrieve the bundle of wood, and Hawk laughed softly. They walked side by side back to the village.

They entered the hut where Lily was working, and Hawk told her what had happened. Then, Lily began to translate for Hawk.

"What you call man who attack you?" she asked Emma.

"Sliced Arm."

Lily told Hawk in Cherokee, and they both grinned.

"Cherokee words too hard for Emma. Hawk say Sliced Arm not honor Cherokee. He tell Sliced Arm must do better or leave village. Lily not send Emma out alone no more. Hawk say if Sliced Arm keep to bother Emma, then Emma have Sliced Arm scarred head to toe." Lily and Hawk both laughed at this. Emma smiled too.

"Hawk say Emma be wife of Hawk. No man bother."

"No," Emma said. "The man I promised to marry is back where I came from. He's the man I love. I cannot marry another."

Lily told Hawk, and Hawk replied. Lily translated again.

"Hawk say he be good to Emma. He here now. Emma need man now."

"Tell Hawk I respect him greatly, but I could never marry anyone but Edgar."

"What respect mean?"

Emma thought. What word would they know that was close in meaning? "Honor," she finally said.

Lily translated, and Hawk spoke again. "Hawk say you like Hawk now. You love Hawk later. Say you honor Hawk and be wife."

Emma took Hawk's arm and looked him directly in the eyes. How did she make him understand without hurting him? She spoke directly to him while Lily translated in the background.

"You are a good man, Hawk. I like you a lot, but not as a husband. If I had never met Edgar, it might have been different, but I have given my heart to him, and I cannot love you as you deserve to be loved. If you really care for me, see that I get back to Edgar. That's my heart's desire."

Hawk looked into her eyes. She hoped he saw the truth of what she said. She hoped he realized she didn't want to hurt him, but she couldn't be his wife.

Lily broke into her thoughts, and she realized Hawk had said something. He gently took both her hands in his, as Lily told his thoughts.

"Hawk is great warrior, leader of his people. Hawk never met woman like Emma. Emma fierce like mountain lion and gentle like baby rabbit. Emma fight Sliced Arm at every turn, but treat Hawk with kindness. Hawk wish he meet Emma first. Hawk say Edgar lucky man. Hawk think on what Emma say."

Hawk released her hands, pulled her to him, hugged her tenderly, and then walked out. What did it mean? Would Hawk consider taking Emma back to Edgar? She didn't know, but something told her it would hurt him too much to do so.

Several days later, Lily told her, "Hawk say Lily and Emma take two deer hide from Hawk to make Emma dress."

Emma needed a new dress. The one she had on had become torn in places on her journey here, and it had become threadbare in other places. Lily had washed it once for her as she sat wrapped in a blanket in the hut until it dried, but it needed washing again now.

"This is good," Emma said. "Tell Hawk I thank him."

Making the dress reminded Emma of when she'd made the coat for Edgar's Christmas present. She prayed he wouldn't be too distressed over her disappearance. She prayed he knew to wait for her, that she would return to him as soon as she could. She didn't know how it would come about, but she believed with all her heart that she would be able to return to him. She had to.

The dress turned out to be shorter than Emma thought proper, but it fit her otherwise. There had been enough hide for them to make moccasins too. Emma did like the footwear because they felt so much better on her feet.

Hawk came in for the evening meal after they'd finished the dress. He stopped in his tracks when he saw her. He looked her from head to toe, his face softened, and he looked pleased before he spoke.

"Hawk say you beautiful Indian woman. Say he give half his years you be his woman."

Emma lowered her eyes to her feet so she wouldn't see the love and admiration in Hawk's eyes.

"Hawk say not worry," Lily continued to translate. "Emma not to feel bad. Emma no can change heart. Hawk know things are what things are. No can change."

Emma looked him in the eye then. "Thank you," she said. He nodded in resignation without Lily translating.

"Hawk tell all, you his woman. No one bother now." Lily told Emma days later.

Emma didn't want anyone to think they were husband and wife. The look on her face must have told Lily what she was thinking because Lily continued to explain.

"Hawk not treat Emma as wife. Cherokee woman can say yes or no to choose man who asks her. Men not try to bother Emma now. Hawk protect. Many men watch Emma. Emma not safe without her man. Hawk be Emma's man, not be husband."

It didn't make much sense to Emma, but as long as Hawk didn't consider himself her husband, she guessed it would be okay.

Apparently he was telling everyone she was under his protection to keep her safe.

He had teased about how she'd fought Sliced Arm, but Hawk had been the one who'd saved her each time she'd fought. Things would surely have ended differently without him. The truth be told, she did love Hawk, but as a dear friend, not as a husband.

The village held a festival to celebrate the end of winter. Emma didn't want to go. She appreciated Lily and Hawk, but she didn't feel a part of the community. The stares of most people made her uncomfortable. Besides, winter didn't feel over, and the weather still often felt biting and cold.

"Hawk ask Emma go for him. This thing please Hawk," Lily told her.

Emma looked at the handsome brave. He'd taken good care of her, and she was unharmed because of him. Surely she could do this for him.

"I'll go because he wants it," she said.

Hawk nodded his head and grinned widely. Either by her tone of voice or expression, he had understood she would go.

The festival lasted for several days. One night there was a dance where women wore turtle shells, formed a circle with the men in a single file, and moved counter-clockwise in a circle. Each dancer took two small branches from the spruce tree and waved them up and down like bird wings.

Hawk wanted Emma to join the Spruce Dance, but she preferred to sit and watch, so he sat with her. Water drums, gourd rattles, and flutes made the strange sounding music. The dancers swayed as they moved in the circle with their arms outstretched, and their movements looked quite lovely.

Emma looked at Hawk and smiled to let him know she was enjoying it. The look he gave her was so like Edgar's look of love that she caught her breath. This may have been a mistake. She didn't want to encourage Hawk's courtship.

The fourth night, they were to make offerings to the sacred fire. Emma decided to stay in the hut. She didn't want to become a part of the Cherokee religion, and she didn't want Hawk to think she was changing her mind about him.

Spring came late to the mountains, but in April the temperatures had begun to warm until there were some mornings without frost. She wondered what Edgar would be doing now. He and Emma had planned to marry in the spring. Did he still believe she would return, or did he think her dead?

Lily began to show Emma plants in the field as they gathered and collected them. Emma knew a few of them already, but many were new to her. She also watched Lily help those who came to her with minor ailments.

Hawk continued to look at Emma with longing, but he didn't ask her to become his wife again, nor did he try to get her to share his bed. He would sometimes meet her away from the village when she'd been sent on a chore. Lily felt sure no one would bother Emma with Hawk's declaration, so Hawk wasn't here so much for her protection as for her companionship.

If she went to get water, he would carry it almost back to the village. Then, he would hand it to Emma. Emma knew he didn't want the other men to see him doing her chores.

If she walked out to gather plants and herbs, which Lily now trusted her to do, he would often walk beside her and watch. Sometimes he would tap her on the shoulder and point to a pretty bird or animal. Once he stopped her movement and, in one fluid motion, threw his knife to sever the head of a timber rattler. After that, Emma appreciated his company even more.

One day, in what she guessed must be around the first of May, she left the village to go look for plants from the forest. The day was warm enough, and she didn't need her cloak, especially with her leather dress.

She carried her basket on her arm and had just gone from sight of the village when Hawk joined her. She smiled her welcome. She didn't want to encourage the man, but she did enjoy his company. She missed his companionship on the times he didn't come.

Hawk had ducked behind some bushes for a private moment, and Emma continued collecting the plants. She rounded some dense growth and came face to face with a bear cub. She knew enough to back off, but it was too late. The mother bear had spotted her and charged.

The creature moved lightning fast for its large size. Hawk came just as fast. He quickly shot three successive arrows into the beast as he ran, but they barely slowed it. As the bear went up to lunge at Hawk, he thrust his spear. The creature knocked Hawk to the ground and landed on top of him, giving an indescribable roar.

Neither of them moved, and neither did Emma. Her breath stopped, and her heart stood still for a split second. Then, she moved to the pile of flesh.

"Hawk! Oh Hawk!" she cried. *God, he couldn't be dead. Please let him be all right.*

She couldn't move the bear. The beast weighed too much to even roll over. She saw Hawk's head appear from under the bear. She grabbed under his shoulder and tried to pull him out. He crawled clear, and Emma wondered if she'd helped or hindered him. He had gashes across one cheek, and he was covered in blood from his chest to below his waist. Emma pulled up his shirt and carefully tried to find the wound, but she couldn't find it.

Hawk tapped her shoulder to get her attention and pointed to the bear. He was telling her the blood was from the bear. She breathed a sigh of relief, and he smiled.

She examined the claw marks on his face. Apparently the bear had raked his face as she fell. They weren't deep, so there'd been no force behind the blow. They should heal fine, without even a scar, especially if Lily applied some of her ointment.

Emma pointed back to the village. She was ready to go back now. The life had drained out of her when she'd thought Hawk might be dead, and she didn't have the energy to collect more plants. Hawk nodded.

Lily took one look at Hawk and thought the worst. He quickly told her what had happened.

"Put some salve on Hawk's face," Emma told the older woman, and she nodded.

When Lily started to apply the ointment, Hawk said something. He looked at Emma.

"He wants Emma to do," Lily told her and handed her the salve.

Emma tenderly applied the medicine as Hawk watched her expression the whole time.

He said something, and Lily put it in her broken English. "Hawk say Emma love Hawk."

"Tell him I love him, but not as a wife."

Lily did, and Hawk nodded. "Hawk go now with men to get bear," Lily said as Hawk left.

CHAPTER THIRTEEN

Changes

Edgar couldn't believe Emma had been gone for about four months. His father had told him time would heal his anguish, but it hadn't. He missed Emma as much if not more now than the first week she'd gone missing. In fact, he missed her more the longer it became.

His heart ached for her with even a physical hurt. His mother said he was making himself sick, but he had no control over it. Emma's disappearance had happened apart from his control.

He'd lost weight, and his skin looked shallow and pale. His mother said his eyes had even lost their spark. He no longer had the zest for life he'd once had. He tried to eat, and he managed to force down some, but he found it difficult. Nothing tasted good, and he had no joy about anything. He had not laughed nor teased since Emma had vanished.

He read his Bible and tried to seek God's answers to his questions. All this had happened for a reason, he told himself. He struggled to find out what that reason could be.

He no longer blamed God. That had been a fleeting notion, created at first from his great distress. He trusted God completely. God could see the big picture and know the future. Edgar couldn't. Yet, Edgar couldn't shake the thought this had something to do with him and his perceptions.

"God," he prayed over and over again, "if there's something I'm missing, if there's something I need to learn, please show me what it is. If I need to change, if I need to do something differently, please let me know what it is. Give me understanding and point me in the right direction."

Over time, three Bible sections and passages stood out in Edgar's mind. It just took him a while to put it all together.

The first came in the book of Job. He read it over and over, and it still called to him. He began to understand Job not only as a patient man but also one of great faith. Nothing Satan did to him could shake his complete faith in and love for God. Yet, it wasn't until Edgar put the two other places with it that it all became clear.

One was where God ordered Abraham to sacrifice Isaac, Abraham's beloved son of his old age and his only child by his wife, Sarah, whom he loved dearly. Yet, God demanded he sacrifice Isaac as a burnt offering. Edgar couldn't conceive of such a request, but as Abraham prepared to stab Isaac to put him out of his misery before he burned him, God sent an angel to stop him. God didn't require the sacrifice. He just required Abraham to be willing to do it.

The other one came in three of the Gospels. Matthew, Mark, and Luke all said the exact same verse, so it must be important. Jesus said, "Love the Lord thy God with all thy heart, and with all thy soul, and with all thy strength, and with all thy mind; and thy neighbor as thyself."

Edgar had probably read those verses over a hundred times. He could quote them by heart, but had he ever taken them to heart? Put with the story of Job and his patience and faith and the story of Abraham's willingness to do anything God required of him, the verse on loving God spoke directly to Edgar.

Edgar had to put God above all else in his life. Edgar had to love God more than he loved Emma. He'd never consciously made the decision to love Emma more than anything else in his life, but that's exactly what he'd done. It had been easier to love Emma, whom he could see, than God, whom he couldn't.

But, God was real to him. He felt His presence in his life. Now, he knew what he had to do. He had to put God first. He had to love God more.

"God, forgive me," he prayed. "Forgive me for allowing Emma more importance in my life than I put on Thee. You are everything to me. Search my heart now. Know that I put You above all else. Only Thou art eternal and never failing. For all I know, Emma may be dead, or she may have found another man to love but, regardless, You will be here for me, loving me. I realize I need You more than I need Emma. I say this, not to bargain or impress so You will send Emma back to me. I say it in love and trust for Thee. I will look to You for my joy, for my peace. Help me, I pray. Amen."

Edgar felt better immediately. He would still pray and ask God to send Emma back to him, but whether that happened or not, he would still put God first.

His parents and sister noticed a difference in Edgar right away. They assumed he had finally begun to get over Emma. His father suggested Edgar might like to call on some of the other young women within a day's ride.

"I'm not interested," Edgar told him. "I'm waiting for Emma. Even if she never comes back, I'll strive to live my life for God. Either way, I put God first."

He could tell his father didn't understand, but his parents said no more to him about it. He began to eat better and no longer seemed despondent, so they let well enough alone.

Toward the end of May, Lily came to Emma. "Lily love son," she told Emma.

Emma knew Lily loved Hawk, so why did she think it necessary to tell her?

"Lily want Hawk happy. Hawk love Emma. Lily want Emma marry Hawk and be daughter. Hawk be happy."

"I love you both." Emma shook her head. "But I can't marry Hawk. Hawk deserves someone who will love him more than I can. Hawk is a good man."

"Emma still love Edgar more than Hawk?" Lily asked. "Emma still want to go back?"

"Yes, I love Edgar more than anyone on earth."

"Hawk must go with men," Lily told her. "Hawk no want Emma here without Hawk. Hawk take Emma to cabin of sister. Husband and sister take Emma home."

Emma stood too stunned to move. Did Lily just say what she thought she'd said? Had Hawk worked out a way to get Emma back to Edgar?

"Home to Edgar?" Emma clarified.

"Home to Edgar," Lily nodded.

Tears formed in Emma's eyes and streamed down her face. She cried from the joy of going back to Edgar. But she also cried for Hawk, for the tall, handsome, gentle, kind man of integrity who had given Emma his heart. She hadn't wanted it, had indeed rejected it and probably broken it. Yet Hawk had defended her against all foes and loved her always, despite her rejections.

She realized how much he loved her now. He loved her enough to give Emma her heart's desire. He would send her back to Edgar and out of his life so that she could be truly happy. He would set her free.

The three of them set off two days later. Lily would go stay with her grandchildren, while her daughter and son-in-law took

Emma home. Emma liked the plan. She didn't want to ride back with only a man she didn't know to accompany her.

They traveled over two days to get to the cabin. Of course, their pace was slower than before, since Lily traveled with them.

Hawk looked at Emma with sad eyes, and her heart went out to him. She realized she caused his sadness, but she didn't know what she could do about it. She knew without a doubt she belonged with Edgar. It felt like an impossible situation either way: she either hurt Hawk, or she hurt Edgar. She loved Edgar so much; she would never choose to hurt him, but how she wished she didn't have to hurt either of these honorable men

What if something had happened to Edgar? What if he had died in an accident, like Luther? What if he had married someone else, although she doubted that? What if he no longer wanted her after he heard her story and knew she'd been with the Indians for this long? Her family had all gone west. She would be all alone without him. Could she accept Hawk as her husband if that happened?

She looked up at the man walking beside her. Could she ever love this man like a wife? Maybe, but would she always love Edgar more? She had to go back to Edgar first. She'd never know another peace until she found out if Edgar still waited for her.

If something had happened to Edgar, she could always return with Lily's daughter and son-in-law. In that case, it would probably be the best thing for her to do.

How rare for a woman to find so great a love from one man, but Emma had found it from two, two very special men. To say she would make Hawk very happy if she returned to him would be an understatement. She knew he would accept her as his wife on any terms, even if she would always love Edgar more.

Emma realized then that she could love Hawk as a wife. She also knew she had to return to Edgar, her first love. She'd promised to marry him, and she intended to live up to that promise.

Her feelings for him had never wavered. He had filled her heart before she ever met Hawk. She would go back to Edgar, but she would come back to Hawk if she couldn't have Edgar. She would leave it all in God's hands. He knew best.

They made it to the cabin by the afternoon of the third day. The log house was not as nice as Edgar's, but it was better than Emma's had been.

The daughter's English name was Sheila, and her husband turned out to be an Irishman named Connell O'Leary. Connell didn't want to take Emma back unless his wife accompanied them. "It wouldn't look right," he said. He was correct, but Emma had been in the woods alone with four Indian braves for over a week. What would Edgar think about that? Would he still want to marry Emma?

Connell O'Leary loved to talk and laugh, and he tended to laugh at himself much of the time. Sheila seemed much quieter, even quieter than Lily. Maybe she would talk more once she got to know Emma.

She had a gentle way, although she went about her tasks in silence, and she noticed everything. She resembled Hawk, but she seemed petite and pretty, where he was tall and handsome. She spoke English much better than Lily.

"My brother looks at you with love in his eyes," she told Emma as they washed up the supper dishes. The O'Leary family lived like the whites.

"He may, but I was promised to Edgar before I met Hawk."

"My brother is a good man. He would make a good husband. He may become a great leader, for he already does well for one so young. Besides his skills as a hunter and warrior, he has wisdom beyond his years."

"I agree... but he's not the one for me." Emma wasn't going to dare mention any other possibilities until she found out if Edgar still wanted her.

Hawk walked in on the end of the conversation to hand them his coffee cup. He asked Sheila something, and she answered. He said something else, and she translated.

"My brother says if you will stay, he will build you a cabin and live like the whites. He says he will learn to speak to you in your own language. He will do these things for you, Emma."

Deeply touched, Emma had to share another concern. "I noticed Hawk still seems to practice the Cherokee religion. As a Christian, I shouldn't be unequally yoked."

Sheila told Hawk.

"Hawk says, for you, he will study your God, but he cannot make promises on matters of the spirit. The afterlife is too important. He will seriously consider your beliefs, however."

"Tell him I appreciate his offers, but I still must return to Edgar."

She did and told Emma Hawk's reply. "Hawk wants to know if Edgar has gone or no longer wants you, would you come back to him?"

There it was, the question she had tried to avoid. Hawk constantly surprised her with his intelligence and insight. He'd thought of every possibility to have her. Now what did she say? She didn't want to give him false hope, but she needed to be truthful.

She thought carefully while both Hawk and Sheila watch her intently. *God, give me the right words*, she silently prayed.

"Perhaps it could be so, but I must see Edgar first. Our love was so great, it knew no bounds. My love is still the same, and I think his will be too." She took a deep breath. "I'll know how he feels before you and Connell leave to come back. If something is wrong, I'll come back with you, but I wouldn't want to marry right away. Hawk would have to be patient with me, but I would see him and think about becoming his wife. I think I might eventually be able to marry him, but I can't consider that now. I must see Edgar first."

Sheila seemed to understand. Emma hoped Hawk would.

"Hawk says he will wait for you. He says now he knows what love is, he will never marry unless he finds someone to love as much as he loves you. He says no matter when it is, if you want him, send for him by getting word to us here, and he will come for you."

"Tell him, if I don't come back with you, not to wait for me. I want him to be happy. Tell him to find his own happiness because that will make me happy. I would be sad to know he was waiting for nothing."

"He says he will wait unless he finds someone to love as much. He will wait."

Hawk would stay with them that night but planned to leave in the morning. Lily would stay at the cabin with her two grandchildren, a girl and a boy.

They were beautiful children, and the thought passed Emma's mind that her and Hawk's children would look much like them. She looked up to see Hawk watching her, as usual. He nodded at her and gave her a knowing smile. It was infuriating how the man could read her mind. They wouldn't need to speak the same language, except she couldn't read his thoughts as well—or could she?

Emma had a feeling Hawk would leave in the night before she got a chance to say good-bye. She didn't stop to think why this mattered so much to her. She just knew it did. She slept fitfully and lay awake more than she slept. She got up early the next morning, well before daylight broke. Hawk had rolled up his pallet. Had he already gone? She hurried to see.

She found him on the porch. He had all his things, but he was sitting on the porch, waiting for the light. The sky must be overcast, because there were no stars or moon to be seen.

She sat down beside him and touched his arm. "I'm sorry, Hawk," she said. She had no doubt he would know what she was saying.

He said something in Cherokee as he turned to her. He had said something like, "Me too."

He put out his hand to her, and she put hers in his. They sat there in a comfortable silence, holding hands. The sun finally peeped up, and Hawk rose. He stepped down to the ground, still holding Emma's hand. He turned and pulled her into his arms. He rested his head on the top if hers, relishing the feel of her. She allowed him this. She owed him this much. She owed him her life.

He released her but held her shoulders and looked into her eyes. "I love you, Emma," he said in his language.

"I know," she said.

He turned and left her then, walking quickly away without looking back. But not before she had seen the tears pool in his eyes and roll down his cheeks.

Her tears also fell, not for the want of Hawk, but for his want of her. She hurt for his hurt.

The rest of them stayed at the cabin one more day. Emma planned to wear her leather dress, but she had packed her other clothes. She might change to them before she got to the Moretzes, even if they were ragged. But she hoped some of her other clothes would still be at her cabin, and they would pass there first.

They left at sunrise. Lily hugged Emma tightly. "You daughter too," she said.

"Thank you for everything," Emma told her, "especially for the lessons on healing. Thank Hawk for me. I didn't even say 'thank you' to him, and he's been so good to me."

"He know."

He probably did know. He seemed to know exactly how she felt and thought, and because of this knowledge, he had helped her go home.

They rode horses back. Emma had never considered this possibility. She sat astride the horse with her leather dress up to her knees, which didn't look very lady-like, but she rode east toward Edgar and home.

Because of the horses, they had bedrolls and a small pot to cook in. This turned out to be a much more comfortable trip than the first one. They made it in half the time.

The terrain began to look familiar, but they came to her cabin before Emma expected it. Hawk must have given Connell good directions.

The place looked sad and deserted. Anything worth taking had disappeared, but the daylight already dimmed, so they would stay here tonight. They would be at the Moretz's cabin sometime in the morning.

Emma's clothes had been taken, so she tried to change into her old clothes. However, when she tried to button the dress, it ripped in two places. The fabric had become too threadbare, and she had grown. She had no choice but to wear her leather one. She also put on the moccasins. She still had her shoes, but they looked strange with the Cherokee dress.

They started out at first light with Emma leading the way. The closer they got, the more nervous Emma became. She prayed her way up the mountain. God had brought her through all this. He wasn't going to leave her now.

She finally chided herself as foolish. Thanks to Hawk, she had someplace to go, even if Edgar didn't want her. She knew how most folks felt about the Cherokee in these parts, but then, Edgar wasn't like most folks—not at all.

She put it in God's hands, sighed deeply, and slid off the horse just before they came into sight of the cabin. If she had to meet Edgar wearing Cherokee dress, at least it wouldn't be pulled up above her knees.

Edgar had just finished the milking and was coming from the barn. He had run later than usual this morning, but he had been up half the night birthing a calf.

He looked up to see Indians. On the second look, there was a white man and two squaws. What did they want? He thought about getting his rifle, but these three didn't look like trouble.

"Edgar?"

The voice came from the past and struck an arrow through his heart. *Emma?* It couldn't be. *It was! Glory be, it was!*

He released the milk buckets, not waiting to see how they landed. He ran to her as she ran for him. He caught her in his arms and lifted her high, letting her ease down the front of him, reveling in the feel of her, and all the while looking into her eyes.

"Oh, Emma, my prayers have been answered."

He kept his arm around her. He might never let her out of his arms again.

"Come, come, all of you," he beckoned to the others. "Come tell me all about what happened to you,"

Emma introduced Connell and Sheila to Edgar, and then to his family. Everyone was shocked but happy to see her.

"I thought Edgar was going to waste away to nothing," Mrs. Moretz told Emma. "I've never seen a man so distraught. I feared I'd lose my last son for a while there."

"You look good now," Emma told him and smiled.

"I feel great now that you're back, but God had to give me a good shaking after you vanished. I've learned to love and trust Him more through all this."

Emma told them her story from the time she had been taken to where Hawk and Lily took her to his sister's, and they brought her home. When she told of Sliced Arm, Edgar clenched his fist and gritted his teeth, but he listened without saying anything.

"Thank you so much for bringing Emma back to us," Mrs. Moretz said to the O'Learys. "You must stay with us for a while."

"We need to be getting home," Connell said.

"Please stay." Emma looked at Sheila. "At least for tonight."

Sheila seemed to understand, as Emma hoped she would. "Yes, for tonight," she told them. Her husband seemed surprised but nodded.

"Could we go for a walk?" Emma asked Edgar. "We need to talk."

"Sure," he said with a puzzled look.

They walked to the pasture behind the barn. The spring flowers dotted the green grass with splashes of color.

"You look so different," he told her, "but the Indian dress suits you. Of course, anything would suit you. You're so pretty, Emma, even prettier than when you left. You look older, even though it's only been a little more than four months."

"It seems longer. So much has happened."

"It does seem much longer. It seems like years." He looked at her carefully. "Were you harmed, Emma? Did you sleep with anyone while you were gone, either by choice or by force?"

"No, Edgar. I would have been forced if it hadn't been for Hawk, but he kept me safe."

"And this Hawk, your voice changes when you speak of him. It grows soft and tender. Did you fall in love with him?"

"No. I care for him, but I didn't fall in love with him. I couldn't, because I still love you so much."

Edgar let out a deep breath from where he'd been holding it in. She could see he wanted to believe her, but he was having a hard time doing so. He still felt unsure.

"And, did Hawk fall in love with you?"

"Yes, Hawk loved me a great deal. He loved me enough to put my happiness above his and send me back to you."

Edgar looked stunned, as if he couldn't quite comprehend it. "That is surprising. I wonder if I could have done the same thing if the situation had been reversed. Perhaps I could, if I thought you loved Hawk more than me. I'm not sure."

What was he telling her? Was he saying Hawk's love for her was greater than his?

"If I'd been killed or something, would you go back to Hawk?"

She took another deep breath. She didn't want to answer this question, but she had vowed to tell Edgar nothing but the truth.

"I told him I would come back if you no longer wanted me or if something had happened to you, but I wouldn't marry him right away. He would have to court me."

Edgar gave a strange little laugh. It had no merriment in it.

"So, you have an alternate plan, and you come out with a lover either way."

"Edgar, don't do this. If you don't want me, I'd have nowhere else to go. My family has left. I wouldn't go with them because I wouldn't leave you. I was waiting for you to come that Sunday. I'd have come home with you, but I was captured on Saturday. At every danger, I fought as hard as I could, but I would have been raped and killed if it hadn't been for Hawk. Without you, I would go back because I have no better place to go, and he would be good to me. He would be so good to me. Still, I wouldn't go back to marry him immediately, but I'd give him a chance."

Edgar listened to her. She could tell he was weighing what she said, but she couldn't tell what he was thinking.

"Talk to me, Edgar. What are you thinking and feeling?"

"Oh, Emma, I'm not sure I know. My thoughts are all scrambled and confused."

"Do you still want to marry me?"

He paused, and that pause told her more than she wanted to know. Why did he have to think about it?

He looked away and began to talk. "I've wanted you back so badly. Besides God, you're all I've thought about, all I've longed for. For over four months, most of my prayers have been about you, and every time I've prayed, I've included you. Now my prayers have been answered. You're back, but are you the same Emma who left? You seem changed, more grown up, more sure of yourself." He looked at her. She saw the confusion, but behind it all, she thought she could see the longing and the love.

"I haven't changed that much, Edgar. I've had some harrowing experiences, and I've come through the dangers unscathed. Through it all, I knew God was with me, and I just trusted Him. Through it all, I thought of you. I always believed I would get back to you. When Hawk asked me to marry him, I told him my heart belonged to you, and if he wanted me to be happy, he'd have to bring me back to you. That's when he began to arrange to have me brought back."

"What was Hawk like?"

Why did he want to talk about Hawk? She didn't, but she sensed some need within him to know and understand. Perhaps she'd feel the same way in his place.

"He was a fine man, strong and courageous, but kind and caring. He was smart too. I could make him understand with just gestures. At the last, he could just look at me and almost know what I was thinking. When we said good-bye, he spoke in Cherokee, and I spoke English, but we each knew what the other was saying."

"He didn't speak English?"

"No, but his mother spoke broken English and understood it better. She translated some. And Sheila speaks good English. She's Hawk's sister."

"Did he ever kiss you?"

"No! Never."

"Did he touch you?"

"He touched my face once, he held my hands, and he hugged me."

"You let him hug you?"

"Yes, he hugged me to say good-bye. I felt I owed him that much." Emma laid her hand on Edgar's arm. "He saved me from Sliced Arm's wrath when I cut him with the butcher knife, from rape twice, and from being mauled by a bear. I wouldn't be standing here before you today if it wasn't for Hawk."

"You sound like you think a lot of him."

"I do. My heart ached when he hurt so badly because I didn't want him for my husband. He had done so much for me, but I had to hurt him to get back to you. I know I broke his heart, Edgar."

Edgar removed Emma's hand from his arm. "Why did you come back to me, Emma? If you care so much for Hawk, I'm surprised you didn't stay with him."

Emma pressed both hands to her pounding heart. "How can you ask me such a thing after the love we shared? Was the deep love just on my part? Was your love not strong enough to see you through? Yes, I care for Hawk. I care a lot about him, but I love you so much more. It's you I came back to, Edgar. If I'd wanted Hawk, I would have stayed there. I didn't have to come home."

Edgar just stared at her for the longest time. Emma didn't know what else she could say to make him understand. She'd said all she could. She'd told the truth.

He gave a sigh, closed his eyes for a second, and then pulled her into his arms. "Yes, you came back to me, didn't you? You came back to *me*." He pulled back and took both her hands in his, so he could look into her face. "Jealousy is such an ugly beast, Emma. Forgive me. Yes, I still want to marry you. I've always wanted to marry you. If you had been raped, I would still want to marry you, but I praise God you weren't. I praise God Hawk was there for you, to keep you safe. I praise God Hawk loved you enough to send you back to me."

"He was my guardian angel, Edgar, but you are my love."

He kissed her lips, lightly, tenderly, lovingly. It sent a shiver through her that shook her to the core. She knew he, like her, wanted a deeper kiss, but he was saving those until they were married. She hoped they could be married soon.

She looked in his eyes and saw they were filled with love. This was the Edgar she knew—the one she'd always loved.

"Come," he said. "We need to get you back inside before they think we've both gone missing."

"I could go missing with you. I could go anywhere with you."

Edgar let out a joyful laugh, one filled with happiness and expectation.

PART TWO

CLIFTON AND SARAH

CHAPTER FOURTEEN

Belinda

NORTH CAROLINA MOUNTAINS, MAY 1829

"Mama did all that really happen to you?" Gracie asked in amazement, as she had in the past. "You were taken by some Cherokees, and a brave named Hawk befriended you and kept you safe?"

Clifton watched his older sister. This story had always fascinated her.

"That's what happened," Mama told them. "Hawk protected me and helped me come back to your father. I've told you this story before."

"I know," Gracie said, "but it's been a while, and I like to hear it. I'd forgotten a lot."

"Do you know what happened to Hawk?" Clifton asked.

"No, I never heard from Hawk again. When Connell and Sheila went back after bringing me home, they knew your father and I were planning our wedding."

"If I remember right, Sheila was Hawk's sister," Clifton said. "It's too bad Hawk didn't come to your wedding, since he had been such a good friend."

"I think Hawk liked Mama too much for that," Gracie said knowingly.

"He was a good friend," Mama told them. "I hope he's happily married and has children as wonderful as mine."

"We're hardly as little as you make it sound, Mama," Gracie said. "I'm married and moving to Salem in a few weeks, and Clifton has finished college, practiced with a doctor, and is ready to start his own medical practice."

"I can't believe how the time has flown, but you'll always be my children." Mama sighed. "We added onto the house to accommodate four children, and soon there'll be just Edgar and me again."

"I'm not going away anytime soon," Clifton said. "You're stuck with me for a while yet."

Mama tilted her head as she gazed at Clifton. "I almost wish you hadn't become a doctor, Clifton. It would be nice if you wanted the farm, since your brothers aren't here."

"We all miss them, Mama," Gracie said. Her two youngest brothers had been born a year apart and were almost like twins. They died a year apart too.

"It's awfully hard to lose a child," Mama said, "and Edgar and I've lost two."

Clifton looked at his sister. "You and I were born a year apart, Gracie. Just like our brothers."

"I know, but we've hardly been like twins, although we are close. I guess we'd have been even closer if we'd both been girls."

"Or boys," Clifton added. He turned to his mother again. "You never heard what happened to your parents, did you, Mama?"

"I never did. They headed west is all I know. I felt my mother would have written to me if she could, but I never heard from her. I used to worry about it, but I've since come to realize she'd be better off in heaven. Living with Papa's drinking made life extremely difficult for her."

"But you did get a letter from your older sister, didn't you?" Gracie asked.

"I did. It was right after Edgar and I were married. I'd had Edgar write her when Christie, our youngest sister, died. Francie wrote back several months later to say she and Martin were living in Philadelphia, and Martin was helping his great-uncle in his clock shop. Martin seemed to like working on watches and clocks."

"You didn't really think they were happy, did you?" Gracie asked.

"I worried about them, certainly. Francie said Martin remained distant and aloof much of the time. I know he had a hard time dealing with his brother's passing when they married and left here in such a hurry."

"I just don't understand how she could marry Uncle Martin so soon after Uncle Luther died," Gracie said. "After all, she was going to marry Uncle Luther until he was killed in that fall."

"She had her reasons, I suppose."

"But, she couldn't have loved him."

"She wrote that Martin had been a good provider, and he never mistreated her. They did have two children, a boy and a girl."

"I remember," Gracie said. "I wish they didn't live so far away. They are my cousins, Luther and Emma."

"Yes, they shortened Emmaline, thankfully. That's a mouthful."

"I don't know," Papa said as he walked in from the garden. "I've always liked the name. It's pretty and different, just like the woman. *Edgar*, now. I've never liked it."

"I never knew that!" Mama twisted her head to look at Papa. "We've been married all these years, and I never knew you didn't like your name."

One corner of Papa's mouth turned up. "Do you like it?"

"I do. I think 'Emma and Edgar' has a nice sound to it."

"They do go together well, don't they?" He grinned mischievously. "I guess I'll just keep 'Edgar,' then."

"What happened to your sister, Papa?" Gracie asked. "I know you told us, but I don't remember the details."

"Hilda married a man who lived over in Meat Camp, close to my relatives there. They lived there for a while, but then they moved to Virginia, near Williamsburg, when her husband inherited some property. I get a letter from her around Christmas time each year, but we've never been that close. I love her, of course."

"Oh, yes, I remember the letters. It's just easy to forget when they are from someone you don't really know," Gracie said.

"When did our grandparents die?" Clifton asked. This willingness to sit down and reminisce was rare, and he wanted to take advantage of this change in his parents.

"When I was expecting you, Clifton," Mama said. "Your father wouldn't let me tend to them for fear I would come down with it. We thought it was smallpox, but where they could have caught smallpox is a mystery. I fixed the medicines and left it outside their door. Edgar stayed with them and wouldn't let me near. I even had to leave his food outside their bedroom door."

"I'd been exposed to smallpox once before and didn't come down with it, so I hoped I wouldn't get it," Papa added.

"Didn't the Cherokee have smallpox epidemics several times?" Clifton asked.

"Yes," Mama said, "but none of us had had any contact with the Cherokee for years."

"The only thing we could figure," Papa continued, "is that your grandfather had gone into Councill's Store, and maybe he'd picked it up there. We never heard of another case at the time."

"Edgar burned all the bedding from the room after he buried them, and he wouldn't let us use that bedroom until you were a few months old. He bathed in lye soap until I thought he was going to scrub his skin off, and he wouldn't sleep with me until well after you were born."

"Maybe I was being obsessive about it, like you thought, but it worked," Papa said. "None of us caught it."

"Where was I during all that?" Gracie asked.

"I kept you with me," Mama told her. "You were a well-behaved child, even as a baby."

Papa changed the subject. "Clifton, weren't you serious about a girl when you were in Chapel Hill?"

"Not really. I courted Imogene Coker for a while. I liked her at first, but she seemed too much of a high society girl for me. I'm not going to get married unless I can have a marriage like yours and Mama's. I want my wife to be madly in love with me," he said with a smile.

"Leave the boy alone," Mama said. "I'm in no hurry for him to leave home."

"Well, he's right about one thing," Papa teased. "My wife is madly in love with me, and always has been."

"That's okay," Mama smiled smugly. "My husband feels the same about me."

"Absolutely," Papa agreed.

Clifton and his parents went to his sister's home to see her and her husband off. Ernest Breyer, Gracie's husband, had accepted his parents' invitation to come back to Salem, where he grew up, and help in his father's gun shop. They planned for Ernest to take over the shop, as well as their house, after they died.

Ernest had never been really happy in the mountains. He'd come to visit friends, met and married Gracie, and moved into Mama's family's old cabin. They'd fixed it up, but Ernest couldn't get used to the primitive way of life. He liked the idea of going back down the mountain to his Moravian roots.

Clifton realized he felt differently. He'd liked college well enough, but life in Chapel Hill didn't appeal to him the way life on the farm did. However, he wanted to be a doctor, not a farmer. He would be happier if he could live on a mountain farm and still have a medical practice, but that would be nearly impossible. One couldn't do two such demanding jobs at the same time. Besides, if he wanted to support a family by doctoring, he was going to have to either move into a town without a doctor, or move to a larger town that could support having more than one.

Maybe he could buy a plantation, hire an overseer, and let the slaves do all the work while he doctored. It would be hard for him to buy a plantation with his meager funds, and he wasn't comfortable with the thought of owning slaves. The idea of owning another human being had never felt right to him.

Well, he'd face all that when the time came. Right now, he just wanted to enjoy being back at the farm with his parents.

He glanced over at his parents. They had been deeply in love with each other ever since he could remember. He wanted to find such a love, but so far it had eluded him. He'd met girls he liked, but he'd never fallen in love with any of them.

"Are you gathering wool, Clifton?" his sister asked. "Come give me a hug and say good-bye. I expect you to come to see us, now. Salem might even be a place you could start your practice."

"I might just come and check it out," Clifton told her, "but for now I want to enjoy being home. I need a break."

"There's an itinerate preacher going to be at the Blankenship cabin for a service Sunday. I thought we'd go," Papa said on the way home.

"I'd like that." Mama smiled at him. "It's been a while since I've seen Oralee." She sighed and leaned against Papa's shoulder. "Remember how she and I became good friends after our wedding?"

"Oh, so you aren't going in order to hear the preacher," Papa teased. He enjoyed teasing Mama.

"That's good," she said, "but I get just as much from our Bible studies at home. I've always thought you would have been a talented pastor, Edgar."

Papa's eyes softened as he looked at her. "I'm happy leading my family in worship," he said. "I don't need a larger congregation. Besides, God never called me to that. You're strong in your faith and trust in God too, Emma. Sometimes, I think you have greater trust than I do, and I know you're more patient. I tend to want to take care of things myself, or else I want God to fix it now. That's what happened when you went missing. I had to read Job over and over before I saw how much I needed to work on patience. And I was so upset, I put my whole attention on you and didn't put God first."

Mama lifted her head. "Sometimes you're too hard on yourself, Edgar. I had it easier at that time in some ways, in matters of faith and trust anyway. I had no reason to believe you were in danger. Yet, you had no idea what might be happening to me. You knew I could very well be facing horrible things. I think God understands situations like that."

"You always know the right thing to say to make me feel better, Emma. Thank you. Anyway, God brought me to the realization that, regardless of how much I loved you, I needed to love Him more."

Clifton listened, enthralled. His parents rarely had such private conversations in front of him. Maybe they'd finally begun to see him as an adult. At twenty-two, it was about time.

Clifton hadn't thought of possibly meeting someone when he'd come to the preaching service at the Blankenships', but here he sat, staring at a pretty young woman with red hair across the way. He'd heard far too little of what the preacher had said.

The preaching ended, and they moved to their wagons to gather their baskets. Everyone would eat a picnic dinner because it would take too long for most people to get home.

"Do you know who the young red-headed woman is?" Clifton asked his mother.

"No, but ask your father. He knows more people around here than I do."

"I don't know her," his father told him, "but she's with the Hodges. Do you want to come with me to talk with them?"

"Sure."

They approached the Hodges family. "Graden." Papa shook the man's hand. "Norma." He nodded at the man's wife. "You remember my son, Clifton."

"I remember him," Mr. Hodges said, "but I remember a little boy, not this young man before me." He turned to the young woman. "This is Norma's niece, Belinda Schreiner, from Greensboro. She's spending her summer with us to escape the heat."

"Pleased to meet you," Clifton and his father said to Belinda.

"Likewise, I'm sure," Belinda replied in a soft, alluring voice.

There seemed to be a coyness about her, but Clifton felt drawn to her anyway. She might be a little on the heavy side, but not much, and she stood out in an attractive way.

"Please bring your quilt and basket over and join us," Mr. Hodges offered. "The young people would probably enjoy getting to know each other better. We're more isolated up here than Bee is used to."

Bee. Clifton didn't much like the nickname, but somehow it suited her. He hoped she didn't sting. He would have said it aloud, but he didn't know how she would take teasing, and he didn't want to offend her at the start.

"What does your family do in Greensboro?" Clifton asked.

"Father owns a furniture shop. He started off small, but now he usually just keeps the books, and workers do all the manual labor. What about your family?"

"We're farmers, like most of the people up here, but I just finished college at Chapel Hill. While I was there, I lived with a doctor and helped him in his practice. I'll be looking to start my own medical practice in the near future."

"Really? A doctor can make a good livelihood, and they have a good standing in the community. Will you stay around here?"

"I'd like to, but probably not. It would be hard to support a family by doctoring around here. I'll doubtless have to move east a ways, but I haven't decided anything yet. I want to spend the summer in the mountains first."

"Where would you move, if you could?"

"I really don't know. I guess it would be Wilkesboro, but I think they have a doctor or two there. I'll just have to look at the possibilities. My sister would like for me to come to Salem."

"You could come to Greensboro. We're slowly growing, and it's not all that far from Salem. Greensboro is now the county seat, you know."

"I'll consider my options when the time comes and decide then. When are you going back to Greensboro?"

"Not until August."

"Maybe we can see each other again."

"I'd like that."

"Why don't you folks come over to dinner on Saturday?" Norma asked. "I would invite you to supper, but it would be hard for you to get home before dark. Of course, you're welcome to stay the night. I wish we lived closer to folks. I feel so isolated and alone at times." She looked at her niece. "I'm so happy to have Bee with me for the summer, since all our girls have married and moved away."

Edgar looked at Emma. "We'd love to come for dinner," she said, "but we'll need to get home for the evening chores. What time?"

"Come about eleven. That will give us time to visit before and after we eat."

"Do you cook, Belinda?" Clifton didn't know why he asked. Didn't every girl cook?

"Not so much. We've always had slaves for that, as far back as I remember."

"How many slaves do you have?"

"We're up to five now in the house, which is probably as many as we need in town. Of course, Father also has some at his shop, but I don't keep up with those. Why don't you have slaves here in the mountains?"

"We don't have the big fields, and the growing season is much shorter here," Mr. Hodges answered for Clifton. It might have been a good thing he did, because Clifton's answer may have been more offensive. He hated the very idea of slavery.

"But, Uncle Graden," Belinda said, "they would be ever so useful around the farm. You could get more done, more planted, and neither Aunt Norma nor you would have to work so hard. You should get a couple of house slaves too."

"Farmers around here couldn't afford even one slave," Papa told her. "I understand they bring a good price."

"I don't really know about things like that," Belinda said. "I'm sure they do, but we own five, just in the house."

Clifton almost wished he wasn't going to be seeing Belinda on Saturday. The more he learned of her, the less they seemed to have in common. She certainly liked to brag.

Saturday, Belinda met them at the door dressed in a soft yellow dress that suited her pale complexion and red hair. Clifton had to admit she looked lovely.

Clifton had toyed with the idea of not even coming, but he couldn't bring himself to snub her like that. It seemed too selfish. So, here he was. He just hoped he had misread the things she'd said Sunday.

"Uncle Graden's cabin is so rustic," she said. "Our house in Greensboro is so much nicer."

This cabin wasn't as large as the Moretz's, since they'd added on the upstairs, but it was well-made. He'd seen much worse.

"I'm rather partial to a log house, myself," he told her. "I guess it's because that's what I grew up in."

"Our house in Greensboro has four bedrooms," she informed him.

"So does our cabin." It came out before he could stop himself, but he smiled to soften the words. *But, I don't usually brag about it.*

"Do you attend church in Greensboro?"

"Of course. All the best families do. It's expected."

Did she never do anything without selfish reasons or for some gain? Was there no topic on which they could converse that her shallowness or snobbishness wouldn't come out? He felt at a loss. This shattered the hope he'd felt when he'd first seen the woman. Imogene, back in Chapel Hill, hadn't even been this bad, although she had been concerned about status and material things too. He looked up and realized Mr. Hodges planned to take his father to the barn to show him something.

"I believe I'll go with the men folk," he said. "I'm sure you women have more to talk about without us around."

His mother raised her eyebrows but said nothing. Mama knew him well and should realize Belinda held no interest for him. Visiting with her would make his summer miserable.

Clifton managed to stick with the men and join their conversations for the rest of the visit. Belinda seemed miffed and said little. She stared at him with questions in her eyes, but how could he explain?

"Well, you weren't very friendly with Belinda today," his father said as they made their way back home. "I thought you might be interested."

"I was when I first saw her, but the more I got to know her, the more she annoyed me."

"*Annoyed* is a strong word," Mama said, "but I can see your point. She seems much too caught up in money, possessions, and social standing. It's sad, really."

"Yes, it is," Clifton agreed.

CHAPTER FIFTEEN

Sarah

A month went by, and Clifton gladly settled into the farm schedule. He liked helping his father with the never-ending list of things to do on a farm, especially in the three warmer seasons. After living in Chapel Hill while attending school, he appreciated the cooler summer climate more than ever. He loved these mountains. He loved being home.

He and his father came in from the farthest field to find three horses tied out front. They had visitors. Surely Belinda wouldn't ride a horse here, especially one without a sidesaddle. Clifton couldn't believe she'd want to see him again, either. He could tell she hadn't liked it when he hadn't paid her special attention the day they'd gone for dinner.

The two men went inside to find three strangers in the sitting room with Mama. Although they were dressed in normal clothing, the two women looked to be Cherokee.

"You remember my husband Edgar, and this is our son, Clifton. Clifton, this is Connell and Sheila O'Leary. I know you remember my story of the Cherokee and how they brought me home. And this is their youngest daughter, Sarah."

Clifton looked at the older couple and saw an Irishman full of fun and laughter and his quieter, composed Cherokee wife. Then his eyes fell on their daughter. His breath caught in his chest.

He'd never seen such a gorgeous woman. Her smooth complexion looked only slightly darker than Mama's, and she had long black hair that fell almost to her waist. She looked at him shyly, but her dark brown, doe-like eyes were so warm they would melt the most frigid man's heart. He knew he'd never seen anyone so beautiful, but anyone this pretty would likely be conceited, he thought. Belinda certainly was, and she hadn't been half this attractive.

"'Tis hoping this'll not be putting you out," Mr. O'Leary said, "but Sheila's been feeling poorly over the things that have been happening to the Cherokee and all, and I thought she needed a bit of a change. Ever since the rumor of gold discovered on Cherokee land has been spread about, there's more and more talk of taking the land from them. She's also been wondering about you two, so I thought we'd just take a trip."

"I'm so glad you did," Mama said. "I've wondered about all of you as well. How is Lily?"

"Lily died several years ago," Mr. O'Leary said, "but she'd lived a good life."

"And Hawk is doing okay on his own," Mrs. O'Leary added. "We're hoping he'll come live with us if the removal ever comes."

"He never married, then?" Mama asked.

"No, he never did," Mrs. O'Leary answered, and a look Clifton didn't understand passed between her and Mama.

"Do you think you will be allowed to stay if they do try to relocate the Cherokee?" Clifton asked.

"I think so, with my being Irish-American and all," Mr. O'Leary said.

"We'll pray this removal never happens," Papa said.

"Things have changed for the Cherokee," Mrs. O'Leary told them. "Most of them are building log cabins instead of the traditional huts. The men farm and raise cattle instead of hunting all the time. The women grow cotton and use it to spin and weave beautiful items. The missionaries have come and opened schools, and our children are more educated. Sequoyah has even developed a Cherokee alphabet for our own written language, and we now have a Cherokee newspaper and books in our language."

"Maybe this will help the Cherokee be seen as more civilized and cultured and help them keep their land," Mama said.

"I surely wish that would be the case," Mr. O'Leary said, "but I don't hold out much hope by what we're hearing. With gold fever spreading and other settlers wanting the land as well, I'm afraid the government will give in to pressure and take the land."

"How many children do you have now?" Mama asked. She seemed to want to change the depressing subject. "I remember seeing the two oldest."

"We had four more. They're all married and have families now, except for Sarah. She's our baby. We have over a dozen grandchildren already. In fact, one of our daughters and her white husband is seeing to our place now."

"Sarah's twenty, Sheila-love. She's hardly a baby."

Clifton definitely agreed with that. He couldn't keep his eyes off this woman. They repeatedly went to Sarah, no matter how many times he reminded them not to stare.

"We had four children," Mama told the O'Learys, "a girl, then three boys, but our two youngest boys were killed in separate accidents. A bear killed the youngest, and his brother was shot while out hunting about a year later. We don't know who did it, but we think it must have been an accident."

"I'm very sorry," Mrs. O'Leary said, and Mama nodded.

"I'm so glad you've come," Mama told her. "How long can you stay?"

"About a week, if you're sure it's okay?" Mr. O'Leary said.

"I'm sure that won't be nearly long enough," Mama said with a smile, "but we'll try to make it work."

"Now I'm remembering your teasing ways and why I liked you so much, Emma," Mr. O'Leary said with a laugh.

Clifton watched Sarah carefully in the days that followed. Her kindness and gentleness amazed him, but he couldn't believe anyone could be so beautiful in body and spirit. She had to be hiding some flaws. Shyness had been the only one he'd found so far.

Sarah and Mrs. O'Leary helped Mama, and Connell O'Leary helped Papa and him. They fell into farm life so easily that no one wanted to see them go.

Clifton tried to pull Sarah into a conversation, but she tended to give one-word answers to his questions, making it difficult. He loved the sound of her voice. It sounded soft and melodic, a cross between an Irish lilt and Indian tones. He began to think he liked everything about her. At least, he hadn't found anything yet he didn't like, unless it was her shyness. However, after Belinda, even that seemed rather appealing.

"Mama said Lily taught her all about herbal healing," Clifton told Sarah one evening after supper. "Did she also teach you?"

"I know some, but I was still a girl when Grandmother died." Sarah paused. "She always said Emma had been her best student."

"Mama does know home remedies." Clifton leaned back in his seat. "She's a big reason I wanted to become a doctor. I saw how she cared for people, and I wanted to help in the same way."

Sarah smiled at him then, the first time she had done so. It captivated him.

"I think it's important to help others and not just think of ourselves," Sarah said.

This had turned into the longest conversation she'd ever had with him. He wanted to keep her talking.

"Are you a Christian?" he asked.

"Yes. I've accepted Christ into my life, and I try to live as He teaches."

"My faith is very important to me. My parents have always emphasized serving God. I think trust in God got them through the time Mama was taken by the four Cherokee braves."

Sarah dropped her gaze for a moment before looking at Clifton. "You do not blame the Cherokee for doing such a thing?"

"I don't blame all the Cherokee, and I don't blame Hawk. He tried to help and protect her. I think I might feel differently about the one she calls 'Sliced Arm,' however."

"I never knew him, but Mother said he was an evil man."

Clifton leaned closer and lowered his voice. "My sister thinks Hawk must have been in love with Mama. Do you know if it's true?"

Sarah shook her head. "I don't know, but when Mother asks Hawk about getting married, he's always said it wouldn't be fair to the woman if he couldn't love her as much as he did his first love. Until he found one he could love that much, he preferred to live with his memories and meet the one he loves in his dreams. I don't know for sure who that was."

"But . . . you think it was my mother."

"I have guessed as much, but I wasn't born when she was with our people. I never saw them together."

"She seems to think a great deal of Hawk, but I know she loves my father. I've never met two people who are more in love, even after all these years. I only hope God will grant me such a love."

Sarah gave him a small smile. "May it be so." Then she got up to retire.

Clifton watched her leave the room and wished she would have stayed and talked to him longer. At least now he had some idea of how to carry on a conversation with her. He had to talk about others and not ask questions just about Sarah, as he'd been doing. He wished he could have talked with her all night. Yet, he felt blessed by the conversation they'd had.

As Clifton lay in bed that night, thinking of Sarah, thoughts of Hawk suddenly intruded. What would it be like to love someone so deeply that you'd give her up to make her happy? Clifton hoped never to find that out for himself. He wanted to love that completely, but he hoped and prayed the woman would love him back like that too.

After their brief conversation, Sarah didn't seem as reticent as before. Clifton set about to make her more at ease with him. He had to be careful because if he became aggressive or pushed too hard, he felt she would withdraw completely.

A week passed, and the Moretzes talked their guests into staying longer. It delighted Clifton when they agreed, but he knew their days here were numbered, and he couldn't stand the thought of never seeing Sarah again.

"How far away do they live?" he asked his mother.

"It's far, Clifton. Too far to get to without days of riding. You like Sarah, don't you?"

"I like her very much."

"Then pray about it, but don't tell God what you want Him to do. Find out what God wants you to do."

"How would you feel if I did end up marrying Sarah?"

"If you love each other, it would make me very happy. Sarah reminds me of Hawk by the way she cares for others. Hawk had a giving spirit. I think Sarah does too."

"Did Hawk love you, Mama?"

She looked at him for a long time. "He did. I think Hawk loved me with the most unselfish, unconditional love I've ever had outside of God's. I don't think many men would have sent me back to your father."

"Did you love him?"

"I probably did, but I loved your father deeply and felt we were meant to be together. All the time I lived with the Cherokee, I wanted to be back here with your father."

"I didn't expect to come in to hear you two talking about Hawk." Papa sounded serious.

Clifton stood up. "I guess I was asking Mama questions I shouldn't have."

"I heard her say she loved me and kept thinking about getting back to me. That didn't sound so bad to me."

His father was joking, so he wasn't upset. Clifton decided this was a good time to see what Sarah was doing. He heard his parents' conversation as he walked away, but he hadn't meant to eavesdrop.

"Have you ever been sorry you came back, Emma?" his father asked.

"No, not for one second."

As he turned to open the door, Clifton saw his father take his mother into his arms.

Clifton took Mama's advice and prayed. He asked God to show him a way to see more of Sarah, only if it was according to God's will. As it turned out, Clifton didn't need to do anything. God had Mama help him out.

"My Sarah has learned all we can teach her," Mr. O'Leary told Mama one night. "She's keen in her books."

"If she reads well, she should be able to teach herself now," Mama said.

"We're concerned about her," Mrs. O'Leary added. "If she marries a Cherokee, they may be forced to leave us, and there's no one around where we live who would be a suitable husband for her otherwise."

"Are there no settlers who would suit?" Mama asked.

"You know how isolated we are, and being half-Cherokee, she's not accepted by everyone."

Clifton felt like raging. How dare anyone reject this amazing woman because of her Indian blood! They would have to be idiots!

"Why don't you leave her with us for a while?" Mama said. "With Councill's Store not too far away, we are less isolated than you, and we'll see she is well taken care of. Besides, I think she and Clifton are getting along quite well, and I know he would like to have someone nearer his own age around. He misses his older sister, who's just moved to Salem with her husband."

Oh, mother! Sarah would never take the place of Gracie and be like a sister to him. But bless her heart for trying to keep Sarah here. He didn't dare look at Sarah during this exchange. He feared his expression of joy and excitement might scare her off.

"That might be a good solution," Mrs. O'Leary said, "but we need to ask Sarah. What do you think, dear?"

Sarah looked at Cliff. She wished she could tell what he was thinking. She liked this kind, wonderful man, but she wasn't sure how he felt. She wanted to stay, but if he'd never be interested in her, it would be better for her to go now. She didn't want Hawk's situation to be repeated. Her feelings would only deepen the longer she stayed around him.

"I think that's an excellent idea," Cliff said, but his voice held no excitement. "She's a big help to Mama, and I like having her around too." He smiled at her then, and that gave her a little encouragement.

Sarah thought carefully. *God, show me what to do,* she silently prayed. She took her time in answering. This decision could have long-lasting effects.

"How would I get home?" she asked to stall things a little longer.

"You could stay until next spring," Mrs. Moretz suggested. "Then your parents could come after you. If for any reason you want to go home before then, Edgar and I will take you back, just like your parents brought me home once. We'd return the favor."

"You do have your own room here," her mother said, "and they even have another bedroom, if someone else comes."

She wished Mother wouldn't be so obvious in wanting her to stay. Cliff might think they were trying to push her on him. She looked into Cliff's eyes. They seemed to be saying, "Say yes, Sarah. Please, say yes."

Still looking at Cliff, she said, "I'd like to stay."

He looked pleased, and Sarah felt relief wash over her. She hoped she'd made the right decision. At least she would get to see if this man could be the one for her, if he could learn to love her.

The thoughts of her uncle Hawk scared her. He'd fallen in love with a woman many years ago, but she had not loved him enough to stay with him and become his wife. She had left him. Her uncle was a fine man, and if this could happen to him, she realized it could happen to anyone. Would it happen to her? Would Cliff ever love her enough to want her above all other women?

These thoughts frightened her. Love and marriage seemed such a gamble. Yet, she knew she had to take a chance on love. How else could she find real happiness?

Mother took Sarah into her bedroom for a long talk the day before she and Father left. Sarah followed along, uncertain about what she would have to say.

"I have some things I need to tell you, daughter," she began. "Your father and I love you very much, and we want the best for you. We want you to fall in love with a good man, marry, and find the happiness we have."

Sarah nodded. She knew all this.

"I need to tell you what we think about you staying here. Your father and I have discussed it."

Surely they weren't going to change their minds. If they wanted her to go back with them, what would she do? She wanted to have a chance with Cliff.

"I have watched you and Clifton. I think you may be well-suited for each other, but only time will tell. This is why we are leaving you here. You must discover if he is the one for you. If you love him, and he asks you to marry him, follow your heart. You will have our blessing. We think a lot of the Moretzes and would like for our families to be united in this way. This is only if it's what you want, however; only if he will make you happy."

Sarah breathed a sigh of relief. This sounded much like what she'd been thinking.

"There are several Cherokee braves who would like to make you their wife, but we think you'll be happier in the white world. Because of the way we've lived, you've grown up more in this manner. When we come back in the spring, we'll either be coming to take you home or coming to your wedding. We'll be prepared for either, but it will be your decision."

Sarah hugged her mother. She loved her gentle, wise ways. Her parents had stayed near the Cherokee because the settlers had often been unkind to her mother. Sarah realized she would now be coming into this same white world. Just because the Moretzes welcomed her, didn't mean everyone would.

Sarah would have been welcomed in love among the Cherokee, but their world continued to change. They were unlikely to be able to keep their land or a place in their mountains. If Sarah joined them, she would be subjected to even more pain and degradation than if she moved to this white world. If the rumors proved correct, she might even have to walk a great distance from North Carolina. It would be hard either way.

"They'll be having one of those mother/daughter talks," Mr. O'Leary said after his wife and daughter had been upstairs for over an hour. As long as nothing caused Sarah not to stay, Clifton would be fine with it.

When Mr. and Mrs. O'Leary rode away the next day, he breathed a sigh of relief. Sarah stood beside him, waving to her parents. She had really decided to stay.

He couldn't say things fell into a routine. Nothing could be routine with Sarah here.

Gradually she grew at ease around them, and she talked freely with Clifton more and more. They might often be apart during the day as each went about their separate tasks, but they sat together at meals and talked long into the evenings.

Somewhere along the way, he had stopped questioning what she might be hiding. Now he believed his interest might be turning into love. Yet, he held himself back. He didn't want to make things awkward between them and didn't want her to feel rushed or overwhelmed. He could be patient, especially when it came to Sarah.

He treated her as a delicate flower that would crumple at his touch if he came too close. He found it difficult to stay back when he wanted to be so near, to become her friend when he wanted to become so much more.

"Sarah, come with me to the barn. I want to show you the new kittens."

"How many are there?" she asked as she came up beside him. She moved with more grace than anyone he'd ever seen.

"Three, I think."

Sarah said nothing, but she carefully picked up a gray tabby and stroked its fur. He watched her hand move gently and lovingly over the tiny creature. He wanted that. He wanted her hand to touch him with love.

"It's so soft," she said and held out the kitten with both hands for him to touch. He touched the baby cat, but in the process, he touched her hand. She looked at him and smiled. *She smiled!* She didn't back away, and she didn't seem to mind. Her skin was as smooth as the kitten's fur. He wanted to tell her, but he kept quiet. They'd made so much progress, and he dared not do something to change that.

"Mama, do you think it would be okay if Sarah and I spent some time alone together?" Clifton asked one day when he found they were by themselves.

"What do you mean?"

"I know it's not considered proper in our society, but what about the Cherokee? Would Sarah think it wrong?"

"I'm not sure. I spent only a few months with the Cherokee, and you couldn't call my situation normal. From what I saw, however, I don't think an unmarried Cherokee woman would spend time with a man, especially if they were alone, although I admit I sometimes did with Hawk. But I trusted him because he'd already proven himself honorable and trustworthy. Besides, Sarah's father is Irish, and he would have taught her our customs as well. Her family didn't live in the traditional Cherokee way."

Still, Clifton pressed for an answer. "Do you think it would be okay, Mama? Here on the farm, where no one else will see us. What's considered proper here in the mountains is not as strict as elsewhere, like in Chapel Hill."

"I think you may be putting too much temptation on yourself if you do this." She looked at him carefully. "Do you think you could control yourself under such circumstances?"

"I do, because I'd never do anything with the potential to hurt Sarah."

"Your father felt the same way with me, but there were certain things we couldn't do, or it would have led to more. He kissed me thoroughly twice before we were married, and both times took us to the edge. We decided it was much too dangerous for us to kiss like that before our wedding, so we didn't, not even when I came back from the Cherokee."

Clifton understood what his mother was saying, and he appreciated that she felt free to tell him something so personal. The older he got, the more he appreciated his parents.

"Was it the same with Hawk?" He asked it before he thought, because Hawk's story bothered him. "I'm sorry, Mama. I shouldn't have asked that."

"No, it's okay. It was different for me with Hawk. I knew all the time I wanted to come back to your father, so I never let feelings for Hawk develop in that direction. I don't know exactly how Hawk felt, but he rarely touched me, and never in an inappropriate way. I assume he respected me too much. We never kissed."

"I'm glad you'll talk about it," Clifton said.

"I know you're an adult now, son, but I probably wouldn't have said much about Hawk if it weren't for Sarah. The fact you and she are getting along so well has made the story more significant somehow."

"If Sarah and I did fall in love and marry, do you think that would compensate for Hawk's tragedy to some degree?"

"The glib answer would be to say 'not for Hawk,' but he's such a considerate person, he might feel differently. It's a difficult question, a question more for God than me. I really have no idea, but I would say it would only have any possibility of doing so, if you and she fall deeply in love, and even then, I doubt it. It shouldn't even be a consideration in why you marry."

"It won't be. I can promise you that, but back to my former question. Do you think it would be okay for me to take Sarah on walks without a chaperone?"

"I trust you, Clifton. I trust you to behave like your father did, if there's a strong physical attraction. Sarah is very special, and I want what's best for her and for you."

"I know, Mama. So do I."

Clifton asked Sarah to go for a walk with him Sunday right after breakfast. He'd only seen her in homespuns. She looked beautiful in any dress, but they'd made plans for a forest walk, and when she met him after lunch in Cherokee dress, her exotic beauty took his breath away.

"This is better for the woods," she said. "I hope you don't mind."

"Not at all," he told her. "You're lovely."

She smiled. He loved her smile, and he wished he could cause her to smile more often.

He hadn't intended to go very far, but they found some old Cherokee trails he'd played on as a child, and they ventured far into the forest and almost up a mountain before he noticed. He'd been too busy noticing Sarah.

Her leather dress hung shorter than her others. When she walked ahead of him in the narrow places, he couldn't help but notice how her dress swished around her body, how shapely her ankles were, and the curves at her calves.

She had wanted to walk behind him in the narrow parts of the trail, but he'd insisted she go in front, and she'd complied. He wished she would have more trouble with the steep grades so he could help her, but she seemed accustomed to hiking mountains.

When they got to the crest, they stood together and looked down at the valley and across at other peaks. With the clear sky and bright sun, they could see for miles and miles. He took her hand in his. She looked at him, but she didn't say anything or pull her hand back.

"There's a lot of world out there," he finally said.

"Do you want to see more of it?" she asked.

"Not really, I'm happy in these mountains. I can't imagine a prettier place."

She seemed pleased with his answer. He guessed she felt much the same.

"Come, let's sit down and rest a bit." He led her to a large rock, and they sat close together.

"I like it here," she said. "I think your farm is prettier than ours."

"How so?"

"Well, our place is more in the woods. You've cleared more land. Our cabin is also smaller. I like the upstairs of yours and all the extra bedrooms. You could have many children and still not fill them up."

It felt like his heart did a somersault in his chest. He would love to fill up those bedrooms with her.

"I'm beginning to care for you, Sarah." He needed to let her gradually know how he felt.

"I care for you too, Cliff."

No one had ever called him that before, but he liked it. He also liked that she had her own special name for him.

He could have said so much more about his feelings for her, but that was enough for today. More could come later.

They talked and laughed most of the way down the mountain. Sarah now walked behind him, because they were on the narrow, top portion of the trail. She'd pick up speed and almost run into him at times. He'd put out one arm to stop her, while he hung onto his musket in the other. She'd run into his arm, and he'd rein her in and hold her for a split second. He laughed in delight, and she joined him. He couldn't remember when he'd had so much fun.

When the trail widened, they walked hand-in-hand beside each other back to the cabin. He loved holding her small, soft hand.

"Well, I don't guess you got too lost, after all," Papa teased.

"No, on a clear day, we would never get lost," Sarah said seriously.

Papa's eyes twinkled in laughter, but he didn't laugh aloud.

Sarah laughed at herself. "Oh, you tease like my father." She laughed again and went to help Mama put supper on the table.

Sarah lay in bed that night and thought of Cliff. This had been a good day. He had seemed close to her on the mountain. Sometimes she felt unsure about what the Moretzes considered improper. When she had mentioned filling the farm's bedrooms with children, she'd noticed some emotion flicker quickly across Cliff's face. She hoped she hadn't shocked him with her comment. She didn't have the same background as Cliff, and some things were just hard for her, but she decided she must be herself, anyway. How else could she and Cliff know if they could live together in love, as husband and wife?

Father had told her some things. He'd explained it was improper for an unmarried woman and man to be alone together here also. She'd hoped it might be different. How could they get to know one another well if they had no time alone? She had been surprised when Cliff suggested their walk in the woods. She'd been afraid he didn't respect her, but she trusted this man and had gone with him. It had not been a mistake.

She remembered their talk on the mountain. She'd thought and hoped he might tell her he loved her, but he didn't. He did tell her he was beginning to care for her. Was that the same as beginning to love her? She didn't know.

She smiled to herself as she remembered frolicking down the mountain. She would gain momentum, and Cliff would turn and catch her to slow her down. She loved the feel of his arm around her. She wished he hadn't released her so quickly.

She hated the feeling of being caught between two worlds, feeling that she didn't really belong in either. Would she ever know what was right and proper here? Would she ever fit in somewhere?

This had been a busy week for Clifton. Besides doing the regular chores, another circuit riding preacher had come and wanted to hold a service at their place. Papa had readily agreed and scheduled it for Sunday. That meant a long list of extra work.

Mama and Sarah had cooked extra food since the preacher would be eating with them. The preacher stood on the porch and delivered his message on loving your neighbor as yourself.

Mr. and Mrs. Hodges had come and brought Belinda with them. Belinda took one look at Sarah and stopped in her tracks.

"Oh, I see you took my advice and got a slave," she said maliciously. "She's rather pretty for a mulatto."

Mama and Sarah had made Sarah a new dress of green calico. She looked even more stunning than usual today, definitely more fetching than Belinda could ever hope to be. Clifton thought it best to try to ignore Belinda's cutting remark.

"This is Sarah O'Leary, the daughter of good friends of Mama's. She's staying with us until spring. Sarah, this is Belinda Schreiner from Greensboro. Belinda is staying with her aunt and uncle for the summer."

"Oh, Clifton, you know to call me 'Bee.'"

Clifton noticed Sarah's confused look out of the corner of his eye. "I don't think we are on such familiar terms," he told the exasperating female.

"Nonsense," she said without batting an eye. She patted his arm. "I enjoyed your attention at the last preaching service and then you coming to my place for supper. I look forward to our next get-together."

Without giving him a chance to reply or acknowledging Sarah, she turned and walked away. He turned around, and Sarah had also disappeared. He looked in the house and around the grounds but couldn't find her.

CHAPTER SIXTEEN

Trouble

Sarah felt confused and hurt, so she retreated like a wounded animal. She had to get away from Cliff and Belinda. How could Cliff have another woman? She'd never have believed he'd be that kind of man. He shouldn't be paying special attention to Sarah if he had an understanding with Belinda. He had wronged them both.

She started toward the barn but saw a couple of young men headed in that direction. She hadn't wanted to go into the house for fear of running into one of the Moretzes, but she needed the privacy of her room. It seemed the best place to hide and sort out her feelings. Tears threatened to trickle down her face as she realized how hurt and jealous she was.

Why did Belinda have to be so pretty? She had ample curves, brilliant red hair, and the whitest skin Sarah had ever seen.

Why did love hurt so much? Even though Cliff had wronged her, Sarah realized she still loved him. That didn't mean she should marry him, not if he turned out to be this kind of man. Besides, he'd probably never intended to marry her anyway. She must be just a dalliance, a summer diversion. He hadn't even thought enough of her to defend her from Belinda's rude remarks.

She made it to her bedroom without confronting any of the family. She leaned against the door and breathed a sigh of relief. But what should she do?

She could always ask Mr. and Mrs. Moretz to take her home. Yes, maybe that's what she'd do. She would go home and try to mend her broken heart. She would survive. Hawk had.

Sarah threw herself across the bed, still fighting tears and refusing to give into a hard cry. She heard footsteps on the stairs and jumped to see if she had locked the door, but the door opened before she got there.

"I saw you run in here," Belinda stepped gingerly into the room as Sarah stepped back. "I'm sorry for what I said earlier. I realize now you're an Indian and not a slave. You're the first Indian I've ever seen, so I'm afraid I misjudged you."

Sarah stared at the pretty woman warily. She still felt the sting of Belinda's earlier remarks. The barbs about her heritage had hurt, but the deepest cuts had come from Cliff. How could she have been so wrong about the man?

"I'm upset with Clifton too. He should have told you about us at the very beginning. He was wrong to play with your feelings like that. I mean, we've even talked about him coming to Greensboro to set up his medical practice." She shrugged. "I guess men will just take whatever they can get from a woman."

Belinda looked at Sarah as if she expected her to confess something, but she had nothing to tell. "Well, I'm going to find Clifton and chide him for how he's handled this. He should know better." Belinda turned to leave.

Sarah drew up strength she hadn't known she had. "Wait. I'll go with you. I want to hear what he has to say about this."

Belinda turned with a hand pressed to her heart. "I don't think that's a good idea." She reached out and placed her hand on Sarah's arm. "Why, it could prove quite humiliating to you. I don't think that would be wise, as upset as you must be."

Sarah pulled her arm away. "I like the idea of us taking some action. If Clifton has wronged us both, he should be the one to be uncomfortable. If we confront him at the same time, then he won't be able to tell you one thing and me another." Sarah spoke with more courage than she felt. She would not give Belinda the satisfaction of seeing her cowed or defeated.

Belinda began to pull at her neckline, although the dress seemed an impeccable fit. "I-I don't th-think that would be the right thing to do. It's much too brash and forward for genteel women." She shook her head. "No, it's just not the way things are done." Were those sweat beads on Belinda's forehead?

"But it makes perfect sense," Sarah tried to reason with her. "Don't you want to confront Clifton for the way he's behaved? He won't be able to talk his way out of it with both of us standing there."

Belinda took her handkerchief and dabbed her forehead. She almost seemed to be searching for what to say. She finally gave a huff. "Well, I won't be party to such a thing. Besides, I'm not feeling well." She patted her forehead again. "I'm going to find my aunt and uncle and have them take me home. I need to rest in my own bed." She retreated without even a cordial good-bye.

Sarah sat down on the edge of her bed. Now what? Should she confront Cliff without Belinda? It didn't seem necessary now that Belinda was leaving. Cliff could say what he thought would placate Sarah. With the two of them together, he would have been forced to choose.

Still undecided, Sarah got up and locked the door. She certainly didn't want anyone else barging in right now.

It was odd how the redhead had become agitated when Sarah had insisted on confronting Cliff with her. Did that mean Belinda hadn't been truthful? Perhaps she just wanted Cliff for herself. Sarah stood at the foot of her bed, struggling to understand the situation. What was true, and what was not? What if Belinda had exaggerated the relationship she shared with Cliff? Didn't she know that this was not the way to win a man's heart?

Sarah rubbed her temples. She didn't know what to think or what to do next.

Clifton hadn't been able to find Sarah anywhere outside. He probably should have checked for her in her bedroom first, but he hesitated to do so. A man at an unmarried woman's door could be judged as improper. He'd try to find his mother and enlist her help. He started inside the cabin when Belinda nearly collided with him as she rushed outside.

"Belinda, have you seen Sarah?" he asked.

Belinda shrugged, and her gaze drifted toward the Moretz's barn. "I heard Sarah arrange to meet a couple of young men in the barn earlier. You might check there. I tried to tell her she was making a big mistake, but she wouldn't listen. "

Clifton stiffened with shock. This didn't sound like the shy, sweet Sarah he knew. Was his first impression of her correct? Was she able to use her beauty to her advantage? Did she need attention from more than one man to feel confident in herself?

"Will you help me look for her?" He regretted asking as soon as the words left his lips. Considering the hateful comments Belinda had made to Sarah when they first met, she should be the last person to help him search.

"I can't," Belinda whined. "I'm not feeling well. I was just going to ask Uncle Graden to take me home."

Clifton didn't really care if his face showed his relief. Without another word, he hurried inside. He knew he should have said something polite, but he felt a sudden urge to be away from Belinda. If she thought him rude and uncouth, maybe she would keep her distance.

"Mama, have you seen Sarah?"

"No, dear. Is something wrong?"

"I think I caught a glimpse of her going upstairs a little while ago," Papa said.

Clifton ran up the stairs. He knew his parents would remain in the house, and that should keep his presence at Sarah's bedroom door from appearing too improper.

"Sarah?" He knocked lightly. "Sarah, are you in there?"

No answer came. He couldn't hear a sound. If she was in there, she wasn't moving around.

"Sarah, I need to know you're okay."

There was silence, and Clifton began to panic. What if she'd gone somewhere else, and he couldn't find her? What if Belinda had been right about her meeting someone in the barn?

"I'm okay. I just need some time alone."

Clifton breathed a sigh of relief when he heard her voice, but he knew something was wrong. The things Belinda had said earlier must have bothered Sarah, and he had just stood there without standing up for her. He told himself Sarah had run off before he had much of a chance, but deep down he felt he should have let Belinda know how wrong she'd been.

"Sarah, I need to talk to you and explain some things. Please come down as soon as you can."

"I will."

Clifton left then. He tried not to worry. Surely Sarah trusted him. Surely she knew he had no interest in Belinda.

Sarah lay on her bed, unsure of Cliff and disgusted with herself. Since Belinda wouldn't help her confront Cliff, nothing seemed settled. How had she gotten herself into this mess? Had she been too eager to find love? Had she given her heart away too soon? Could Cliff be that much of a philanderer? Her questions spun around in her head. She told herself he wasn't worth crying over, but she had barely managed to hold back her tears.

Sarah wished she'd never stayed in the first place. It had been a huge mistake. Now she needed to pack her things and get Cliff's parents to take her home.

She took in a huge breath of air, got up, and began getting her things together. The sooner she got back home, the better.

Another knock at her door interrupted her thoughts. Sarah certainly didn't want to see Cliff now, and she didn't want to explain why she had begun packing.

"Sarah, it's me," Mrs. Moretz said. "We're all getting worried about you, and I wondered if you needed to talk."

"No, I'm fine." Sarah wondered if her voice sounded normal.

"Could I please come in for a few minutes?"

Sarah didn't want to see anyone just yet, but how could she refuse Mrs. Moretz? This was her house. Sarah might as well make her wishes to return home known. She opened the door.

Mrs. Moretz stepped inside. After one look at Sarah's face, she closed the door. "I can see you're upset. Oh, Sarah, I'm so sorry. What can I do to help?"

Mrs. Moretz gently put her arms around Sarah. Sarah put her head on the kind woman's shoulder, and silent tears came.

Mrs. Moretz just stood there, holding Sarah and stroking her back, and it felt so good to be cared about. When her crying had stopped, Mrs. Moretz led her to the bed and sat down beside her.

"Did someone frighten you?"

Sarah shook her head.

"What is it then?" Mrs. Moretz's voice wrapped around her like a soft blanket.

"I need to go home. I want to go home right away."

Sarah could feel the shock and concern in Mrs. Moretz's body. This woman had been like a second mother to her for the time she'd been here.

"Why, Sarah? Is it Clifton? Are you running from Clifton?"

"I think he's interested in Belinda, and . . . I don't want her to think there's anything between Cliff and me. I don't want to be a hindrance."

"Clifton is not interested in Belinda. I'm sure of that."

Sarah looked at Cliff's mother. She felt certain the woman wouldn't lie, but she might not be aware of the situation.

"I see the uncertainty on your face. Let me tell you what I know. We met Belinda in May at a service like we had here today. Clifton thought he might be interested in her at first, so we went to dinner at her uncle and aunt's the following Saturday. The more Clifton got to know her, the more she bothered him. He called it *annoyed*. I don't think he would mind my telling you that he found her to be selfish, money-hungry, and prejudiced. She likes owning slaves, a practice which Clifton can't condone, and she's snobbish and self-centered. They have nothing in common, and he never wanted to see her again. He hasn't laid eyes on her again until she appeared today."

Sarah blinked. "You're sure of the way Cliff feels about her?"

Mrs. Moretz smiled. "I'm very sure, because he told his father and me on the way home from eating with the Hodges. In fact, Clifton stayed close to his father and Mr. Hodges most of that Saturday and didn't give Belinda much attention at all. She seemed to be peeved over his actions. In fact, I'm sure Clifton cares much more for you."

Sarah blinked again. "He has told you this?"

"Not in so many words, but from the questions he's asked, I'm sure it's where his thoughts are."

How could anyone, even a mother, know someone's thoughts? Sarah wanted to believe her, but the things Sarah had seen from Cliff and Belinda didn't fit with what Mrs. Moretz was telling her.

"Give this more time, Sarah. Give Clifton a chance. I think you would break his heart if you left."

"My heart might get broken if I stay." As she said it, Sarah realized her heart was already breaking. It would shatter even more if Sarah rode away. But what if she stayed? Would things get even worse?

"Just stay for two more weeks. Wait at least that long and see what happens."

Sarah didn't believe staying two more weeks would change anything. But, oh how she wanted to believe it might!

"All right. For you, I'll stay two weeks, but you promise to take me home then if I ask?"

"Yes, I would take you home now, if that's your final decision. I've already promised you."

"I'll stay two weeks and see."

"What happened today?" Mama asked Clifton. "What did you or Belinda say to Sarah?"

Clifton told her what Belinda had said and done when she met Sarah. Mama sucked in her breath.

"Sarah must have run straight to her room," Clifton continued. "Belinda said Sarah had arranged to meet a couple of men, but I can't believe that about her. Besides, I don't think she'd had the opportunity. I was with her until Belinda's words hurt her and she disappeared."

"I don't believe it, either. I think Belinda is hurt by your lack of interest, and she's trying to stir up trouble."

"She seems to be doing a good job of that. Did Sarah tell you anything that happened?"

"No, she didn't. I think Sarah is more concerned about your feelings for Belinda right now."

"My feelings for Belinda! I'm having a hard time not hating that girl, and I know hate's a sin."

"You're going to have to tread softly with Sarah. She's ready to go back home, but I've talked her into giving us a little more time."

Clifton hadn't expected that. "I'll explain things to her right away."

"You can try, but I'm not sure she's ready to listen. She seems deeply hurt."

"Then what do you suggest?"

"I don't know, Clifton. I'm afraid I'm not that wise. Pray to God and let Him be your guide."

Mama went to the kitchen, and Clifton got out his Bible. He began with prayer first.

Sarah didn't come downstairs until Mama called her to supper. When she came, she wouldn't look at Clifton.

"Are you feeling okay?" he asked, and she just nodded.

Supper turned out to be more awkward than any Clifton had ever had. Sarah didn't speak unless asked something directly, and then she gave the shortest answer possible. He needed to talk to her in private. He didn't hold much hope she'd go with him, but he had to try.

"Sarah, go for a short walk with me. Just around the farm. We need to talk."

She shook her head to decline.

"Let me tell you how I feel, Sarah. Don't close the door on me without hearing my side."

"It's been an exhausting day," she said. "I need some rest first. I'll talk with you in the morning."

He watched her rise and turn for the stairs. She looked lost and defeated, and his heart cried out to her. How had things become so twisted? *Belinda.* He could wring that redhead's neck!

Sarah had told Cliff she needed rest, but she got none. She lay quietly in the dark, but sleep wouldn't come.

Scenes from the day rolled through her mind over and over again. Belinda had seemed intentionally cruel when Cliff introduced them. She'd been nicer here in the bedroom, when she'd put Cliff in the wrong.

Was Cliff really like Belinda painted him, or was he more like Sarah had seen him before today? How could Sarah know the truth?

She remembered their day on the mountain. Cliff had been so attentive then. He'd told Sarah he was beginning to care for her. Had he meant those words, or did he already care more for Belinda? Perhaps he wasn't serious about either of them.

Sarah had agreed to talk with Cliff tomorrow, but she dreaded that talk. She felt he would try to convince her he cared more for her, but how did she know she could trust him? How would she know if he told the truth or not? She would want to believe him. Oh, how she would want to believe him!

Sarah heard the bed squeak across the hall as Cliff turned over. Apparently he couldn't sleep either. She'd heard him toss and turn all night.

Sarah turned over and began to pray. She would take it to the Lord. It was all she knew to do.

Sarah went down for breakfast late, but she doubted she could eat anything. Everyone else had already eaten, but they'd left plenty for her.

"I've kept it warming on the hearth," Mrs. Moretz said as she swept the floor.

Sarah nodded. She tried to get a bite down, but it stuck in her throat. She sat sipping her tea instead. Perhaps she could manage some of it.

She hadn't been able to sleep at all last night. Still, this morning, she'd stayed in her room until she heard the men go outside. She hoped to postpone talking with Cliff as long as possible.

She heard him coming through the larder door now. He looked to her immediately when he entered the kitchen with the milk from the morning's milking. He handed the milk to his mother before he came to the table. He didn't look as if he'd gotten any sleep either.

"How do you feel?" he asked kindly.

Her gaze fell to her uneaten breakfast. "Still tired." She glanced up.

He nodded. "Come." He held out his hand to her.

She put her hands on the table to rise rather than take the offered hand. He dropped it to his side. He went to the front door and held it open for her.

"This way," he said after following her out, and he walked toward the road.

Sarah tried to follow behind him, but he wouldn't allow it. He'd stop and wait until she walked beside him again.

"There's a natural meadow over here," he said. "I thought it would be a good place for us to talk."

He motioned for her to sit on a huge rock on the roadside of the meadow, and she did. He sat down beside her.

"Yesterday was a horrible day," he began. "Belinda was mean and vindictive and said horrible things to you, and I apologize. Her anger should have been directed at me, because I'd been the one to snub her when we went to dinner at her uncle's."

"Belinda didn't seem to be upset with you," Sarah pointed out. "She seems to adore you. I saw her face when she looked at you."

Cliff shook his head. "I think Belinda would like for me to pay her attention, but I know she doesn't care for me. She's more interested in the position of a doctor. If she thought I would stay here and farm, she'd never give me another thought."

Sarah looked Cliff in the face for the first time. He sounded sincere, as if he believed what he was saying, but she couldn't be sure.

Clifton looked into Sarah's eyes and saw pain and confusion. How could he make her understand? How could he show her the truth?

It hurt that Sarah had a difficult time believing him, but he couldn't let that affect him now, not if he wanted to keep Sarah from leaving him. Hadn't he had doubts too, when Belinda had told him Sarah went to meet someone in the barn?

"Belinda told me you had gone to the barn to meet a man," Clifton said.

He saw the horror and shock in her face. At that moment, he had no doubt Belinda had lied.

"It's not true. I would never do such a thing."

"I know that."

He put his hand on her arm, and she didn't pull away. She looked into his eyes to try to determine the truth.

"Tell me what has you so upset, Sarah. There seems to be more than the cutting remarks Belinda made."

Sarah's gaze fell to her hands as they lay clasped in her lap. "Belinda came to my room to tell me you were hers. She said you had made a commitment to her, and you were going to move to Greensboro to start your medical practice."

Cliff was stunned speechless for a moment. Then he found his voice. "That was an out and out lie. Nothing could be further from the truth. As I told Mama, I'm struggling not to hate that woman."

Sarah still looked into his eyes, but he couldn't tell if she believed him or not. "Did you talk to Belinda again after I left?" Sarah asked.

Clifton took a deep breath. He hoped the truth didn't get him in even more trouble. "I saw her rushing from the house right before I came inside. I had been looking for you. Belinda told me that she wasn't feeling well and was going home. That's when she told me you had gone off to meet a couple of men in our barn. I had actually seen a couple of young men headed in that direction earlier."

Sarah gasped at Belinda's outrageous lie. "I can't believe she said that, because she'd just left my room. She knew exactly where I was." Sarah reached out and touched his arm, but he knew she didn't realize what she'd done. "Did you believe her?" She retracted her hand.

"No. I didn't go to the barn at all. I came inside hoping I would find you in your room." He paused, deep in thought. "I think part of the problem is that Belinda is jealous of your beauty."

Surprise flickered across Sarah's face. "You think I'm beautiful?"

Did she honestly not know? Had she never seen herself in a mirror?

"You're the most beautiful woman I've ever seen, but that's not even the best part. It's your character and personality that draw me to you. You could be the ugliest woman I'd ever met, and I'd still be interested because of your inner beauty."

He could have added this was the real reason he loved her so much, but he didn't want to overwhelm her. He just wanted her to give him a chance to prove himself.

She seemed to soften for the first time, and he knew he'd said the right thing. He pushed his new standing.

"Sarah, just give us a chance. I think we have the possibility of finding something very special together. Don't throw that away by believing the lies of a jealous, spiteful woman. You don't have to make up your mind about me this minute. Just give me a chance."

Sarah began to waver. He could see it in her face.

"You know Belinda told me lies about you meeting someone in the barn. Don't believe her over me. Have you ever caught me in a lie? Before you met Belinda, would you have thought I would toy with the affections of two women? Surely I have more credibility with you than she does."

She gave him a tiny smile. "You would make a good attorney. You argue your case well, and I can see reason in what you say. I'll give us a chance. I'll wait and see what happens."

"Thank you."

He got up and offered her his hand. She took it, but she pulled her hand away as soon as she stood. At least she had put her hand in his for a moment. He would take heart in that.

"I wish I could keep people like Belinda from hurting you, Sarah, but I can't control what they say," Clifton said as they walked back to the cabin. "What I told you on the mountain is true. I do care for you. I care a great deal for you."

He looked into Sarah's face and realized she still felt unsure of him. He could see questions in her eyes. She seemed to be trying to assess if he really did care for her.

"How do you feel now?" he asked.

"I feel much better than I did before we talked."

"I'm glad. I hope we can always talk through our problems."

When they got to the front door, he took her hand again. He brushed his lips across the back of her hand, and she responded with a tiny shiver. He opened the door for her to go inside.

"I'm going to spend a little time talking to God now," he told her and turned to leave.

CHAPTER SEVENTEEN

Decisions

Supper was neither the uncomfortable meal the previous supper had been nor like the easy, warm meals they'd shared before. Clifton tried to be as he'd been before, but Sarah didn't try. She still appeared quiet and guarded, much as she'd been when she first came. Clifton felt as if he needed to start all over again, but at least Sarah hadn't packed up to go home.

"Let's go for a short walk before dark," he said to Sarah as they finished eating. "We won't stay out long."

"I need to help your mother clean up."

"That's not necessary, Sarah," his mother said. "You go talk with Clifton. I don't have much left to do here."

Sarah reluctantly came. He picked up her hand to hold as they walked, and he thought she was going to take it back, but she didn't.

"Remember how we held hands as we came back from our walk on the mountain? I need that now, Sarah. I need that much reassurance things have a chance of working out for us. Please don't make us go back to the beginning, where you were so quiet and shy around me."

She didn't say anything, but neither did she withdraw her hand. Without any purpose other than to just be with her, he led her toward the barn.

"No, Cliff." She stopped short.

"It's just a barn, Sarah. Don't make it into anything more. Just because Belinda told lies about you meeting someone here doesn't mean you should avoid it. I know you're not that kind of woman. Don't you want to go in and check on the kittens?"

She hesitated before she stepped inside. The kittens weren't where they usually were. Their soft mews came from the loft.

"Can you make it to the loft in that dress?" Clifton asked.

Sarah gave a slight smile. "My Cherokee dress is much better for climbing, but I'll come, if you go first."

He wanted to send her up first, so he could help her from below, but Clifton realized her dress could cause a problem with him beneath her, so he took the lead. She came slowly, being careful not to step on her hem. He extended his hand and supported her up the last step.

She immediately went to the kittens. She picked up the black and white one, cuddled it in her arm, and stroked its fur.

"They're growing so much," she said.

He sat down on the edge of the loft and let his lower legs and feet dangle over the side. She came to join him. She handed him the kitten until she seated herself. He helped Sarah balance as she sat down and then handed the small cat back to her.

"I like the view from here," she said. "It's a good way to see the farm."

He watched her pet the kitten, which had quickly nestled in her lap. Soon it fell asleep. Sarah seemed more comfortable with him now. She glanced at him, and he smiled at her. She returned his smile.

"I'm sorry I listened to Belinda's lies, Cliff. You have never shown me anything but kindness, but Belinda was vicious from the start. I should have trusted you over her all the time."

"Yes, you should have, but if you see that now, my prayers have been answered. I'm just glad you listened to me this morning and gave me a chance. I was terrified you'd leave me and go back to your parents."

"I had planned to do that very thing, but I told your mother I would wait for two weeks. I've thought about what you told me today, and I see the truth in most of it."

Clifton raised his eyebrows. "And, what part do you still doubt?"

A sheepish look came into her face, and she looked down at the kitten asleep in her lap. "The part about my beauty and goodness," she said quietly.

He put his arm around her shoulders and pulled her closer. "Oh, but that's the most solid fact of all."

They stayed in the loft until almost dark. They talked some, but it was enough just to be together.

Clifton thanked God Sarah had realized the truth and had started to relax with him again. It had happened quickly. Yes, he thanked God from the bottom of his heart.

Breakfast saw their relationship almost back to normal. Sarah came down early and smiled at him when he came to the table. They talked easily through the meal.

Clifton wanted to tell Sarah how much he loved her, and he thought of taking her back up the mountain today, but something cautioned him to give it more time. After all, she had been ready to leave him yesterday.

He waited all week. By the end of the week, Sarah seemed to treat him the same as she had before the incident with Belinda. He could find no uneasiness about her.

"Let's walk up our mountain again," he told her Sunday after dinner.

"The leather or homespun dress?" she asked without hesitation.

"Whichever you prefer," he told her. He secretly hoped it would be the leather Cherokee dress, where he could see her shapely form better.

She came in the homespun. "I need to learn to be more civilized," she said.

"I like you any way you dress," he told her, "and you're the most civilized young woman I've ever met. You're Sarah, and that's what I like."

"If I didn't know better, I'd think you had some Irish blood. You have the gift of gab and smooth talking, much like my father does."

He laughed and felt delighted that she chose to tease him. He hadn't seen this side of her before.

They walked up the trail side by side where it turned wide enough to do so. He put his arm around her and pulled her close to his side. He could feel the soft curve of her hip against the side of his upper leg. They climbed to the top and sat on the same rock as before.

"I like it when you call this 'our mountain,'" she told him.

He took a deep breath. This might be too soon, but he didn't think he could wait much longer. He picked up her hand and looked into her eyes.

"I love you, Sarah. I love you so much it hurts. I love you more than I ever imagined I could love someone."

"I love you too, Cliff."

She loved him too! Hallelujah, she loved him too! He took her in his arms and held her tight. She put her arms around him and clung to him.

"I don't want to rush you, Sarah," Clifton whispered in her ear. "Do I need to slow down? I know Belinda caused problems. Do you need more time before you'd consider marrying me?"

His breathing stopped with her pause. She pulled back and looked at him. A smile played around her lips, and he could breathe again.

"If you're sure of your heart, then I don't need more time."

He released her and knelt down in front of the rock, where he had a clear view of her face. He took both her hands in his and looked into her lovely eyes. He could get lost in those eyes.

"Sarah, I hadn't planned on proposing so soon, but I'm going to ask you to marry me. However, I need to tell you something first."

She looked into his eyes intently. He hoped she would understand.

"I would like to open a medical practice and use the doctoring skills I learned in Chapel Hill, but that's going to be hard to do in these mountains. To support a family, I'll need to go to a town. As much as I love these mountains, I need to leave them to do what I feel God is calling me to do. I'm hoping you will marry me and go with me to find our new place. Will you marry me, Sarah? Will you become my wife?"

The smile she gave him rivaled the radiance of the sun. "Yes, Cliff. I will marry you. It's my heart's desire to be your wife."

"Can you leave our mountains? Will you go to another place with me?"

"It's important for you to do what God wants of you. If you feel He wants you to help sick people, then we must go where you can do this. What was it Ruth said in the Bible? Something like 'whither thou goest, I will go; and where thou lodgest, I will lodge: thy people shall be my people.' Your God is already my God, Cliff. I will go anywhere you want to go. I would even go to the ends of the earth with you."

"Are you sure, Sarah? It won't always be easy. People won't always treat you as they should."

"It would be the same here. We saw evidence of that earlier at the preaching service. Mountain people hate the Cherokee because of the raids they remember. I can handle the scorn much better with you there for me."

"I love you so much, Sarah. I can't wait to make you my wife. When can we be married?"

"I would like to marry you right away, but we need to wait until my parents return in the spring."

"Oh, I completely forgot." Cliff clapped a hand to his forehead. "I need to ask your father's permission."

She laughed lightly. "It's not necessary, because he has already given it. That's what Mother and I were talking about the day before they left. She said it was too early to tell, but if we fell in love and you asked me to marry you, I was to follow my heart. When they returned, they would either be coming to my wedding or to take me home."

"That's great, except for having to wait so long."

"Is it all right that you must postpone your doctor's practice? I feel I owe it to my parents to wait for them."

"Of course we can wait for your parents. We'll take pleasure in our time together at the farm, and I'll enjoy this time with my amazing, wonderful fiancée."

"You do not want to go ahead, start your practice, and then come back for the wedding?"

"No, I don't. I couldn't stand to leave you, Sarah. When I go, I want you to go with me."

"This pleases me," she said. "You know, I wonder if my marriage wasn't the real reason my parents came on this trip. I know Mother did want to see your mother again. She has often talked of 'Emma,' and I think Mother wanted to make sure she was happy with your father. But, I think they wanted me to find the right husband too. What Mother said is true. All the Cherokee people may be forced to move far away, according to the talk in Washington. Some of our leaders are working to change this, but they aren't having much luck. In addition, none of our white neighbors are both single and would treat me with respect. Mother and Father have been worried about my future."

"Well, I'm so thankful they brought you here. Did they know of me? Did they know my parents had a son a little older than you?"

"No, they didn't, but I think they hoped. Perhaps God had a hand in all this."

"I'm sure He did, darling Sarah. I'm very sure He did."

Sarah descended the mountain, but she felt as if she floated down. She didn't remember her feet touching the ground at all.

This man she had come to love loved her back and wanted to marry her. Cliff had asked her to become his wife. She would keep reminding herself of this over and over again, because it seemed to be too good to be true.

She no longer distrusted Cliff. After she'd thought about what he'd tried to explain, it confirmed everything his mother had already told her. Belinda had been jealous and wanted to lash out. She had wanted to break Cliff and Sarah apart. Sarah regretted she'd almost let it happen.

Sarah couldn't blame Belinda for wanting Cliff, however. But now this special man had chosen Sarah. He loved her! Her joy knew no end!

Mrs. Moretz joyfully hugged Sarah and then her son when they shared the good news. Mr. Moretz congratulated them.

"This wasn't totally unexpected," Cliff's mother said. "I've seen how Clifton has looked at you, Sarah, and I knew much love lay behind those looks. I also saw how tenderly you looked at him when he turned away. I'd thought it would be just a matter of time until it all worked out. You had me worried, however, after Belinda came and seemed to spoil everything."

"My observant wife informed me of what was happening," Mr. Moretz said. "I couldn't be happier things have finally worked out for you two. Great love is rare, but we've found it in our family for at least two generations. I pray to God He will grant its continuance."

Three days later, Clifton came from the barn to see a young Cherokee brave ride up. He glistened, bronze and handsome, and his unbound hair floated out as he stopped and reined in his horse. He jumped down in one fluid motion.

Sarah came running out of the house to meet him, and Clifton's heart turned to cast iron in his chest. He first thought he needed to stop this man who dared to come to Sarah here. He immediately reprimanded himself. He didn't even know what was happening. Perhaps the brave was bringing Sarah important news.

They were speaking in Cherokee as Clifton strode up, so he couldn't understand what they said, but Sarah didn't appear happy to see brave. Clifton hoped it wasn't bad news from her family.

Sarah looked as Clifton approached and smiled at him. "Cliff, this is Standing Bear. Standing Bear, this is Clifton Moretz, the man I was telling you about—the man I have agreed to marry."

Standing Bear said something in Cherokee. Sarah stopped him.

"No, we'll talk in English so Cliff can understand what we say. English is also my first language, the language that is spoken in my home."

"You left before I had a chance to present you with the deer meat," Standing Bear said in English. "I was disappointed you did not return with your parents. I should have shown you I wanted you to be my wife earlier, before you left. We could be taking it before our family clans now."

"That is the old way," Sarah replied. "Those ways are changing. I would not have accepted the meat, anyway."

Standing Bear frowned. "I would gladly ask your father for your hand, if that is how you would like it done. I will go to him and ask him now, and he can come get you, if you would prefer not to travel back with me alone."

"No. I'm promised to Cliff, and it's my wish to marry him. I hardly know you."

"You know of me. You know I am a good man and a brave warrior who brings honor to his people. You know I have traveled all this way east for you."

"You don't know me, either. We may not suit each other at all. I know Cliff and I are meant for each other. I'm happy with Cliff."

Cliff stepped up and put his arm around Sarah's waist. He wanted to show this brave that Sarah was his. She glanced at Cliff and smiled.

"I may not know you well, but I have seen you many times. I know of your beauty and grace. I know you would make me a good wife."

"You know wrong. I'm sorry you have come all this way for nothing, but I would never make you a good wife. I think I have been created to be Cliff's wife."

"This is your final word?"

"Yes. I am happy to become Cliff's wife. He's the man I love."

Standing Bear mounted his horse without saying a word and rode away. Sarah turned to Clifton.

"I can't believe he came here to get me. We've never had any contact. I didn't know Standing Bear even noticed me. I never dreamed he might choose me for his wife."

Clifton's words had fled him, as if they'd also ridden off. He had stood and watched Sarah refuse Standing Bear. She had told this Indian, in no uncertain terms, she was Cliff's and Cliff's alone.

"Thank you for that," Cliff told her as he took her hand to walk her inside the house. He moved her hand to his other and put his arm around her.

"I was so afraid you might be jealous," Sarah said as she looked into his eyes. "I don't want anything else to come between us. I couldn't stand the thought you might be jealous and think I had something to do with Standing Bear coming here."

"I admit I was jealous when I first saw him, but I decided to wait and see why he'd come. You dispelled any negative feelings I had as I listened to your conversation. You were amazing, Sarah. I love you so much, and I'm so happy you've agreed to be my wife."

"As I am happy you want to marry me."

His father had always warned Clifton to put God first in his life, and Clifton had always tried to do so. After he'd proposed to Sarah, Papa explained again the struggles he'd had after Mama had been taken hostage.

"I loved your mother so much that, without realizing it, I actually put her above God. I knew something didn't feel right. I felt a need to straighten out my life, but I had to work to find the answer. I didn't even know what was wrong at first. By studying my Bible, praying, and having battles within myself, I finally realized what had happened and switched the order of things. God showed me what I needed to do."

"Mama came home soon after that, didn't she?"

"Yes, but I did this, not because I thought it would cause God to send Emma back to me, but because I wanted and needed to put God above everything else in my life. When I talked with God and prayed over it, I had some peace for the first time since Emma had been taken. It gave me the patience to wait for God's will to be revealed.

"I tell you this, son, because I can see the love you have for Sarah is similar to mine for your mother. I caution you not to let it be greater than your love of God. That would be a great sin."

"What about Mama? Didn't she love you in the same way?"

"She loved me greatly, maybe as much. I don't know, but she always looked to God first. Even though I had helped lead her to Christ, her faith seemed stronger than mine. She put complete trust in Him. She always believed He would lead her back to me. She just didn't know how or when."

The end of summer, a time of plenty, allowed Clifton and Sarah to be together. They hoed weeds from the garden, picked vegetables, and took some to the root cellar to keep for later. Clifton cut wood, and Sarah would help move and stack it. They milked the cows, fed the hogs, and gathered eggs.

Sarah would wash clothes, and Clifton would carry the water from the springhouse for her. They'd go to the creek to take baths; Clifton washed quickly first, while Sarah waited out of sight. Then, Sarah would bathe with Clifton standing guard a distance from her. He always kept his back turned until she called it was okay. He knew this allowed him to show her how much he respected and honored her. Sometimes they got caught in a summer afternoon shower, and if the day had been warm, they would frolic in it.

The rest of the summer passed quickly, and autumn fell upon them. They gathered nuts, grapes, apples, and persimmons and took treks through the forest to enjoy the bold splashes of color nature had painted for them. They breathed deeply of the cool, crisp air and went arm-in-arm through the cool days. They set tubs of water behind the woodshed in the sun and bathed in the warm water that afternoon. Sarah would go first and then sit by the fireplace to let her long hair dry while Clifton took his bath.

Clifton and Edgar killed a hog and butchered it. Sarah and Emma stood outside on a makeshift table and rubbed salt into pieces to be hung in the smokehouse. They ground and stuffed sausages and rendered lard to cook with and to make cracklings.

Edgar and Clifton went hunting, and Sarah asked to go along. She donned her leather dress and moccasins and followed along soundlessly. She could pick up signs the two men missed and proved to be a big asset.

"A Cherokee brave could do much better," Sarah told them. "I know only a few of their ways."

Winter hit with a fury. A great blizzard blew in and lasted for days. The snow drifted up so high on the outside door to the larder that they had to use the front door to get out. When it first started, Papa looked at the sky and strung a rope from the house to the barn. It proved a smart idea, because it became so hard to see through the dim light and blowing snow, they could have become lost as they went to milk the cows.

They stayed indoors most of the time. They read the Bible and had long discussions. They poured over Clifton's books, and Sarah learned so quickly, she amazed him. They read novels and analyzed characters, each one taking a turn to read a chapter aloud. Clifton taught Sarah how to play some games, and she often beat him.

He had thought the time would drag by as they waited for spring, but as the time neared, Clifton realized the days had flown. He treasured these days at the farm, because he knew things would change when they left here. Not only would they go out as a couple with different heritages, but he would also be hard at work establishing his place as a doctor.

The time he regretted the wait the most was when they went to bed at night. He longed to take Sarah into his own room. He would lie in his lonely bed for hours thinking of her before finally drifting off to sleep and dreaming of her.

CHAPTER EIGHTEEN

Down the Mountain

Sarah's parents rode up the first week in April. "Intending to wait until later in the month, we were, but we couldn't wait any longer, so here we are," her father announced.

She hugged them both and drew them inside the cabin. Mama looked happy to see them, but Clifton knew she dreaded to see Clifton and Sarah move away.

"You don't have to tell me," Mrs. O'Leary said with a smile. "I can see it in your face."

"Then, we've come for a wedding," Mr. O'Leary said, nodding his head wisely.

Clifton and Sarah were married the next week with only their families there. It turned out to be the only week the preacher would be in this area until late in May.

Sarah came to Clifton on her father's arm. She wore the most beautiful dress of sky blue silk. This vision surpassed any of his dreams.

The preacher joined them for their wedding supper. Mama and Mrs. O'Leary had outdone themselves on the food, but neither Clifton nor Sarah ate much. They were interested only in each other.

The newlyweds retired early that night. Clifton finally got to lead Sarah into his bedroom.

"Are you nervous?" he asked. "I want everything to be perfect for you."

"No, I'm not nervous or anxious," she said shyly. "I've longed for this from the day you asked me to marry you."

"I love you so much, Sarah Moretz. I love the sound of your new name."

He gently took her in his arms and kissed her. Suddenly a burning passion exploded in them, and time ceased to exist. The only thing that existed was them uniting with God's blessing and becoming one.

They stayed at the farm through the summer. Clifton hesitated to leave this bliss. Now he and Sarah could bathe together in the creek. They could unleash their passion on the mountain and sleep in each other's arms every night. They'd found a refuge together on the mountain. Clifton didn't want the honeymoon to end, but they couldn't live away from the world forever.

Sarah's parents stayed until the beginning of June. Clifton could understand their reluctance to leave their daughter, but they said they must. None of their children had been available to watch their place this time, since they all had their own farms, but Hawk had agreed to stay until they returned. They worried there might be trouble, however, if they stayed away for long.

"We're hoping he can stay with us if the village's lands are taken over," Mrs. O'Leary confided one evening. "He should be able to, since he's the brother-in-law of a white man. He's not so young anymore, and marching all the way to the West—or hiding out in the hills in the winter, like a few of my people have talked of doing—could be rough on him."

"Hawk getting old? I just can't imagine that," Mama laughed.

"Hawk is still fit, but we're all getting older."

"You and I are on that same bridge, Emma," Papa said. "I'm in my forties now, and I'm guessing Hawk's about the same age as I am."

"We may be, but I don't feel old," Mama said.

"You don't look it either, dear," he told her.

Clifton could better understand Mama's story since Sarah had come into his life. If something took him from her, he would do everything he could to get back to her, and he would reject any other woman along the way.

He felt sorry for Hawk, however, for he sounded like a special man. Clifton couldn't help but be sad Hawk had never found anyone else to love. Sarah said he'd sent word to her to be happy with the son of the woman he couldn't have. "Hold on to the happiness and love with all your being," he had told her. So Mama had been the woman he'd loved.

"I wish he could have found someone else," Clifton shared with Sarah.

"I do too, but Hawk recently told Mother his great love for Emma filled him, and the memories had been enough. Even if he could never be with her, his love had sustained him through the years, and it had led him to her God. He says he will see Emma again in heaven, where there are no husbands and wives."

"I'm glad you preferred me over someone else."

"I feel the same way about you, Cliff."

Sarah and Clifton left at the end of September. He had postponed the move as long as he could, but he wanted to be settled before winter. They would ride down the mountain to Wilkesboro and spend the night there.

Sarah took the horse she'd ridden to the farm with her parents' blessing. Clifton would buy them a wagon in Wilkesboro, since it would likely be cheaper there than around Councill's Store. Sarah would not ride sidesaddle, and it wouldn't be considered proper for her to ride astride. Clifton's and Sarah's mares were also trained to pull a wagon, so they had their team.

Each had a travel bag with clothes and personal items. They would buy what else they needed later. Clifton also had his medical bag, but he'd need to purchase the ingredients for his medicines when they got settled.

His parents had given them money for a wedding gift, and so had her parents, although not as much. If they were careful, it should do them until they had money or goods coming in from his practice.

Sarah proved to be a good companion and easy to travel with. She never complained, always tried to see to his comfort, and wanted to do whatever he wanted.

"You're spoiling me," he told her.

"I hope so," she said with a smile.

Bad news assaulted them in Wilkesboro. President Jackson had signed the Indian Removal Act of 1930 into law in May. The Cherokee would likely lose all their lands in the East.

Sarah pressed a hand to her heart. "I feel intense sadness for my mother's people. Do you think they'll be forced to move right away?"

"I don't know, but I'd think it would take some time to get everything planned, organized, and set up. Besides, maybe they'll begin with the relocation of some of the other Indian nations first."

He put his arms around her and pulled her close to comfort her. She held onto him as if he were her one consolation.

The following morning, he checked Wilkesboro for doctors, and discovered that the town did indeed have a doctor. So, Clifton bought a light wagon and hitched up the two horses to travel on to Salem. He hoped they wouldn't need a cover, because, without one, this wagon cost much less. It didn't tend to rain as much in the fall, he reasoned, and besides, his wife wouldn't complain if they got wet. She proved to be as tough as he when it came to enduring what came.

Clifton had traveled through Wilkesboro many times before, but now he saw it through Sarah's eyes. The growing little town had its charm, but more so through her joy and excitement.

At Salem, Clifton and Sarah stayed with his sister, Gracie, in the pretty little clapboard at the edge of town. Clifton liked this town. The village appeared neat and clean and, being a settlement of Germans, a Moretz would be more welcomed than some.

"Why, she's lovely!" Gracie exclaimed when she saw Sarah. Gracie tried to chatter away to her new sister-in-law, but Sarah, although pleasant, remained quiet, as she had at first with Clifton.

"Salem already has a firmly established doctor," Gracie's husband told Clifton over dinner, "but Dr. Vierling is getting old. We may have to look for his replacement soon."

"Do you think the town would be interested in one who's not a Moravian?" Clifton asked, placing his fork on his plate. "At least I'm of German descent."

"I don't know. That's a valid question. Salem tried a doctor outside our religion once, but he didn't work out."

Clifton picked up his fork again. "That doesn't sound very promising, does it?"

"You could always try it."

"Please do," Gracie implored. "I miss having any of my family close by."

Clifton wondered if that would be a good idea. Dr. Vierling had a good reputation in the community, and the Moravians tended to be a rather closed group. They would be friendly to outsiders but wouldn't always accept them as one of their community. Besides, he didn't want to simply wait around for Dr. Vierling to give up his practice or die. It just didn't seem right. There was also the matter of income. He and Sarah would need some soon.

Gracie showed her delight at having Clifton and Sarah visit with her and her husband. They stayed four days. They left with Gracie asking them to come again and stay longer next time. Then they headed south toward Salisbury.

Salisbury proved more promising. It had already grown to be the largest town they had visited. There seemed to be enough people in the area for one more doctor.

At first, the Moretzes stayed in an inn. On the third day, after talking with some men in the stores and gathering leads from them, Clifton and his wife found a charming little three-room house to rent. Clifton could use the larger front room for his office, and they'd still have a bedroom and spacious kitchen. They could put a sitting area at one end of the kitchen and still have room for a table and chairs. The property also had a small stable for the horses.

"What do you think, Sarah?" Clifton asked after they'd looked at the place.

"I think it's just what we need for now. It'll be a good place for you to start your medical practice and for us to have our first home on our own."

They moved in with few furnishings. Gracie and Ernest had given them a table and four chairs as a wedding present. The craftsmen in Salem were known for their fine work. They sat two of the chairs at the table in the kitchen and the other two in Clifton's office.

They purchased pots, a few dishes and utensils from a store in town, and bought bedding from a nearby farm. To start with, they slept on a pallet on the floor.

They bought used furniture when they could. More people were coming to the area than leaving, but there were some who wanted to move on and needed cash. Clifton got a desk, a cabinet for his office, a bed, and a wardrobe this way. He also added to their kitchen wares and other household goods.

Clifton bought some medical supplies and put out his sign. At first, business moved like a slow drip, but it eventually began to pick up. However, some of the visits required house calls outside the town, and those patients were often very sick because they'd waited too long to call a doctor.

Rarely did someone pay him with money. Patients usually gave him produce, meats, linens, or other items. The townspeople were more likely to pay in cash than those on the farms.

Clifton began to worry he might not make a go of it. "If this is where God wants us," Sarah reasoned, "things will work out." If not, Clifton knew they could always go back to the mountain farm. It felt good to have that security.

Sarah supported and helped. She cooked, sewed, made whatever she could, washed clothes, and kept house. She would also mix, make, and organize his medicines. She helped keep his books and soothed the crying children he treated.

Some people impolitely stared at her, but few people were rude or openly hostile at their office. Since he usually called at the homes of his patients, however, Clifton hesitated to take Sarah. She always proved to be a great asset when he did so, but he cringed at the cruel remarks many made, and at some houses, she was asked to leave.

He would have loved to never treat the bigots again, and to speak his mind about their behavior, but he couldn't afford to adopt that policy. He also knew that no matter where they went or what they did, it would be the same. Americans were not nearly as accepting of others as they should be, although all of them were descended from foreigners or had been foreigners at one time, except for the Indians. How ironic!

Sarah never complained. She put on a stoic face and pretended not to hear the snide remarks, but Clifton saw her body stiffen or her jaw clench, and on rare occasions, her eyes would get watery. Despite what she pretended, the words stung.

Clifton hurt for her. He wanted to rave at the perpetrators, punch their faces, silence their tongues. Instead, he followed his oath as a doctor as well as Christ's teachings and treated them or their families to the best of his ability. He learned humility, but it came as a hard lesson.

Clifton chose a downtown church near their house to attend. He saw right away that some of the people here would mistreat Sarah too. The women often snubbed Sarah, if they weren't blatantly rude and ugly to her.

"I can't believe Dr. Moretz married an *Indian*. It's downright disgusting," they heard a fat, well-dressed woman say to her companion. Clifton thought the woman acted disgusting.

"We shouldn't even let that kind in our church," another said. "They'll never be anything but *savages*." Clifton knew Sarah acted much more civilized and well-mannered than this malicious gossip.

"Who does she think she is, trying to fit in with good, Christian people? She should stay with her own kind." *She's not a hypocrite, like you,* Clifton thought.

Such comments were widespread at first. As the newness wore off, talk went to more current gossip. Nasty comments about Sarah, however, never entirely disappeared.

"Let's try another church," Clifton suggested.

"It wouldn't do any good," Sarah said. "It would be the same, and the talk about me seems to be dying down here. If we moved, it would just start all over again."

Clifton saw the truth in what she said, but he hated it for her. That she had seemed to expect it almost made it worse.

"I just hate that your medical practice might be hurt because you married me," Sarah added.

"It won't be, darling. People can tell I care for them well, but I hate it that you have to put up with such maliciousness. I think part of the problem is that you're so pretty. It makes many jealous—the women especially but also the men that you're my wife."

"I don't think that's true. You just see me so differently than others do."

"That doesn't mean it isn't true."

The men might call her "half-breed," "Injun," or "squaw." When she was nearby, they would tell tales of raids, scalpings, or killings. But when their eyes followed her in a silent appraisal, it made Clifton's blood boil. He could guess their unchaste thoughts, yet they claimed to be Christians. In fact, it was disheartening how many of the "Christians" treated Sarah unkindly.

Hearing of the abuse, a handful of women went out of their way to be kind to Sarah. Clifton appreciated these godly women, but he wished Sarah would be more at ease with them. Sarah remained quiet, almost withdrawn, until she got to know someone better.

He noticed Joyce Knight seemed too persistent to be put off. She looked to be several years older, probably at least in her thirties, but she had an optimistic attitude and gentle ways. She would bring by baked goods, accept a cup of tea, and calmly talk to Sarah. Her husband had been killed in a riding accident, and she'd had several potential suitors. She would talk to Sarah about them and the positive and negative attributes of each. This brought Sarah out, for Sarah always preferred helping others to talking about herself. Joyce made life in the community tolerable for Sarah.

Joyce had a daughter who usually attended school, but the little girl loved Sarah as a second mother. Sarah seemed drawn to little Amy, and Clifton knew his wife longed for children of their own.

Clifton would have liked for them to have a baby, but it would be all right with him to wait until his practice grew. He wasn't ready to see Sarah in that danger yet.

Clifton had feared he would be too busy establishing his medical practice to spend much time with Sarah, but it hadn't been a problem. He stayed busy, but he had Sarah's company much of the time.

They arose in the morning around seven, and Sarah would prepare their breakfast. After eating, Clifton went to his office to catch up on any paperwork or research he needed to do, while she cleaned up. The items people gave him for his services kept them stocked in such things as candles, soap, preserves, pickles, and produce in season, and Sarah didn't have to work so hard because of it.

She would join him within an hour, and they would talk and laugh as they worked. Sometimes a patient might come in with a minor ailment, and Sarah could tell by the way the person looked at her whether she should leave or stay and help. On rare occasions, a few men might bring in a serious case. Then, Sarah would spring into action right beside her husband. He felt certain no doctor ever had a more efficient assistant. Sarah would prepare dinner, which they usually had a chance to eat together, though sometimes dinnertime would find them both out on a call.

Clifton closed the office for supper, but that didn't mean he never had to leave. A doctor stayed on call twenty-four hours a day. Sarah didn't seem to mind, and she often kept the same schedule he did. She wanted to go with him, even late at night in the dead of winter. She amazed him.

She thrilled him in their private moments too. Her passion often matched his, and she showed no shyness or reserve there. This surprised him more than anything else about her, but it also delighted him. He felt as if God had opened the portal to blessings and drenched Clifton with them. Except for the prejudice against Sarah, his life would have been almost perfect.

Clifton helped Sarah into their wagon after having made an emergency house call. The dark, lowhanging clouds added to the gloom lodged in Clifton's heart. Sarah searched his face as he slipped into the seat beside her.

"You did all you could, Cliff. They waited too late to call you."

He rubbed his forehead as if he could massage away the memory. "It's hard to lose a mother and baby like that. I can't help but wonder what the family will do now. They'll have it hard."

"I know. Seeing someone die is never easy but, I repeat, it was not your fault."

He reached over, took her hand, and squeezed it to let her know he appreciated her reassurances. Somehow the words were caught in his throat. He did hate losing the mother and child, but his blood ran cold with fear that it could happen to Sarah. Too many women died in childbirth, and it hit rich and poor, well-to-do and the lower classes indiscriminately.

"You're thinking it could happen to me, aren't you?" His wife knew him too well.

Clifton picked up the reins and gave the signal for the horse to move forward. "Giving birth can be dangerous for a woman. Today proved that."

"God will take care of us. Nothing is certain in this world, but if I go before you, I'll be waiting for you in the next." Sarah swayed as the wagon wheels rolled through a puddle.

"I know you're right," Clifton said, "but I can't help but be concerned."

"Cliff, you know people typically only call you out for the problem cases. I'm healthy. My mother delivered six healthy babies with no problem. There's no reason to believe I won't be able to do the same. Besides, worrying about it won't change anything. It's best not to let your mind dwell on what might be. When you do, you cease to enjoy what is."

He knew she was right, but he prayed there would be no complications for her. Thankfully, he delivered more healthy babies whose mothers recovered nicely, and he took hope in this.

Clifton's parents came to visit after Christmas. They'd spent Christmas with Gracie. Now they would stay with their son through most of January.

He and Sarah moved their bed to the office for his parents. He and she planned to sleep on a pallet on the floor of their bedroom again. However, when his parents arrived, they had a wagon loaded down with extras. There were vegetables from the root cellar, meat from the smokehouse, additional pots and pans, quilts, sheets, pillows, a mattress, a bed, and more chairs.

"You look as if you've moved from the mountains," Clifton said and laughed.

"Well, with just the two of us, we have plenty," Mama said. "There were still things Edgar had moved to the farm from my family's old cabin. Besides, I thought I might buy some new things to take back. This is the first time I've ever had the opportunity to do some serious shopping. I'd especially like some nice furniture for the sitting room."

Mama also brought some dried herbs and helped Clifton with some home remedies. A few of her medicines proved more effective than the ones he bought, and others seemed to be close to the same thing.

"Who's minding the farm?" Clifton asked.

"We sold your Mama's old place," Papa told him. "A man with a family came and offered us a decent price. He asked if I had any livestock to sell. Your mother and I had been trying to figure out a way to come visit you and Gracie, so I let him borrow the cows and the chickens to get milk and eggs. I told him anything born on his place, he could keep, and I promised him I'd give him a spring pig, regardless."

"That worked out well, didn't it?"

"Yes, it certainly did."

"And, it gave me some funds with which to buy new furnishings," Mama added.

"Well, there's some more of those mountain people," a woman in church said with a snicker to her companion. "At least *they* don't seem to be half-breeds."

Mama faced her and said, "Mountain people are the salt of God's earth. They have the independent, persevering nature that helped form this country. Furthermore, the Cherokee were original inhabitants in this land. They are a noble people who aren't hypocrites. I've always thought Christians should strive to be more like Christ, but I guess you haven't understood His messages."

The women stood with their mouths agape. Finally one said, "Well, I've never!"

"Oh, yes, you did, but I wish you had never," Mama said, and the woman flounced off.

"I doubt if that did much good," Papa told Mama.

"You're probably right," she agreed with a sigh, "but it came out before I could stop it. I hope I haven't made matters worse. Sometimes my jaws have a tendency to flap like sheets in a strong mountain breeze. I know speaking one's mind rarely does anyone any good, except maybe for the speaker, and that's often questionable."

"I thought it well-deserved," Clifton told her, "but I've never seen you like that, Mama."

"Oh, she's always been brave and outspoken, and she can be ferocious at times. Her parents called it 'gumption,'" Papa said with a twinkle in his eye. "You should have heard what she told Belinda Schreiner, the next time we saw her after the preaching at our place. Your mama gave her quite a tongue-lashing."

"Really?" Clifton looked at his mother in a new light. "I would've liked to have heard that. When did this happen?"

"At another preaching service, not long after you and Sarah married. Your mother and I had gone alone. I believe you wanted to keep Sarah away from further such comments, and I suspect you wanted the house to yourselves for a little while too."

"Good for you, Mama."

"I'm sure God often shakes his head at me," Mama said. "I do need to learn to control my tongue. As I get older, it seems to get worse instead of better."

"I think if that's the worst of your sins, Emma," his father said, "God will still smile at you as you walk through those pearly gates. After all, Christ said some stern words to the Pharisees and Sadducees. That doesn't give us the right to be obnoxious or hurtful, but we are to stand against injustice, which is what you just did."

"You always know how to make me feel better, Edgar." She moved closer to Papa.

Clifton wished he could stand against injustice as Mama so freely did. If only he had some of her gumption. He shook his head and smiled, his gaze still on his parents. Their love had always given him a warm feeling of security. He glanced at Sarah. She looked at him with the same expression Mama used for Papa. *Thank You, Lord,* Clifton silently prayed. He felt overwhelmed by how much he'd been blessed.

Now that Clifton's parents were staying with them, Sarah stopped accompanying Clifton on his calls, and he missed her. For the most part, the couple had learned in which homes Sarah would be welcomed and in which she wasn't. She always went with him to the places where no one minded her presence, and she pitched in to help.

Sarah had been a quick learner, and Clifton couldn't imagine a better assistant. Nothing made her flinch or turn away. Outwardly, nothing seemed to bother her or upset her, although Clifton knew differently. Like him, she cared for people, and she hurt for their pain. Still, she had the backbone and nerve to do what needed to be done.

He also missed Sarah joining him in his office, but he loved seeing his parents. Instead of working in the office, he often left the door open between it and the kitchen. The four of them would sit around the dining table and talk until someone came for him.

He knew Sarah enjoyed his parents' presence. She and Mama visited the shops around town. Mama had become Sarah's champion. Few dared say anything derogatory in Mama's presence. Clifton would have liked to be more like that, but he dared not and still try to practice medicine in the town.

"Do you wish you'd gone to medical school in South Carolina, Virginia, or Kentucky?" his father asked one day.

These were the colleges with medical schools closer to North Carolina, and Clifton had considered attending them. He'd finally decided to go to the University of North Carolina in Chapel Hill instead.

"No, I feel I've received good medical training," Clifton replied. "By taking what biology and medical courses I could at the college, and assisting Dr. Thomas for the practice and experience, I feel good about my education. Having a degree from a medical school would have been more important had I wanted to specialize or practice in a state that has licensing requirements, but for general, private practice, the degree I have and the experience I've gained have given me a good foundation. North Carolina hasn't shown any interest in licensing physicians, so I have no need for a degree from a medical school. In addition, many of the states that had initiated licensing requirements for doctors have since repealed them."

Sarah smiled at him. "Cliff is an excellent doctor," she told her in-laws. "As you can tell, he keeps up with things in his field. You can be very proud of him. I am."

"I think we should be thinking about returning home," Papa said toward the end of January. "In another week, we'll have been here a month, and we were already at Gracie's a couple of weeks."

"You need to stay as long as possible," Sarah said. "With the farm, you may not have the chance to come again."

"Besides," Clifton added, "you can never tell what the weather might do this time of year."

"If we wait on the certainty of better weather, we'll be waiting until spring," his father said, "and we can't do that."

"Why not?" Clifton asked, and they all laughed.

"I thought Gracie would have had a child by now," Clifton heard Mama tell Papa one day.

Clifton had come to his office to do some paperwork, and his parents sat in the kitchen while Sarah went to the bedroom to change her dress to go uptown with Mama. They didn't know he could hear them.

"I would have thought so too. I think I'm ready to be a grandfather. Emma, do you think Gracie and Ernest are as much in love as we are?"

"I'm not sure. From what I've seen, they're happy and well-suited for each other, but their love doesn't have the depth or intensity ours does. They seem more comfortable with each other than deeply in love."

"I agree, but Clifton and Sarah seem to have our kind of deep, passionate love."

"Yes, they do," Mama agreed. Clifton could imagine her pleased smile. "Who do you think will give us a grandchild first?"

"Only the Lord knows, but my money would be on Clifton and Sarah, if I were a betting man."

Clifton grinned to himself, both because his parents sensed the deepness of his and Sarah's love and because they thought

Sarah might become pregnant soon. It surprised him his parents knew what was going on in their adult children's lives so well.

The older couple ended up staying until March. They seemed comfortable staying with him and Sarah, even in their small house. Of course, his parents had always lived in a small cabin—before they'd had four children and added the upstairs. They planned to go back to Salem and spend some more time with Gracie before heading back up the mountain.

"This has been the mildest winter I've had since I left the flatlands at fourteen," Mama said.

"It's the mildest I've ever spent," Papa added.

"To have never been out of the mountains, you seemed to have adjusted fine," Clifton told his father.

"As long as I'm with your mother, I'm fine anywhere," he said as he looked at his wife. "The good Lord had better take me first. I'd be lost without Emma. She could get along without me much better than I could without her. Her abduction proved that."

"You don't know what you're talking about, Edgar," Mama told him. "I think the good Lord should take us together, because that's the only way we'll both be happy."

"Now, don't go trying to tell the Lord what to do, Emma," he teased.

"I never tell Him what to do, Edgar Moretz. I was just telling Him my thoughts, and I do that all the time."

Sarah and Clifton looked at each other and smiled.

"You'll have to arrange it to come spend the winter with us every year," Sarah told them.

"I doubt if we'll be able to do that, Sarah," her mother-in-law said, "but I'd like to."

Clifton truly hated to see his parents go. It would be strange not having them around. At least Sarah would be with him more, and that made him miss his parents less than he would have otherwise.

CHAPTER NINETEEN

Abducted

One cool spring morning, Clifton and Sarah worked in the office. Mid-morning the sheriff and a deputy came in, half-carrying, half-dragging a bleeding man between them. Since Clifton had left the extra bed in the office, the men deposited the injured man there.

"This one got drunk, got into a fight, and got himself sliced open," the sheriff said. "He's on his way to jail, but I thought we'd better bring him in and get him put back together first. I'll leave my deputy here and be back later."

Sarah began preparing what Clifton would need, and he started to swab away some of the blood so he could sew up the gash. It looked like a deep one, but it didn't look as if any vital organs had been touched.

The man wouldn't have been bad looking, if he'd been cleaned up. Clifton guessed him to be in his late twenties or early thirties. He had a lean body, but at the same time, his muscles looked toned from hard work. He had several days' growth of beard on his face, but he must normally be clean-shaven. His brown hair hung in clumps and looked so dirty that Clifton couldn't tell if it would be light or dark if clean.

While his hands worked, he thought what a shame this man had chosen a life-style of drinking and fighting, and so early in the day. He'd heard the sheriff say the patient had an alcoholic father, and he'd caused all kinds of problems for the family. He wondered what caused a man to turn to liquor instead of God, and why a man would make the same bad choices he'd seen his father make.

"What's his name?" Clifton asked the deputy, who was sitting in one of the chairs.

"Alan Bryne."

Clifton helped hold the patient up while Sarah started wrapping the bandage around his waist and chest. The patient regained consciousness. His eyes lock onto Sarah.

"Am I dead and gone to heaven?" Alan Bryne mumbled. "You sure do look like some kind of angel, darling."

"That's my wife you're talking to," Clifton said. He didn't try to keep the disgust from his voice.

"If you were dead, Bryne, it wouldn't be no angel you'd be seeing," the deputy added with a laugh.

The wounded man looked at Clifton for the first time. "You the doc?"

"I am."

"You sure got a real purty wife."

"I know."

Clifton lowered him gently down to the bed and finished tying off the bandage. Sarah had left for the kitchen on the last remark. Clifton turned his back to Bryne.

"He can be moved to the jail now, deputy. He may be weak for a time. Keep him as still as possible to prevent further bleeding. See that he gets some meat or broth to gain his strength back. I'll come by and check on him in the morning, but if there're any concerns before then, come for me."

The deputy had just stood up when the sheriff came in the door. The sheriff paid in cash, got a receipt, and then the two lawmen escorted Alan Bryne to jail.

Clifton sat down. He felt a little weak himself. He knew other men had admired Sarah, because he saw how they looked at her, but this was the first time anyone had said something improper. Clifton couldn't believe the man had called her "darling." The others who'd said things they shouldn't to her had referred to her Indian blood. Bryne was the first who'd talked openly about her feminine beauty, and Clifton didn't like it one bit.

He realized being so attractive had the potential of putting Sarah in great danger. When he went on calls where the people didn't welcome Sarah, he left her home alone. His thoughts frightened him.

Maybe he was letting his imagination run wild, but he couldn't get the misgivings from his mind. He would caution Sarah about keeping the doors locked, pray, and let God take care of things. He would put his trust in God, as he always had.

Their following days were uneventful, except for the cases every doctor has. Clifton began to relax, but he still told Sarah to lock the door behind him every time he left her alone. Thankfully, those times had been few.

"Doctor, Papa sent me to fetch ya," the teenage boy said when Clifton answered the door. He and Sarah had just gotten up, and she had started breakfast.

"It's Mama," the boy continued. "She's having trouble birthing the baby."

"I'll be right there," Clifton told him. "I'll just grab my bag. Sarah, lock this door behind me."

He kissed Sarah lightly on the lips. The farmer whose wife Clifton was going to help was extremely prejudiced. To avoid trouble, Clifton would have to leave Sarah behind.

"I'll be back as soon as I can, sweetheart."

The labor turned out to be a difficult one. For one thing, the woman was getting too old for this. For another, it was a breech birth. Clifton finally got the baby turned, and things turned out well. The family had a hefty, new baby boy and a completely exhausted wife and mother.

Clifton went home tired and ready for something to eat. He hoped no one called for him this afternoon. He could use a nap.

As he rode up their street, he saw a group of men milling around his house. His blood ran cold. Something must be terribly wrong.

The sheriff came and met him as he dismounted. The man looked worried.

"We've got a problem here, Dr. Moretz," he said. "Alan Bryne kidnapped the little Knight girl as she headed to school, and he used her to get into your house. The little girl escaped and ran home, and her mother alerted us to the situation. If she hadn't, Bryne might have gotten away. As it is, he's got Mrs. Moretz in there. He's probably boozed up again and not thinking straight."

"What can we do?" Clifton's fear left him weak and stiff. He felt as if his blood had turned to ice and life had been drained from his body.

"Well, I'm trying to talk him out, but it's not working so far. I've got extra men with me, but I hesitate to storm the place for fear of what he might do to Mrs. Moretz. Right now, you stay back and pray. I'll try to keep him talking. If he's talking, he's less likely to harm her."

Clifton wanted to ask if Bryne had hurt her already, but he knew the sheriff wouldn't know that. He backed up against a tree and stood watching the house. He said a prayer, but he didn't close his eyes. He stared straight ahead, seeing little.

"Dear Father," he whispered, "I need Thee now more than I ever have in my whole life. Protect Sarah, I pray. She's such a good wife, and she loves Thee as much as I do. She serves well by ministering to the needs of others, even when they treat her poorly. Please keep her safe and bring this awful situation to a speedy resolution, I pray in Jesus' name. Amen."

"Bryne, you can't stay in there forever," he heard the sheriff call. "Send Mrs. Moretz out right now, and I won't charge you with kidnapping. I'll just take you to jail for disorderly conduct and let you sleep it off."

"But I want this woman, sheriff. Have you seen her? She's the purtiest thang I ever laid eyes on. I've got ta have her."

Clifton's stomach lurched, his palms became sweaty, and his whole body turned as weak and wobbly as a newborn foal. He called to God again in agony and despair. Then, it dawned upon him the man had said, "I've got to have her." That meant he hadn't had her yet. It gave Clifton hope.

He also realized his emotions must be similar to those his father had felt when his fiancée had been taken by the Cherokee. Was history repeating itself? If it was, he sure hoped things would turn out well this time, and he would have Sarah back unharmed.

He saw the sheriff motion for his deputy and whisper something in his ear. The deputy went to each man and told them something. They began to silently fan out and circle the house. Most of them eased toward the back. Something was about to happen.

The sheriff kept talking. "No woman is worth dying for, Bryne. If you don't get killed today, you'll die by hanging later. Is that what you want?"

"This woman might be worth even all that, if I can spend some time with her, private like, you know. My life hasn't been all that easy, anyway. I don't guess it's worth much."

"Your life is hard because of your own choices, Bryne. You can change all that."

Clifton heard a commotion toward the back of the house, and Bryne came through the front door. He pushed Sarah along in front of him, holding her tightly with one arm and holding a knife to her throat with the other. Clifton rushed forward toward his wife.

"Don't do it!" Bryne warned, and the knife tightened enough at Sarah's neck to break the skin. The thin, red line of blood glared at Clifton. Bryne looked straight at him. "Stop right there!"

Clifton froze in his tracks. He looked at Sarah, but she couldn't see him because she couldn't move her head or neck. She looked calm and collected. She showed no sign of terror, but he knew she hid her feelings well. He knew she was crying and screaming on the inside.

"Sending those men in the back was a stupid move, sheriff," Bryne continued. "I will slit her throat if you try anything again. If I can't have her, the doc there won't either. By the look on your face, Doc, I'd say she'll be worth it."

When Bryne said "Doc," Sarah tried to turn enough to see him, but she couldn't. A small steam of blood trickled down her neck. Clifton backed up and tried to walk around where he would be in her direct line of sight.

"You stay right where you are, Doc. Don't you move a muscle. Brang that horse over here, Murphy."

Clifton guessed Bryne had been drinking, but he showed no signs of being drunk. He seemed to be managing himself pretty well.

The man named Murphy untied Clifton's horse and led it over to Bryne. Bryne shifted around and looked uncertain.

"This ain't going to work," he said. "I can't get her on the horse and get on myself with all you men standing around ready to jump me."

"Let her go, Bryne," the sheriff said. "You don't want to do this."

"Oh, yeah, I do. Y'all stay back now, or I'll kill her."

He turned and backed up, still dragging Sarah with him. Sarah could see Clifton now. He saw the recognition in her eyes. Her anxious gaze never left him as Bryne dragged her down the street. Clifton couldn't tear his gaze away from her either, not until she and Bryne disappeared somewhere down the way. He wanted to follow them in the worst way, but he feared Bryne would use his knife on Sarah if Clifton took even one step after them.

The sheriff sent the other men to get their horses, and he took Clifton's. Clifton ran to the stable to saddle Sarah's horse. He planned to go too. He'd go insane if he had to wait here.

He must have saddled the horse in record time, but he hardly remembered. He suddenly realized he rode in the direction the sheriff had gone. Somehow he'd manage to beat the sheriff's men. He actually didn't feel as helpless now that he had some action to take.

He found the sheriff up ahead, walking around, leading the horse, and looking for signs. He looked up when Clifton approached.

"I checked an empty house in this direction, but they weren't there. No one seems to have seen them, but he could have taken her into a stable or outbuilding anywhere around here. I figure he might try to steal a horse too."

Clifton hoped Bryne would put Sarah on horseback, because that might give her the best chance of escaping. She could ride better than most men. However, Clifton feared that Bryne would take her to a secluded place right away. *Just don't let her die, Lord. Whatever else happens, don't let him kill her.*

Sarah tried not to panic. She needed to stay calm and think through the situation. She needed her wits about her if she was going to get away from this attacker.

She'd wanted to escape out the door in the house, but Bryne hadn't given her a chance to do so. He stayed within reach of her, and he held the knife in his hand. Sarah had the feeling he wouldn't hesitate to throw it in her back if she made a run for the door.

After he'd forced his way inside, Sarah had managed to keep him at bay before the sheriff got there by offering him the bottle of whiskey Cliff used to make his tinctures. It had worked. Then, the sheriff had come and kept the kidnapper busy talking.

When the men stormed through the back of the house, Bryne grabbed her, put his knife to her throat, and ordered them to stay back. He'd pushed her out the front door but gave her no chance to make a move. She could feel the pressure from the knife getting tighter on her neck. She knew better than to try to swallow, but her mouth felt like cotton fields in a hot summer drought.

Sarah had heard Bryne call to Cliff. She'd tried to turn her eyes in that direction, but she still couldn't see her husband. He would be even more distraught than she. He loved her more than she loved herself.

When Bryne called for the horse, she became alert. If he put her on the horse, she might have a chance to break free.

He'd been drinking, but she wished he were drunker, so he would be less in control. The drinking hadn't affected his movements that much so far.

Her hopes fell when Bryne decided he couldn't put her on the horse and mount himself without the men overpowering him. She'd planned to ride quickly away as soon as she was seated on the horse, leaving the sheriff's men to overpower Bryne before he could throw the knife or else he'd miss her.

Then Bryne turned her around to pull her down the street, and she could see Cliff for the first time. He looked as upset as she feared he'd be. This might be the last time she ever saw him, so she locked her eyes on him and didn't move them until she could see him no more. Even through his distress, his expression had told her how much he loved her. It renewed her courage.

Bryne turned and ran with her arm still tight in his grip once they left sight of the others. The knife was no longer at her throat, but he still held it in his other hand as he forced her to run by his side. His fingers held her upper arm so tightly that she knew they would leave bruise marks.

Sarah tried to trip Bryne as she moved, but he evaded her foot every time. He ran so fast that she had no chance to try to kick him. He almost dragged her along anyway, and he had threatened to stab her, if she didn't keep up.

He frantically looked for a place to take her, and she knew her strongest fear so far. If he found an empty structure, she had no doubt what would happen. He'd made it very clear he wanted her body.

She had a decision to make. If he threw her down and fell on top of her, should she lie beneath him without moving, or should she fight with everything she had in her? If she fought, she had little doubt she would end up dead. If she did the first, her life might be spared, but he might keep her as his prisoner and force her again and again. She couldn't endure that, so she chose the latter.

Bryne pulled Sarah into a barn. Once inside the barn, Bryne stopped and listened. Sarah heard talking. It sounded as if someone was headed in this direction.

"Don't you make a sound, woman," he hissed. "I still have the knife, and I'm good with a knife."

He shoved her into a stall with a horse and pulled the horse out. He positioned the horse in front of the gate to the stall so she couldn't get out and then slid the halter over the horse's head, tied it to the top rung, and began to saddle it. Sarah quickly tried to climb over the side of the stall, but Bryne knocked her back down.

"I will kill you if I have to," he said. "It'd be easier for me to escape without you, so don't try me."

He grabbed some nearby twine and tied her hands together in front of her. Then, he shoved her on the horse and tied her hands to the saddle horn. He untied the horse and climbed up behind her. She knew he must be pushed to the back of the saddle, like she had been pushed to the front. As they rode out of the barn, a plan began to form. Since she couldn't get off the horse with her hands tied to the saddle, she would have to try to get Bryne off.

She wiggled her hands and gripped the saddle horn as tightly as she could. She pulled in her knees slightly and tightened the muscles in her thighs to hold on better. Moving her upper legs as little as possible, she shoved her heels into the sides of the horse as she pushed back against Bryne to unseat him.

The horse jumped and moved even faster. Bryne wasn't expecting such a move from Sarah, and he toppled off the horse and hit the ground in a cloud of dust. Sarah had done it! She was free!

Now, how could she stop the galloping horse without her hands? They were heading away from town at a fast pace. She leaned over and spoke softly to the horse. She loosened her legs as much as she could and still stay balanced on a runaway horse. She couldn't take a chance of falling and being dragged along.

The horse gradually slowed. What a relief! Sarah knew the Indian ponies would turn with just pressure from the rider's legs. She hoped this one would too.

It did! She turned it to head back to town, back to her house. She hoped Cliff would be there. If he wasn't, she would find someone to untie her, but right now, she didn't want to see anyone but Cliff.

What the townsfolk would say about her being astride a horse with her legs hanging below her skirts crossed her mind as she traveled down the road. The situation would just add to the scandal. For now, she focused on getting back to her husband.

A man ran out of his barn and called to the men. "Sheriff, a man came by, dragging a woman by force! He took her toward the Baker place."

The sheriff mounted and took off with Clifton right behind him. Clifton heard other men on horses not far behind them.

"I see him," the sheriff called.

Clifton saw him too. He was running toward a patch of woods in the distance, but Sarah was nowhere in sight.

The sheriff rode in front of Bryne and cut him off. Clifton dismounted, grabbed Bryne by the shoulder, and spun him around. Bryne must have dropped the knife, for it was nowhere to be seen. He prayed the lunatic hadn't left it in Sarah's body.

"Where's Sarah?" he yelled. "What did you do with my wife?"

Bryne threw up his hands as if to fend off a fight. "I didn't do nothing to her. In fact, I . . . I had already decided to bring her back when she—she took off without me!"

"Now why don't I believe that?" the sheriff asked Bryne.

Clifton didn't stay to hear the rest. He jumped on his horse, swung it around, and headed for the Baker place, calling Sarah's name as he rode.

She wasn't there. Wild with worry, Clifton turned his horse around and scanned the area as he rode back the way he had come. Where could Bryne have hidden Sarah? What had he done to her?

His fruitless search led him back to his house. Helplessly, Clifton glanced around, debating whether to stay there and wait for the sheriff or deputies or go back and look for his wife, when he saw her riding toward him on horseback. He quickly tied his horse and ran to meet her. Her hands were tied to the saddle horn. He pulled out his pocketknife and slashed the cord. As soon as she was loose, she fell into his arms.

"Oh, Cliff."

She couldn't say anything else, because his kisses became too intense. He had never felt such relief and joy.

"Come, darling," he said.

He picked her up and carried her into the house. The sheriff would be by soon—for the horse Sarah had ridden if nothing else—but Clifton didn't want to let her out of his arms. He carried her to the office, sat on the bed, and held her in his arms. She wrapped her arms around his neck, rested her head on his shoulder, and clung to him as if he were her life source. They sat like that for several minutes.

Clifton broke the silence first. "I have never been so frightened in my life, Sarah. I was so terrified for you that I became sick."

"I shouldn't have opened the door, but when I heard Amy Knight's voice, I didn't think. I should have looked out the window."

"Oh, darling, this was Alan Bryne's fault, not yours."

"I was afraid he was going to force me right here in our house. I gave him the bottle of whiskey we use to mix our tinctures, and by the time he had drunk it, the sheriff had come. The sheriff kept him talking enough to keep his attention off me some." She rested one hand over Cliff's heart. "You know what happened after that. I wanted to get back to you so badly. I was afraid I might never see you again."

"Oh, darling, you feel so good in my arms, but I need to let you go while I get something for the cut on your neck. Your wrists look chaffed and also in need of doctoring."

Sarah shook her head and nestled closer. "Not now. Just hold me a little longer. They're just minor scratches."

"Did he hurt you otherwise, Sarah?"

"No, I wasn't harmed at all, other than a few bruises. I thought he was going to force me in a barn stall, but then he started saddling the horse to escape. There was never a moment when he could try to have his way with me."

Clifton pulled his wife closer. "I love you so much, Sarah. I prayed so hard for your safety, and now I praise God you are safe and back in my arms."

"I love you too, Cliff. Besides God, you are my everything."

The sheriff gave a quick knock and came in. Clifton had left the front door half open.

"I have Bryne in jail on kidnapping charges and a few others. He won't be going anywhere anytime soon. I think I have most of the information I need, but I just need to ask a couple of questions.

"Mrs. Moretz, I'm happy to see you here! Did he hurt you in any way that I need to add other charges to the kidnapping?"

Sarah shook her head. "No. Thankfully, I'm fine."

"I'm glad to hear that." The sheriff turned to Clifton. "You've got quite a little lady here, Dr. Moretz. She handled herself well to keep her head about her and get away from Bryne. It looked bad for a while, but I'm glad everything turned out okay." He extended his hand.

Clifton shook his hand. "I am too, sheriff. Very glad. Thank you for all your help."

"That's what I'm here for. Just nail up that back door for tonight, and I'll send someone to fix it for you first thing in the morning."

"You haven't had anything to eat today, have you?" Sarah asked Clifton after the sheriff had left. "I'll fix you something."

"Let me put some ointment on your neck and wrists first. Then, you can fix us something quick and easy. Eggs will be fine. I'm going to put a sign on the front door that we're closed for the day so we can eat in peace. Then, I think I am tired enough to go to bed. What about you?"

She smiled a delightful smile. "I'd like that," she said. "I'd like that very much."

Joyce came the next day to see about Sarah. "Amy cried and cried that she'd helped that man get into your house," Joyce told Sarah.

"She must have been petrified," Sarah said. "Tell her not to worry. I'm fine. Why don't you bring her over after school so she can see for herself?"

They hugged, and Joyce stayed with Sarah while Clifton went out on a call. It wasn't out of town, so he wasn't gone over an hour. When he came back, they were laughing and talking. His heart jumped at the sound of Sarah's laughter.

After the harrowing ordeal, Clifton and Sarah were closer than ever, if that could be possible. Clifton knew he could have lost her that day. That scoundrel Bryne seemed capable of taking what he wanted and leaving her dead. Clifton winced every time he imagined it, but it hadn't happened. God had taken care of her and brought her back unharmed. Now he realized all over again how precious Sarah was, and he basked in her presence and their love.

For her part, Sarah seemed to need him more than ever. She wanted to be close to him, to feel him, to hold him close. Her security had been shaken, and she clung to Clifton to keep the anxiety at bay.

Clifton understood this and did all he could to reassure her. He'd walk up behind her, put his arms around her, and kiss her neck or cheek. She might walk by him, and he'd pull her into his lap and hold her. In private moments, even in the office, he gave her long, passionate kisses that left both of them breathless. They were together and a part of each other. They were one.

"Sarah, would you like to leave here and go back to the mountains?" he asked her one day. "Maybe it would be better if we went back to the farm. I know my parents would love that."

"I love the mountains, Cliff, but you are an excellent doctor, and you have built a good practice here. Why would you want to leave?"

"It seems you're always doing for me, and I want to do something for you. I want you to be happy and live without fear and away from prejudiced people."

Sarah wrapped her arms around Clifton. "I'm tremendously happy, Cliff. I meant it when I once told you I would be happy anywhere with you. Every place has its good and bad, and every place has its dangers. Things can happen in the mountains, just like they can here. Look at what happened to your mother before she and your father were married, and what happened to your two brothers.

"The farm is where we met and fell in love," she continued. "It will always be special to me, just like the time we spent there, and it remains in my heart. I don't need to go back to remember it. We're building other happy memories right here.

"Your mother once told me there were many fields to be cleared in life, so better things could be planted. I think we may be helping to clear some of those fields right here in Salisbury. More people seem to accept me than at first."

Clifton kissed Sarah's forehead. "How did you get so wise, and how did I end up with such an amazing wife?"

"I think maybe God created us for each other," she smiled, "and He does good work."

Clifton's practice had taken off, and he could begin to be more selective. He informed his prejudiced patients that he would not be coming to their houses anymore, unless Sarah could also come.

"I need her assistance," he explained, "and as you must have heard, she was kidnapped when I was on a call where she wasn't welcome. I won't take that chance again."

Surprisingly, he lost the business of only six families. He liked to think the others recognized the good care he gave them.

A month after Bryne's attempted kidnapping, Clifton noticed changes in Sarah. "You show all the signs of expecting a child," Clifton told her as they finished breakfast one morning.

"I know, but I hoped it wouldn't happen for a couple more months."

"Why?" Clifton couldn't hide his surprise. He knew how much Sarah had been praying for a baby. A scene from the past flashed through his mind.

"Cliff," Sarah had said one night as they lay in bed listening to the nighttime songs of crickets and frogs, "do you think something's wrong with me? Is that the reason we haven't started our family already?"

He had wanted to tell her the only thing wrong with her was an extreme case of beauty inside and out that drove her husband to love her to distraction, but he knew she felt strongly about wanting his children. He didn't want her to feel he made light of how she felt, although his first thoughts held a lot of truth.

"No, I don't. It could be me, you know, but I don't think anything is wrong with either of us. I really feel we'll have a child when the time is right. In the meantime, I'm happy to have an outstanding assistant by my side and have my wife all to myself much of the time."

She lay still. "Will you be jealous of a baby?"

"No! I could never be jealous of our baby, created in our love. I want a son or daughter too, but I can wait on God's timing."

She had rolled over in his arms, and he knew he'd said the right thing. She was God's greatest gift to him and the joy of his heart.

Now, Sarah stood staring at the kitchen towel in her hands and said, "I am worried that what happened to me may affect our baby. Bryne wasn't gentle with me. He even left bruise marks on my arm where he dragged me away, and when I tried to climb over the barn stall, he knocked me back." She swung her gaze to Clifton. "Do you think it could have hurt our baby?"

The desperate look on her face tore at Clifton. "I don't think so, darling. If that had happened this early, I think you would have been bleeding and perhaps lost the child. The fact that it didn't happen is a good sign."

She gave a tentative smile, but he could tell she was still worried. How could he comfort her when worry nagged at him too? He had thought they'd come through the incident with Bryne pretty unscathed, but that wasn't true. With Sarah's pregnancy, Bryne's shadow hung over them like a moonless night, and what should have been a joyous time had become tainted.

Clifton would have been worried about Sarah regardless of these added concerns, but now they tried to consume him. What he had told Sarah had been true, but her fall could have also injured the fetus. There had been studies that even the stress of a harrowing situation could affect both the mother and the unborn child. Yet, Clifton tried not to let Sarah see any of these concerns. It would only add to her stress and anxiety. He had to carry on as if he was certain that everything would be fine. In fact, Sarah seemed to do well with her pregnancy. She had morning sickness for about a month, and then it cleared. When she felt better, Sarah was able to continue helping Clifton in his office.

As his business grew, Clifton was able to purchase some things Sarah and he needed. He bought an enclosed carriage, which would be more maneuverable than a wagon, and they wouldn't have to worry about the weather and the elements as much.

They also began looking for a house of their own. They wanted a house with a sitting room and a bigger space for the doctor's office, as well as room for all the children they hoped to have.

They found a nice home on a quiet street. The two-story, white clapboard had been recently built, and it had a garden area in the back. It seemed perfect for their needs.

Clifton secured a bank loan, and they moved in. Sarah threw herself into furnishing the house. They started with the sitting room and office and furnished them completely. They moved their furniture in for the rest and would add to the rooms as they were able. Gradually, the house took shape.

Clifton discovered Sarah had very good taste. She included comfort and practicality with style and elegance for a pleasing combination.

He wanted to start on their appearance next. He bought himself a new suit and tried to get Sarah to buy new dresses.

"I don't need new dresses," she said. "There's still plenty of wear left in the ones I have."

He would have to make it seem like she was doing it for him. He thought about it and came up with a plan.

"Since I've become an established doctor here," he said, "I have a standard and reputation to keep. I don't want us to change or become snobs, but we have an image to uphold. It's not a good reflection on me if my wife wears homespun dresses to church. Do this for me, Sarah. You can still wear your older dresses around here. You are a beauty in anything you wear."

She complied. She ordered one dress from the seamstress and bought material to make three more. Always practical, she said she would make them so they could be let out some as she thickened.

CHAPTER TWENTY

Luke

As more people got to know the doctor and his wife and they became established citizens of Salisbury, the cruel remarks about Sarah became less frequent—at least in their hearing. Many still didn't include Sarah in their social events, however, but they should have. Clifton decided they would have to take matters into their own hands.

"We should host some small dinner parties of our own," Clifton told her. "We can invite only those we want."

"I'm not sure, Cliff. I don't know all the social graces a good hostess should know."

"Nonsense, darling. You have natural instincts. Just be yourself. You're always kind and giving. I think you'll be the perfect hostess."

"But, Clifton, you're biased. You always say I'm perfect, and I know all too well how untrue that is."

"I don't want to push you into doing something you really don't want to do, but I think you'd love having some friends over to dinner. I want you to give it a chance."

She thought carefully. "Okay. We'll invite only two couples the first time and see how it goes. Joyce and her new husband can be one of them."

"I'm going to hire someone to help you on that day. Do you want me to take care of it, or would you like to do it?"

"Oh, Cliff, I don't need extra help. I can manage fine."

"Nonetheless, I'm going to hire someone. In your condition, I certainly don't want you to overdo."

"Sometimes you're too stubborn, Cliff Moretz."

"But, I take very good care of you." He smiled, and she smiled back.

He hired a girl to come in the day of the supper. Jane would not only help Sarah prepare and serve the meal, but she would do some extra cleaning and dusting as well. Jane was fifteen and from a large family. As the oldest child at home, her family needed any money she could earn because she had seven younger siblings.

The dinner went smoothly, as Clifton knew it would. Even Sarah seemed to enjoy herself, and if he hadn't know how reticent she tended to be, he would never have noticed her shyness, because she talked and laughed as much as anyone. It didn't surprise him that she turned out to be an excellent hostess.

Sarah liked Jane. The pleasant girl worked quickly and efficiently. She seemed eager to please and looked up to Sarah. Jane turned out to be so helpful that Clifton talked Sarah into having her come in the mornings on weekdays. Sarah spent more time on the upkeep of this bigger home than Clifton liked. Having Jane there freed up his wife to spend more time with him.

He also had some patients who wanted Sarah to clean their scrapes, apply the ointment, and wrap their wounds. She had a gentle touch that soothed, and they appreciated her competent, caring nature.

Clifton knew that Sarah didn't like the medical practices of bleeding and blistering. He had been taught to rely on them for certain illnesses, but Sarah refused to participate in them. Coming from some knowledge of the medical practices of her Cherokee grandmother, she could not understand the presumed benefits.

"How can causing new wounds on the body help heal anything?" she asked.

His mother would agree with Sarah, Clifton realized, but of course the same Cherokee woman that taught Sarah had taught Mama, so that was to be expected. Yet, when Clifton performed the procedures and a patient died, he couldn't help but wonder if there might be some truth to Sarah's opinion.

Keeping up with developments in his field was important to Clifton. In doing so, he came across an essay written in 1815 by Dr. Ennalls Martin about an epidemical outbreak in Maryland. Dr. Martin had done his own study of bleeding and concluded that bleeding did more harm than good, and many of his patients who died might have lived had they not been bled.

After consideration, Clifton became more skeptical of the procedure and used bleeding sparingly and only when the patient or the family requested it. The patients he didn't bleed seemed to recover better than those he did, so he began to recommend skipping the use of bleeding and blistering altogether. Sarah grinned widely when he told her, as he had suspected she would.

Sarah had no trouble for the few first months of her pregnancy, allowing them both to relax. As her husband, Clifton wanted her to sit around and take it easy. Of course, Sarah laughed and would have none of that. As her doctor, Clifton believed activity, within reason, could make the delivery easier in a normal pregnancy, and the doctor, along with Sarah, overruled the husband. He certainly hoped this would be a normal pregnancy.

Still, he had Jane come all day during the weekdays and half a day on Saturday. Sarah agreed after he told her Jane's family really needed the extra money.

He asked Sarah if she'd like to hire a nanny to help in the nursery when the baby came. She looked at him in dismay.

"I will take care of our baby myself, as I should," she said.

"Will you allow me to help some?" he asked.

She laughed and agreed. She seemed pleased he wanted to be involved, and he did. He had a feeling he would find it hard to keep away from his offspring. He wondered if a parent could love a child too much for its own good.

One humid summer afternoon, Clifton came into the house from a call and saw Sarah sitting in her rocking chair. She didn't seem to notice him, and that was unusual. He hurried to her.

"Is something wrong?"

She reached out and put her hand on his arm. "I'm bleeding just a little." She must have seen the confused look on his face. "Internally," she added. "I noticed it when I used the chamber pot a little while ago." Her hand tightened on his arm, and he felt her worry. Fear gripped Clifton's heart, but he struggled not to let her see it. "Let's get you to bed so I can examine you."

"Yes, doctor." Sarah tried to make it sound like a joke, but he could hear the tremor in her voice.

As Dr. Moretz, Clifton helped his patient to the bed so that he could begin the examination. He forced himself to be detached, as if it was someone else's wife and not his own that he examined. For the moment, Sarah needed a professional doctor and not an anxious, shaky husband.

"It's not bad." He told her as he checked her over. "You're not losing the baby now, but you're going to have to stay in bed to prevent that."

Sarah winced, and Clifton realized he should have been less direct.

"Do you think that will happen?"

Sarah swallowed hard. She was probably swallowing back some tears, Clifton thought. He had no idea, but he prayed not.

"No, it just means you need to stay horizontal as much as possible. I've had this happen to women before. Most of them were just fine and gave birth to a healthy baby." He wouldn't mention how many hadn't.

Clifton tried to relax his face and body and give no indication of how worried he had become. He would take his anguish and petitions before God privately. Right now, he must try to keep his wife from worrying.

"How will we manage if I must stay in bed?"

"I'm sure Jane would like to come and stay fulltime. We can give her the far bedroom. She'll be in much better conditions here than at her family's home, and they won't be as crowded or have to furnish her support."

Sarah reached up and clasped Clifton's hand. "Couldn't we just have her come during the day . . . so we could have the house to ourselves at night?"

"I don't think that would be wise, darling. You know I'm called out at night too. Besides, I don't think we're going to be making much noise in the bedroom until we get this little Moretz into the world." He kissed her lovingly on the forehead to soften that piece of news.

"You won't sleep in another room, will you?" The desperate look she gave him cut at his heart and warmed it at the same time.

"Not unless you ask me to." Clifton patted her hand. "I still plan to go to sleep every night holding you in my arms."

"Until I get too bulky."

"Then, I'll just hold you with your back against my chest."

Her smile told him he had alleviated most of her concerns—for now.

"Do you think this trouble is coming from the rough handling Bryne gave me?" Sarah asked him later that night as they cuddled in bed.

"I don't know," he answered truthfully. "It could, but it could also be the result of any number of things. The important thing is that we take care of you, so there are no further problems."

"D-do you think our baby might be born with a problem from this or what happened with Bryne?"

"There's no reason to think that. You need to take your own advice to me and not be worrying about what could happen. Let's just take things as they come, and God will be with us through it all."

"Yes, He will." But Clifton heard her voice shake.

Clifton felt as if he had a dual personality. He forced the optimist out in Sarah's presence. But, in his alone times, he felt fear grip him and the what-might-happen press down. With God, he sometimes cried out "why?" but he also begged and pleaded for Sarah and their child's lives. It was agony to have this great burden and not be able to share it with Sarah—to have to hide it instead.

They both breathed a sigh of relief at the baby's first movement. It had to be a good sign, but so much could still go wrong.

Clifton considered getting another doctor or a good midwife to help with the birth. A college professor had once said it wasn't wise for someone to doctor his own family for anything but the most minor things, but he couldn't bring himself to do it. He wanted to be there with Sarah and for Sarah. He wanted to make sure everything went well, and he wanted to be there to offer her his support. As much as he wanted the day to come, he also dreaded the thought of it. So much could go wrong, and the spotting made that even more likely. Would he end up blaming himself? Would Sarah blame him or herself? Would he think he should have done more or called in a different doctor? The mere thought of something going wrong made him shudder.

Time continued to roll on, and soon Christmas arrived. Christmas held special meaning this year, and Clifton prayed it wouldn't be the last one he had with Sarah. They figured the baby would make its appearance sometime this month, but it hadn't come yet. At least Sarah hadn't bled profusely or lost the baby. The spotting had continued on and off, enough to be worrisome but not a tragedy—not yet. Clifton forced his thoughts away from where they were headed.

Clifton had put a small Christmas tree in their bedroom and had Jane decorate it. He had even bought a toy for the baby and placed it under the tree. Sarah loved his thoughtfulness.

"You're going to be the most wonderful father," she told him as he sat in a chair pulled close to the bed. "You're already the most marvelous husband."

"I can't help myself with you for a wife."

Clifton had bought Sarah a pretty emerald ring surrounded by brilliant diamonds and some emerald silk to make a matching dress. He'd never bought her jewelry, and he didn't even know if she would appreciate it, but he wanted something special. When he saw the ring, he knew he'd found what he'd been looking for.

She loved it and the fabric. She liked to sew, and she had propped up in bed to continue sewing a wardrobe for the baby. Since the bleeding hadn't worsened, Clifton had let her, because he knew how hard it continued to be for her to remain in bed.

She had also made Clifton a new suit for Christmas. He had mixed feelings when he opened the package.

"How did you manage this without getting out of bed?" he asked, trying not to sound accusatory.

"I had started it before the doctor assigned me to bed." She gave him a quirky little smile. "I took one of your old suits, got the measurements, and sewed the pants, coat, and coordinating vest while you were out on calls or working in your office."

He had no idea how she had managed all this. The workmanship looked flawless, and he grew almost speechless when he saw it.

After they opened their presents, Clifton remained seated beside the bed. They drank spiced hot cider and shared memories of childhood Christmases.

Their celebration seemed to tire Sarah, so Clifton chose to turn in early. As he lay beside her, he held her close. The next morning, they discovered that her bleeding had worsened. Clifton could tell his wife didn't feel well, although she tried to hide it. When she couldn't force any of her breakfast down, he became alarmed. He stayed home with her all day. The few patients who came to see him were sent to another doctor.

Sarah didn't feel like talking. Clifton managed to get a few liquids in her, but she would eat nothing. "My stomach feels too unsettled," she said.

She slept some that night, but she tossed and turned and couldn't seem to get comfortable. The room felt cool, but she perspired, and yet she didn't seem to have a fever.

Clifton couldn't sleep at all. He got up and sat in the chair beside the bed, hoping that would enable Sarah to rest better, but it didn't seem to help. He paced the floor for a while, but that brought him no relief either.

God, what am I to do? Things don't look good, and I'm worried.

Sarah's condition continued to get worse. Clifton called in the doctor who had been taking care of his patients for him, but the man had no advice to offer. "You're doing all you can," he said. "I wouldn't have done anything differently."

Sarah's labor began just after Clifton lay down beside her on December the twenty-eighth. At first, the contractions were mild and far apart. Sarah seemed so worn out and distraught, however, that Clifton panicked.

About five hours later, her water broke, and then the pains became severe.

Clifton feared Sarah's strength would give out, but when he held her hands through some of them, she squeezed his so hard he felt bruised. Still, she closed her eyes and never cried out. She would moan in relief sometimes as they began to subside

"I love you," she whispered once. How a woman could be in the midst of all this agony and still love her husband baffled him.

He checked, and the baby seemed to be coming head first, as it should. Relieved to have something good to report, Clifton shared the news with Sarah and received a slight nod and smile in return.

After about two hours of hard labor, baby Moretz pushed out. "It's a boy!" Clifton said joyfully to his wife. "We have a son!"

Clifton cut the cord and started to clean up his son when he noticed Sarah seemed to be having difficulty. He lay the baby down in the nearby cradle and turned to help his wife. The afterbirth came out, but the bleeding didn't stop.

Lord, n-o-o! The mother always died when excessive bleeding couldn't be stopped. *God, help me!*

Sarah seemed to be unconscious. Clifton worked quickly doing everything he could to stop the flow. It seemed like hours, but could have only been a few minutes, when the worst appeared to be over.

"Lie still and don't move, darling," he told her, but he didn't know if she heard. He tried to clean up around her the best he could without disturbing her.

The baby started crying louder, and Sarah aroused.

"I want to hold my baby." Her voice sounded weak yet determined.

Her bleeding had slowed to a normal amount. Clifton turned his attention to the newborn as he answered. "In just a minute. Let me get him cleaned up some first."

His son cried the whole time he washed him. He wrapped him up and put him in Sarah's arms. The baby stopped crying immediately.

"I see how this is going to be," Clifton teased. "He's a Mama's boy already, but I don't blame him." Sarah smiled, and that made Clifton feel so much better.

"He's beautiful," she said as she gazed into the face of their baby boy.

The baby did seem healthy. He had a head full of black hair and eyes so dark they appeared navy.

"Yes, he is, and so are you."

Sarah blinked. "I must look a wreck. I know I feel like one."

"You've been through a lot. Are you hungry? You haven't had anything to eat lately."

"A little, but I'm too tired to eat now." She kissed the baby's head as he snuggled against her.

"Rest then, and I'll have Jane bring you up some broth and a little bread when you wake up."

Both mother and baby slept. Clifton felt drained, but he didn't want to leave them, so he sat back in the chair and watched his loved ones sleep. They weren't in the clear yet, but the situation was looking better.

Thank you, Lord. Thank you.

"We need to decide on a name," Sarah said later as she looked at her precious son. Clifton had kept her in bed after her ordeal. She had gained strength and looked much better. No longer did he fear for her life.

They'd chosen Rebecca for a girl's name, but they had yet to agree on a boy's name. Sarah had wanted Clifton or Cliff, but Clifton didn't want to call his son Clifton, and he wanted Sarah to continue to call him Cliff, as she did now. Besides, his parents had liked the name because it reminded them of the majestic peaks and cliffs around the farm. No mountains loomed like that close to Salisbury.

"What about Edgar after your father?" she asked.

"I love my father, but Edgar isn't my favorite name. What about Connell?"

"Not with Moretz," she answered. "Like you, I love my father, and I even like the name Connell, but it's awkward to say Connell Moretz. They just don't seem to go together."

"I guess you're right."

"I know." A spark came to Sarah's eyes. "We'll name him Luke. Wasn't the Luke in the Bible a physician? Luke Moretz. It even sounds right. Let's name him Luke Clifton Moretz. That sounds nice, and Luke suits him."

Clifton liked the sound of it too. "Luke Clifton Moretz it is."

He guessed his parents had been right. He and Sarah had given them their first grandchild.

Luke turned out to be a hearty baby. He took milk well and rarely had colic. He came in a healthy size. By the time he turned three months old, he had brown eyes to go with his black hair.

"I had hoped he would have more your coloring," Sarah said.

Clifton shook his head. "The more he looks like you, Sarah, the better it will be. Besides, I think he's perfect."

Sarah smiled. She couldn't argue with that. Now that Clifton had lifted all restrictions on her, she glowed with happiness. She had recovered completely.

Sarah had spent this entire week out of bed, but Clifton had kept Jane fulltime, although she returned to her own home in the evenings. He hadn't completely resumed his practice yet, but he would do so next week.

Now he and Sarah sat in the parlor, as he liked to do in the evenings. Luke had already been put to bed, and Clifton had Sarah's undivided attention and she his.

"If you could have three wishes, three things for Luke's future, what would they be?" Sarah asked. She seemed to be partly toying with him, but Clifton suspected a seriousness beneath that.

"That's a difficult question."

"Don't take a long time thinking about it. Just tell me the first thoughts that come to your mind."

"Well, let me see. That he has a strong faith and a close relationship with God. That's the most important thing for anyone."

Sarah nodded. "I think so too."

"Then, I'd want him to be happy, of course."

"Of course." Her smile was so big it made him wonder if she might be secretly laughing at him. Probably not. Not Sarah. "And last?"

"I'd have to want him to find a woman to love as much as I love you and for her—"

"To love him as much as I love you." She finished the sentence for him.

"Exactly. And that brings another thought to mind. Since your doctor has lifted *all* your constraints, and I have the rest of the day off, why don't we go prove that love to each other? It's been far too long."

"I agree," Sarah replied. The corners of her mouth turned up slightly. "I think you should have a talk with my doctor. He has been quite unreasonable about certain matters."

"I may just do that, Mrs. Moretz, but right now, I've got something else entirely on my mind."

Clifton stood and held out his hand. When Sarah placed her hand in his, he pulled her up into his arms and gave her the first unrestrained kiss he'd given her in months. He hadn't wanted to tempt his fortitude when it came to stopping the passionate nature Sarah brought out of him. But suddenly, all thoughts left his mind. He lost himself in that kiss and then led his wife upstairs to enjoy more.

Author's Note

I did as much research as I could for this book, but information prior to the end of the Civil War is often sketchy in the South because many of the records were lost or destroyed. My parents were both born in Watauga County, and I came from Wilkes County, so this area is also part of my heritage.

My characters are entirely fictional and are not related to any historical families. Only Dr. Vierling in Salem was a real person. I did use some real places, such as Tucker's Barn, which would become Lenoir. Councill's Store would later become Boone. The Linville River is real, but the Moretz farm on the mountain and the Cagle place are imaginary locations. Of course, Wilkesboro, Salem, and Salisbury are real locations.

I hope you enjoyed reading *Cleared for Planting* as much as I enjoyed writing it. Look for the second book in the series, *Sown in Dark Soil*, which is mainly Luke Moretz's story.

For more information about
Janice Cole Hopkins
&
Cleared for Planting
please visit:

www.JaniceColeHopkins.com
wandrnlady@aol.com
@J_C_Hopkins
www.facebook.com/JaniceColeHopkins

For more information about
AMBASSADOR INTERNATIONAL
please visit:

www.ambassador-international.com
@AmbassadorIntl
www.facebook.com/AmbassadorIntl